THE KORNILOV TERROR

OWEN HOLLISTER

This is a work of fiction. Names, characters, places, incidents and dialogues depicted are products of the author's imagination or are used fictitiously. Any resemblance to actual people, living or dead, events or locales is entirely coincidental.

ISBN: 1979517479
ISBN 13: 9781979517478

ACKNOWLEDGMENTS

I would like to thank my friends and associates who assisted me during the production of this novel.

CHAPTER 1

It takes a lot of physical and emotional effort to beat someone to death but the figure at the centre of the room was doing it. A great bull of a man with a flat face and black hair swept viciously back. Each successive swing fed the anger surging through his body with bolt after bolt of pure malicious energy. The next blow landed square in the remains of the victim's face, once beautifully symmetrical, now gashed up and bloody. The impact sprayed wet matter towards the assembled bystanders. The nearest man recoiled then calmly brushed the sprinkling of scarlet droplets off the fabric of his dark military tunic as he struggled to conceal any outward display of revulsion. The assailant's nostrils flared as he inhaled a massive hissing lungful of breath. This fuelled another volley of punches of such visceral savagery that even the hardened spectators were momentarily cowed.

This was a man whose wrath was never to be underestimated. They had seen his brutality before but never quite this frenzied. Then it was over. The grunting executioner collapsed into a nearby chair like a lover whose lust was finally sated. His frantic breathing slowed and the thick vein in his sinewy neck gradually stopped pulsing. He glanced down at the brass knuckleduster wrapped round his right fist. His expression was quizzical. He narrowed his eyes and pursed his lips like a child inspecting a new toy. He lifted it up to examine the glistening ornament now bejewelled with flecks of human flesh. Then he looked back at his victim to survey his handiwork. A trace of a smile broke across his big flat face. He was happy.

The athletic body hung limply from a ceiling pipe. Its rib cage had stopped its heaving. The stomach protruded from beneath a blood soaked shirt. A smashed nose and an eyeball bulging from its socket were now the only prominent facial features.

None dared speak. Then the man said.

'Get this piece of meat out of here.' He breathed heavily from his nostrils as the torn carcass slowly twisted in front of him.

'And make sure there are no traces. Disappear it, like the others, you hear me.'

The four uniformed men in the room responded instantly to the instruction. This was an act at which they were well practiced. One of them undid the knot keeping the rope taut. As the rope went slack the legs crumpled first. The rest of the body followed with a loud crack as skull and concrete met. The carcass collapsed into the pool of blood and other fluids that had collected beneath it. A blackish rivulet trickled its way along the cambered floor towards a drain in the corner. There was a hose conveniently attached to some pipes further down the wall next to a single metal table covered with an assortment of gruesome looking implements. With its bare concrete walls and strange features, whoever had designed this room must have had such scenarios in mind. A tinge of disinfectant completed the ambiance.

One of the attendants had already made themselves busy unzipping a body shaped plastic sack. Two others grabbed the corpse's legs and started to drag it towards the waiting receptacle. Its head scraped along the concrete leaving a deep scarlet daub in its wake from where it had slid through the blood pool. They shoved the head in first. Then two of them lifted the end of the sack up while the third stuffed the remainder of the torso inside and pulled the zip closed.

'Personal interrogations' were not an infrequent occurrence in this stark chamber of horrors. Usually they were just interrogations, albeit exceptionally violent ones but in those instances there was at least some information to be extracted. Occasionally though, as had just happened, the proceedings got a lot more intense and the 'questioning' became murder. And the man doing the murdering was always the same.

Whilst it was not unprecedented for someone with his background to commit such gross acts, what made the situation unusual was his continuing to do so even when he had reached the highest rank of office. Others in his position might have delegated such tasks to 'overzealous lieutenants' who could, if necessary, be blamed for 'misinterpreting' orders, in a way that was wholly deniable. Not this man. Not Alexei Kornilov.

He was an artist. He took pleasure in his craft and he saw no reason to give up his vocation just because of what he had become. They deserved it, he always told himself. It was the law of nature, him or them. No one else could be trusted to carry out the task quite as thoroughly as he would. They were cowards lacking the guts to do what was necessary. But deep down he knew it was all about the sheer pleasure of it, the tingling thrill. The pain and fear he inflicted was sensuous to him. He liked the way his victims screamed and pleaded as he hurt them. He liked it more when they kicked and struggled. Sometimes that gave him an erection. It didn't matter whether the victim was male or female. The brutality was a kind of release. He knew it was wrong. He just didn't care. This was what he was. This was what he did.

He rose from his steel chair as the attendants cleaned up. He could leave them to it. He sensed that even though they had seen him do this on many previous occasions, this time he had shocked them. This was a matter of supreme indifference to him.

'Make sure my car is ready,' he muttered as he left the room. One of the men made a hurried call from a telephone on the wall.

Now he strode purposefully down a long featureless corridor until he reached the service elevator at the end. He was alone. His security detail would be waiting when he exited at the ground floor. Normally he would never be unaccompanied but this building was one of the few locations that he felt truly safe. The elevator heaved its way slowly to the surface where it disgorged its lone occupant into the building's main lobby. His armed guards quickly fell in at his side as they made their way outside to where his convoy was already assembled. The three heavily armoured black SUV's were designed to be not only bullet proof but also to survive small explosions. The man and his bodyguards climbed into the middle vehicle. Assorted flunkies most of whom were also armed, were already populating the vehicles in front and behind it. The steel gates of the heavily guarded building swung open to release the entourage.

The drive back to his own compound was a short one but it didn't do to take chances in a city like Caspov. First, the cars moved slowly as most of the side streets were still heavily potholed. As they turned onto the main thoroughfare the pace quickened. A few of the central streets had now been extensively rebuilt. This one, 'Victory Boulevard' was intended to be a flagship. It was smoothly surfaced and flanked on either side by brand new high-rise office buildings. Most were still empty or in some cases not quite finished. The man glanced out of the window and frowned as he noticed the scaffolding on one of the unfinished buildings. His mind instinctively leapt to the myriad of potential threats the scaffolding might conceal. Why wasn't it floodlit and patrolled he thought, wondering why he hadn't noticed this before. Then he remembered the 'Victory Boulevard' had only been completed the previous week. It would be officially opened in a few weeks at a ceremony that would be witnessed by a crowd of carefully corralled well wishers and foreign dignitaries. He had even managed to procure the services of a couple of gullible celebrities. Amazing what people will do if you pay them enough, he thought. The celebrations would be another fine example of the magnificent revival and reconstruction that his country was now enjoying. And of course his own immense personal authority and achievement as President of the Republic of Caspia.

He spent the final minutes of the journey enjoying the thought of the fawning foreign dignitaries. He loved the idea of all those straight- laced diplomats and business chiefs exchanging pleasantries with him, oblivious to the truth. 'We really admire the firm leadership and stability you have given your people,' they often said. And other shit like that. He imagined their reactions if they were to learn how exactly he had been amusing himself that evening. Or better still, maybe some of them had already seen the Amnesty reports and chose to see no evil. Even if they had, he could be confident that they would be too beholden, professionally diplomatic or just too damn scared to say anything. Either scenario was wryly amusing as far as he was concerned.

Suddenly, his private phone emitted a jarring peel of rings. Only a handful of people had this number and all were under very strict instructions only to ring it in circumstances of the utmost urgency. He recognised the distinctively harsh tones of a man he had known for over a decade. There was no ceremony in the conversation.

'We have a big problem' the caller said. 'You need to get to the command centre. I will meet you there and explain,' the caller said.

'Fuck that. Tell me now Romanov,' he spat back, but the line was already dead. He punched at the keypad but the other phone was engaged. He was not used to being hung up on let alone defied. It was always the other way round. The other man, Romanov, had sounded strange too. As he tossed the phone aside in exasperation, the motorcade entered his heavily fortified presidential compound.

CHAPTER 2

2012: Present

'Whose cock did she suck to get this break?,' the slickly jacketed media executive muttered into his colleague's ear. The recipient of the comment smirked and scribbled something on a post-it note, which he carefully folded and pushed back across the hardwood table towards the sotto voce question's originator. The slick jacket man unfolded it immediately and the smirk became mutual. The scrawled note simply said, "I hope mine's next!"

The woman who had provoked this exchange had just walked into an editorial meeting at the headquarters of the International Media Corporation. Her day had begun just a short while ago on arrival at their New York offices. These occupied a prime position on Avenue of the Americas and like so many of their kind epitomised 1980's commercial chic. Visitors were greeted by a cavernous atrium all decked out in a black marble finish. Then they encountered a vast reception desk surrounded by minimalist leather sofas. A Starbucks coffee concession was doing a brisk trade in a far corner. A phalanx of electric turnstiles, now a ubiquitous feature of any large North

American office building since nine eleven, guarded the elevator bank situated at the back of the lobby. A steady stream of the building's occupants started to trudge through the Perspex gates. Some were already embroiled in loud conversations about 'focus' and 'reaching out' on their various communication devices.

This was the scene that greeted Tatiana 'Tanya' Georgievna as she arrived in the IMC building's lobby less than an hour earlier. Sweating a little more than was comfortable, she approached the reception desk to announce her arrival. The lady behind the counter made a point of studying her computer screen very intently before looking up and taking Tanya's details.

There was more earnest tapping on her keyboard. A metal nozzle was pointed in Tanya's direction.

'Look into the camera please' the receptionist said brusquely. A few moments later Tanya was handed a temporary pass complete with a photograph that could have been anyone. It certainly did no justice to the striking brunette that had posed for the shot. The blurry snap hardly captured the elegance of her beautiful long face with its mixture of Slavic cheekbones and softer Italianate features. This was framed by a cascade of long dark hair from a tight bunch on top. With her slender legs and statuesque frame she was not unaccustomed to getting second glances, jealous ones from women and lecherous ones from men. Judging by her look of icy hauteur, the receptionist definitely fell into the first category.

'Go through the barriers, third elevator bank on the left, twenty second floor. Report to reception up there, they are expecting you', she informed Tanya crisply before resuming her scrutiny of the terminal.

The express elevator surged skywards bypassing the low floors to reach its destination in a little under a minute. She emerged into a much more compact reception area than the one that had greeted her at street level. It was heavily carpeted and well populated with the kind of light beige easy chairs normally found in airport lounges. Matching beige lamps with brushed cotton shades completed the scene. Unlike the lobby, this area had a more elegant feel about it and positively reeked of executive chic. Tanya guessed this floor must be reserved exclusively for corporate meeting rooms. A glance right confirmed this with signage for boardrooms number three and four. That was a whole lot of boardrooms. This was serious shit. The immigrant girl from the suburbs hits the big time. Her train of thought was broken by the appearance of a woman in her early forties who introduced herself as Cathy from HR.

'Hi, how are you? Really pleased to meet you,' Cathy trilled. 'I hope you had a good journey last night. The meeting's already in progress but you probably won't be called in for another forty minutes or so. I thought you'd want to get here early and relax. Follow me, there's an empty meeting room where you can have a bit of privacy. There's coffee and cookies too. Restrooms are at the end of the corridor if you need them.'

They walked down the thickly carpeted corridor and halted at a door about two thirds of the way down. Cathy ushered Tanya in and pointed towards the refreshments waiting at the centre of a glass table.

'Make yourself at home. I will be right back to collect you when they are ready.'

Tanya poured herself a coffee trying extra hard not to spill a single drop. The room had an impressive view of the Manhattan cityscape facing towards midtown. She instantly recognised the distinctive profile of the Empire State Building. Further to the left she saw another spire shaped tower that also looked familiar. The Chrysler but she wasn't quite so certain. This really was like being in a movie, she thought for moment before scolding herself for having such a non-serious thought. That was not the kind of thought a professional should be having. Her own office in Chicago had a handsome view of Lake Michigan so this wasn't something that should impress her. She needed to focus hard. Focus on success. That's what her father had always told her. This was going to be the most important meeting of her short career and at this moment all she wanted to do was to succeed at any cost. Every ambition she had nurtured since a child was about to culminate in this, a moment of great opportunity. Just thinking about it was making her heart pound.

Her mind wandered back to the last meeting with her boss back in Chicago.

'I believe in you Tanya. Totally. This is your story and it's totally right that you follow it but I am not going to bullshit you, Tanya. They are going to question you: your age, your experience, the story itself. It's down to you to sell it to them, like you did with me. Can you do that Tanya?'

Sure she could. Her short pitch was now deeply en-grained in her head. This was it, she thought. You will never get another break as good as this. Do not fuck this up. She abandoned any further attempt to drink the coffee and closed her eyes. Suddenly, she was back home again, a child standing before her father. 'You can do this. You can do anything, now we are in America,' he said. His presence felt so real she almost started to answer. Then she took a deep breath and opened her eyes. He was gone but she felt so much stronger now, the memory lingering like a sweet aroma that never quite fades

Meanwhile, further down the corridor in a much larger room, the most important meeting in Tanya Georgievna's career was already firing up.

The chairman of the editorial management committee of IMC cleared his throat. 'Perhaps we can move on to the main items of business.'

There were about a dozen people around the board room table who largely consisted of editors of IMC's main broadsheet newspapers, printed journals, on line content and of course the director of their TV news channel plus a couple of the usual hangers on. All the men were wearing pricy chinos. A couple of the younger ones wore designer jackets. Some older guys wore dark blazers with fat brass buttons. Most didn't. No one wore a tie. The chairman of the editorial committee was responsible for news content across all of IMC. He was one of the blazer wearers. Just in case anyone doubted his status as a 'media guy' he sported a trademark pair of bright red socks under his Italian suede loafers. He also wore a large pair of glasses that he liked to think made him look erudite and serious, a big hitter in every sense. He peered down the table over the mesh of cables sprouting from the access points that fed the dozen fancy laptops. It was time to get things moving. He cleared his throat. 'Perhaps we can move on then to the first main item of business.'

There was some further shuffling of papers and clicking of keys as the journalists and executives flicked through their papers.

'As some of you know' he continued, 'we are looking to develop a new investigative story that we could break across all our media channels. The initial article would appear as a major exposé in our 'Global Affairs' weekly magazine. If it catches like we think it will, we can follow through on all our TV and digital channels. We then maintain our story leadership by controlling the release of revelations at our own pace.' He opened his mouth to elaborate further but was interrupted.

'Err, sorry, what is the story?' a lean man with turtleneck sweater but no blazer squeaked from the other end of the table. The much fatter guy opposite failed to disguise a snigger. Someone was out of the loop.

The chairman held up his hand.

'The story is Caspia,' he went on. 'And the chief subject is President Alexei Kornilov. Several other faces round the table were already looking blank. Sensing that he was losing people, the chairman hastened his elaboration.

'There are in fact two major individuals in this investigation. The second subject is a certain Nicholas Petrovna.' This time there was a universal murmur of recognition round the table. Nicholas Petrovna was one of the wealthiest men in the world. His name featured prominently in Forbes and indeed IMC's very own 'Global Plutocrats' rich list. His $20 billion dollar fortune along with extensive US business interests ensured that the notoriously secretive tycoon made brief but regular appearances in the financial press whether he liked it or not. Judging by the ferocious jabbing of keyboards and exchanging of glances, the introduction of Petrovna into the equation had caught the committee's interest. Now all those expectant eyes were trained back on the chairman. What scandal could be so hot that it would dominate all channels? their expressions said. With the initiative back, the chairman pressed ahead quickly.

'Caspia is a pretty god forsaken dump. Surprise, surprise, it's on the borders of the Caspian Sea. The population's small, only about one million and most of those are in the imaginatively named capital, Caspov. Also a dump, but here's the thing folks. The ground beneath Caspia is full of oil and gas, and lots of it. Most of those countries around the Black and Caspian Sea are. Georgia, Azerbaijan, Caspia, no one would give a shit about any of these places if it weren't for the energy reserves. Caspia was part of the Soviet Union since its inclusion in the 1920's. When communism collapsed in ninety one, it became a nominally autonomous republic albeit under the wing of Russia. Unlike most of its neighbours, the majority of the population of Caspia are essentially ethnic Russians who speak a variant of Russian known as Caspian. However, there is a minority Muslim population. When the republic first broke away there was a brief Islamic insurgency but the former Soviet army commander there, a certain Colonel Alexei Kornilov, quickly suppressed this. Some say he provoked or even initially colluded with the rising just so that he could turn round and crush it. There was talk of atrocities at the time but no one took much notice because the second Chechen war was kicking off next door. He seized power a short a while later after his predecessor was killed in a freak helicopter crash. Again, probably engineered by Kornilov. This guy's a real piece of work with a collection of some very scary personality disorders. Anyone who has opposed or criticised him has been killed, imprisoned or just disappeared. He's always been a hard man but rumour has it that even though he is in the presidential office suite now, he still enjoys personally torturing political adversaries. The Kremlin tolerates him because of the gas and because he does exactly what they tell him.'

'OK', it was the fat guy. 'So far, so CIA fact book. Boo hoo Caspia and all that but why exactly is the antics of some minor Russian despot no one has ever heard of in a country no one outside of Langley has heard of, a big story for the US public? I am thinking commercial here. It's a fine story for one of our Sunday editions but it's hardly "hold the front page"' stuff is it?'

The editor held up his hand again as if to signal that he anticipated the objection. 'This is where Petrovna comes in. He is effectively Kornilov's money man. He's a former apparatchik who used to manage the energy infrastructure down there in the Soviet Union days. His links with Kornilov go right back. That connection seems to be the original source of Petrovna's fortune, even though we don't know the details. One minute he's some middle manager technocrat in the Soviet bureaucracy, next thing we know he owns a multi billion dollar petrochemical enterprise. There's no clear explanation as to how he could acquire that much dough so quickly. In fact, the same can be said of most of the other Russian oligarchs. Presumably Kornilov's got a well-stocked Swiss bank account too.' He paused, met with silence, then continued.

'The point is, Petrovna has substantial business interests in the US. We are talking huge property and stock market investments worth well over five billion dollars US alone. He's even got his own private hedge fund based a few blocks down from us here. He uses these companies to make political donations. The largest of his holding companies all have at least one Congressman on the board. What we could have here is a direct link between American companies and politicians to the leader of an oppressive regime. Nicholas Petrovna is that link.'

'Sounds interesting', the editor of their Boston broadsheet entered the fray no doubt smelling that the tide of opinion was on the turn. This guy was an old school member of the blazer faction. With his grey hair and gravel-voiced Bostonian accent, he looked and sounded it. He liked to do things by the book. 'But how do we progress it from here? I assume we use one of our crack foreign correspondents.'

'Not exactly,' replied the chairman. We are proposing to put a young reporting talent on this case. Her name is Tatiana Georgievna from the Chicago office. She likes Tanya for short.'

For the second time in ten minutes a wave of mild disbelief reverberated around the table. Several people could be seen mouthing the word 'who' to each other.

'Tanya's been working on this story for months and she is real keen to pursue it,' said the chairman.

Boston wasn't satisfied. 'But with all due respect sir, would it not be more sensible to use an established name on a story like this? Surely Doug Mountjoy would be a better choice? All credit to this girl, Anna, Tanya, whatever her name is, for developing the early angle but Doug is better equipped to move it forward. He already has the profile. He won an award for his reporting from Bosnia for Christ's sake and he is used to working in dangerous environments. If this story is half as important as you think it is then this girl's just too green.'

There were tentative nods of agreement round the table, but the chairman had foreseen this objection too. 'Actually she's not green. She's done some pretty exciting work up in Chicago on that corrupt senator who just got jailed.' He turned to the head of HR who had been lurking silently in a corner. 'Carol, can you run through Tanya's details so that everyone's up to speed on this?'

There were more barely muffled groans as the HR head prepared to give her little piece. It was bad enough that Muppets like her were even allowed to attend editorial management meetings let alone that they were permitted to speak. It certainly would never have happened in the good old days, Boston thought. He wasn't the only one. Nevertheless, endure her opinions they must.

'Tanya Georgievna is twenty-seven years old,' Carol bleated. 'She joined our graduate training four years ago in our Chicago office straight from Harvard where she graduated Magnum cum laude in liberal arts before taking a master's in Journalism. She's been one of our highest flying young journalists since she completed her basic induction and as the chairperson has just explained, she already has one major investigative story under her belt. Oh, one more thing. As some of you might have guessed from her name, she speaks Russian and is of partial Caspian ancestry.'

'I would like to second that', the editor of the Chicago Mail chipped in. He was Tanya's immediate boss.

Quite why it was necessary to drag the head of IMC's global HR department in to the meeting to give a thirty second biography when the Chicago capo could have done the job was escaping most people, some of whom were now suspecting funny politics. Then the chairman played his final card. 'I can see that some of you are still sceptical about this, so maybe you should hear from this young lady herself. Carol, could you fetch Ms Georgievna please.'

Carol returned a few moments later with a young woman in tow. Although conservatively dressed in a dark skirt, white blouse and court shoes, the pure simple elegance of her face was catching some people's attention. The brunette was blissfully untroubled by these silent yearnings and if she was nervous, she was doing a damn good job at concealing it. Tanya stood up at the end of the table and after a word of introduction from the chairman began that carefully rehearsed pitch.

'Thank you all for giving me the opportunity to talk to you today' she began. 'I am an American citizen born and bred. My mom is from Illinois but my father is from Caspia. He fled to this country just before the Soviet Union broke up. He wanted to escape repression and seek a better life. He was a journalist like me. He sought the truth but spent the day peddling lies to please his political masters. He risked his life to flee to the United States because he admired its values and hoped that one day the people of Caspia would enjoy those values too. I have spent months researching this story about my father's homeland. I believe I have uncovered a major scandal that links US businesses and politicians to one of the most oppressive regimes in the world run by one of the most vicious dictators in the world with the help of one of the richest men in the world. I believe with my knowledge of Caspia, command of Russian and the experience I have already gained from my time at IMC, that I am best positioned to make and break this story. I believe I can do this by getting close to Nicholas Petrovna.'

She paused for a moment and then she continued in tighter voice 'My father died last year. I want to do this to honour his memory and to highlight the plight of Caspia. I hope I have this committee's support.'

'Hey, maybe you should run for congress' someone quipped. The chairman shot them a dirty look.

Persuasive though she was, several members of the committee were still unsure whether this story was really as big as the chairman was making it out to be. It wasn't like this Petrovna guy was behind the Kennedy assassination. However, she had sounded genuine and sometimes it didn't make sense to rock the boat when there was shit going on behind the scenes you didn't know about.

The Chairman spoke again. 'Well, thank you for that Ms Georgievna. We now need to discuss some other matters on the agenda. I am sure you will be hearing from your editor about this very soon.' With that, Carol escorted Tanya from the meeting room. She was still tightly clutching the phone in her pocket like some lucky charm, just as she had been throughout the meeting.

CHAPTER 3

MOSCOW 2000: Past

An ageing Moscow winter was doing its brutal worst to Nicholas Petrovna as he waited for the tram to arrive. He clutched his tatty overcoat into an ever tighter embrace, his cap already tugged down as far as it could go to protect the crop of short dark hair beneath. It was a bitingly raw winter night and most of his fellow travellers already resembled hunched-up statues. Barely visible pinched faces hid beneath large hats and mufflers that concealed their ears from the gusts of searing wind. In a Moscow February, anything not covered freezes and people are no exception. He observed their blank expressions and wondered if they were people at all or just frozen spirits with frozen souls. His sombre thoughts were broken by the appearance of the tram, already rammed with tired and huddled masses. Being a short man, he allowed the others to jostle their way on board first then stepped inside last. At least it was warm.

This wasn't the usual tram he took home. Tonight he had other business to attend to first and it was this that now occupied his mind for the remainder of the journey. He had taken the call that morning at his office. It was from an old acquaintance called Modest Gorky. They had served together as conscripts in the Russian Navy where they had been friends of sorts for a while. After their military service was complete they had gone their separate ways. Petrovna had pursued his career as an engineer. Modest had continued his in the Navy. He had been vague about his current circumstances on the call but had been extremely insistent that they should meet as soon as possible, preferably that evening.

Seeing as with most nights, he had no social engagements, it had seemed foolish to decline the offer. The call had aroused his curiosity and if nothing else it would be interesting to see what exactly his former 'comrade' had been up to for the last ten years.

The tram was approaching his destination. Petrovna braced himself for the cold once again and stepped gingerly onto the icy pavement. They had agreed to meet at a small bar further down the street. The establishment was situated on the ground floor of a 1950s block and was typical of the sort of traditional drinking den so often found on a Moscow side street. Dingy, utilitarian, designed for a man to get seriously hammered in and nothing more.

Petrovna stepped inside the dimly lit lair and peered through the fug of cigarette smoke in search of Modest. The floor felt tacky under foot, no piece of upholstery was unstained or ripped, no patch of wall unscarred. The room was about half full of assorted drinkers, almost exclusively male. Most were seated at the tables round the edge of the room. A few stood at the bar. Most were smoking heavily as they stared intently into their glasses of beer or vodka. Their taut faces hinted at an anger beneath that could explode at any moment. Petrovna guessed that this was not the best place to make new friends or for that matter pick a quarrel. Finally, he noticed a familiar old face sitting at a table in a far corner of the room. Modest cut a nondescript figure amongst the inhabitants of the bar. His slight build, short hair and badly fitting suit blended easily into the smoky scenery. The lean face and small eyes were as Petrovna remembered them, but perhaps a little gaunter. As Petrovna crossed the bar towards him, Modest rose from his seat and greeted him so effusively that Petrovna felt a twinge of awkwardness.

'Nicholas, my friend,' he said, seizing Petrovna's hand with a cast iron grip far stronger than you'd expect from a man of his stature. 'I don't think we have spoken since that final farewell drink in Astrakhan. It must be nearly ten years. What have you been up to comrade?'

Petrovna flashed a nervous grin. 'This and that. Ten years is a long time my friend. What have you been doing?'

Modest had already made a start on a bottle of Vodka and slid a second glass across the greasy Formica table top. He instructed Petrovna to help himself, which he did. A cigarette was proffered but rejected. Guessing that it was his turn to go first, he knocked back a large slug of the Vodka. The sharp kick of the tasteless liquid burnt his mouth and set his nerves tingling. He leant forward.

'After I left the Navy, I returned to Moscow where I was immediately assigned a position as a trainee engineer at the Ministry of Energy. You may recall that my original degree was in mechanical engineering. I spent a year as a duty engineer at a power station just outside Moscow. Then I was reassigned to a refining unit in Caspia. Presumably they saw on my record that I had been stationed down in

Astrakhan during my military service and realised I was already familiar with that part of the world. Not that I had any say in the matter.'

'Which of us did,' said Modest shrugging his shoulders.

'Then I spent seven god forsaken years down there. I was managing various refineries and eventually most of the storage and pipeline infrastructure. Two years ago, all the shit started and I got recalled to Moscow. Been pushing paper here ever since.' Petrovna paused and waited for a reply. He felt he had said enough about himself given he wasn't even sure yet why Modest had summoned him.

'Married?' asked Modest. 'No' replied Petrovna. 'No time for that yet.'

'Ah, no time no ties. You are a lucky man Nicholas, a lucky man.' Modest drew heavily on his cigarette, seemingly deep in thought.

'You know Nicholas, sometimes it's good to have nothing. Means you've got nothing to lose. That makes you a free man. You can take any opportunity life has to offer.' Then he suddenly let out a burst of laughter. 'I have a confession to make. I already knew your life story before you walked in here. I just wanted to hear you say it. The truth is, after you left the Navy I was transferred to, how shall we say, other duties. I think you understand what I am saying.' Modest grinned.

Petrovna nodded. He required little imagination to deduce what line of business his old associate might have been in.

'While you were stationed in Caspia working at your little refinery, I was responsible for monitoring political activity in Caspia. So, you see, I know all about you, your career, your acquaintances, who you have been screwing or in your case, who you haven't been screwing. That's why I asked you to come here this evening.'

'So,' Petrovna said coldly. 'You are KGB or at least ex KGB. You have had a case file on me for years and now you drag me here to tell me about my sex life. Why, is this some kind of joke? What exactly is it you want from me Modest?'

Modest cackled. 'Relax my friend. I have come to make you a proposal. This is the situation. Russia is changing by the day. Since Gorbochev fucked it all up, everything we understood and believed in is finished: the Soviet Union, the Communist Party. They are all finished. Game over. Take me. I was a committed communist since school. I really believed in it then. I was in Komsomol as soon as the young pioneers would take me. Now though, even I see that it's all over. We have this drunken fool Yeltsin in charge of us and meanwhile our enemies laugh at us from behind their hands. But then I see the beauty in the chaos and I think to myself, Modest, this is your chance. Empires are built in crises and there is no greater crisis than the fall of an empire.' He took another swig of his Vodka, looking pleased with his turn of phrase. He topped up his glass and continued. 'Do you remember our old friend Alexei Kornilov? I am sure you do.'

Petrovna did remember. He shuddered at the very mention of the name. During his time as a navel conscript he had been assigned to duty on a small cruiser in the Caspian Sea. Kornilov was also a conscript on the same vessel but at a slightly higher rank due to his being one year advanced in his service. Russian military discipline is

23

harsh at the best of times but in addition to this the young conscripts were forced to contend with a culture known as 'dedovshchina'. This was an especially savage form of hazing imposed on young conscripts by older ones. It was tacitly accepted by the officers as an unofficial form of discipline and a means of toughening up the young recruits. At its mildest it took the form of low level bullying and exploitation. At its worst it could involve savage beatings and various other forms of abuse. Alexei Kornilov had been a notorious exponent of the latter. The young conscripts had been terrorised by Kornilov and were forced to act like petty serfs in his presence for fear of the violent consequences.

One hapless victim had once tried to stand his ground and was beaten almost senseless for his pains. The incident was glossed over by the authorities that secretly liked Kornilov's knack of asserting authority. Petrovna himself had only escaped the worst of it due to his own age, which having had temporary exemption for university was actually a little older than Kornilov's. Petrovna certainly remembered Kornilov. You don't forget a man like Kornilov.

Modest was obviously enjoying himself now. A broad grin spread across his face as Petrovna's countenance visibly darkened at the mention of Kornilov. 'Like me, Kornilov stayed on at the end of his military service but not in the Navy. He switched to land forces where his, how can I put this 'special talents' were more highly prized. He was quickly promoted. Then, two years ago, just as you were returning to Moscow, he was posted back to Caspia as commander of a unit sent to deal with the

Islamic insurgency there. Remember, he was born and bought up in Caspia even though his parents were ethnic Russians. The Kremlin were desperate for the situation not to degenerate into another Chechnya-like scenario so they sent him in the hope that his local knowledge and methods would be able to contain the situation quickly. They were right. It just wasn't subtle. When it was agreed that the Republic of Caspia would separate from Russia, our friend Alexei became head of the armed forces under a puppet President by the name of Bakov. I doubt you've heard much about him. No one else has. About two months ago President Bakov had a little accident in his helicopter whilst flying to inspect one of Kornilov's military bases. It has not been widely publicised yet but our old friend Alexei is now the effective ruler of the Republic of Caspia. President in fact.'

'How in the name of hell did he manage that?' Petrovna exclaimed. 'I can understand him rising through the army ranks but politics. Let alone President. Well that's something different. I mean President, seriously, how?'

Modest looked momentarily pained 'I am not going to give you any more details Nicholas. I told you it was a helicopter crash, in Caspia. Kornilov inherited the crown. I think that's all you need to know. I will leave the rest to your imagination.'

'OK, OK, I think I get it. This is all very interesting Modest but what has any of this got do with me?'

Modest leaned forward conspiratorially. 'Are you familiar with the concept of privatisation?' Petrovna nodded again despite being unsure where this was going.

'Kornilov, President Kornilov as perhaps we should now call him, is most anxious about the Caspian economy. In particular he is determined that the country's main industry which as you very well know is the extraction and processing of oil and gas, is efficiently run. President Kornilov believes that this is best achieved by selling these assets to a private company who will be better placed to invest in them. This is where you come in.'

Modest obviously had in mind some kind of crooked deal. There were a lot of deals going on in Russia at the moment but this was the first time Petrovna had encountered one face to face.

'So, are you interested' barked Modest, suddenly banging his vodka glass on the table, attracting furtive glances from fellow drinkers.

'Well yes, but what exactly are you proposing?' Petrovna asked.

'I will explain that in due course but there is someone else you need to meet first. It goes without saying that we are assuming your absolute discretion in this matter. I must warn you that the gentlemen you will be dealing with do not take betrayal of a confidence lightly. You do understand that don't you?' Petrovna nodded.

'Good. In that case come to this address tomorrow at 3 o'clock and ask for this man,' he said, pushing a business card across the table. 'I will be there. Don't be late.' Then Modest stood up, drained the last traces of vodka from his glass and walked out of the bar, donning his heavy coat as he left.

Petrovna remained at the table with the half empty bottle of vodka and the small piece of card, which he gingerly plucked off the table and examined. It was printed on expensive material and bore the name of a Yevgeny Golitsin, who was apparently 'Managing Director' of Credit Bank of Siberia. Petrovna wasn't familiar with this particular financial institution. It was not a household name in Russia. It did seem to have a very fine address a block or so away from Tverskaya Street. Placing the business card carefully in his pocket, he abandoned the half-finished vodka and the bar, relieved to escape its smoky confines.

The frozen night air hit him hard as he stepped outside. The dimly lit street was largely deserted now. He hastened towards the nearby tram stop. Fortunately he did not have long to wait and he was soon inside the vehicle as it lumbered its way towards the edge of the city. As the tram juddered and squealed past the monotonous apartment blocks outside he nervously turned the business card over in his hand and pondered the evening's events.

When he arrived at his stop he crossed the road to reach the entrance of the apartment block he called home. The stairs could sometimes be icy in this weather so he trod carefully. It was with some relief that he opened the door to his apartment and entered its cold sanctuary. Petrovna's apartment was typical of what Moscow housing had to offer. It was small but did at least have two bedrooms and its own bathroom. By no means everyone had that luxury. In fact, this was the apartment where he had grown up. He had somehow managed to use some connections in the Party to hang onto it after his mother had died. It was amazing what could be done with a single phone call if you knew someone in the Party. He quickly turned on the lights and the stove. He always did this first. Even though the apartment was tiny, the rooms always seemed strangely empty now that only he inhabited them.

Usually he would turn the television on as well to generate an aura of companionship but tonight he didn't bother. He simply sat down and surveyed his surroundings: a grey room with a water stained ceiling and some battered 1970s furniture. There were no other decorations as such, just a single faded photograph of his parents on the mantelpiece. Was this really all that life had to offer him? He didn't like the smell of what Modest was hinting at and he definitely didn't like the idea of having anything to do with Kornilov again. However, maybe, just maybe, this really was his big chance to escape this apartment and this life. It would be foolish not to at least investigate what was on offer. He looked at the business card again and resolved to find an excuse to leave the office early tomorrow afternoon.

———

At proximately 2.30pm Nicholas Petrovna announced to his secretary that he was feeling quite unwell. He had a migraine and not for the first time. When this happened he just had to call it a day. She voiced her concern and inquired if he needed assistance getting home. He politely declined.

It was snowing ferociously outside so he walked only a short distance and caught a taxi cab to Tverskaya Street, which was quite an extravagance for him. He decided not to get the cab all the way to the address. That felt a bit obvious. Like most Russians he was still imbued with a sense of paranoia and although the bad old days had supposedly passed, the instinct to look over his shoulder had never entirely dissipated. Something about this meeting felt vaguely illicit to him. Maybe it was Modest's choice of sleazy bar or perhaps the involvement of Kornilov. Probably both. In any event he chose to complete his journey on foot. He soon found himself walking along Tverskaya's busy thoroughfare. It was still quite early so there were a fair few people about. He strode purposefully, watching carefully for the sign for Probiesky Street, where the offices of Credit Bank of Siberia were situated.

The Credit Bank of Siberia turned out to be inside a converted 19th century building. The premises were shared with several other companies whose names were listed on a plaque in the small reception area. A young woman with a tightly braided blond pony tail greeted him at the desk and sent him straight upstairs without bothering to check his name. CBS had the whole of the second floor of the building, although this was not large and didn't look as if it could accommodate many people. Maybe it was just the Moscow corporate base for a much larger organisation. He pressed the entry button and was buzzed in.

Modest appeared almost immediately and ushered him into a very elegant meeting room decked out in the imperial style, all velvet swags and gilded Louis XIV chairs. Presiding over it all was an over-sized bohemian glass chandelier. A faint chemical aroma rose from the carpet whose thick squishy texture underfoot screamed new. A man sat at the end of a table with his back to the window. Petrovna guessed correctly that this man was Golitsin.

The financier wore a noticeably more expensive suit then Modest's cheap outfit. He was sporting a very extravagant watch. Suddenly Petrovna felt horribly provincial. Golitsin gestured that they should both sit down, which they did.

'Right,' Golitsin began with a business like air. 'I believe my friend Modest Gorky has already explained to you a little of what we have in mind. I take it that seeing as you are here you are interested in listening to our proposal. I must tell you that what we discuss in this room is in the strictest commercial confidence. I think you already understand that don't you?'

'He understands,' Modest added as he pushed a piece of paper across the table. 'It's a confidentiality agreement. You need to sign it before we continue.'

Petrovna glanced over it to ensure that this was indeed the case and then placed his scrawl at the end of the page.

'We have a unique business proposition for you Mr Petrovna. We understand that you are already familiar with our mutual acquaintance Alexei Kornilov, now recently elevated to the Presidency of the Republic of Caspia. We also understand that you are an engineer by training and are currently a manager at the Department of Energy. Before that you spent five years in Caspia running the country's refinery and storage facilities. That experience is of very great interest to us. We need a man who understands how these industries work and is capable of running them. We also need a man who understands the politics of Caspia and who is sympathetic to President Kornilov's policies and objectives. Your name came to our attention for these reasons.'

'I am very flattered,' said Petrovna guardedly.

'I am sure you are,' Golitsin continued. 'As you know, most of the energy infrastructure in Caspia is severely dilapidated. It requires huge investment. Unfortunately the State of Caspia does not have the funds to do this at the moment, so President Kornilov is proposing that the entire State Energy Company be sold off to a private enterprise. That company will be in a better position to invest in and develop these assets. A potential bidding company has already been established. Let's call it Caspoil. Mr Gorky and I are both directors of it. The plan is that Caspoil uses finance provided by CBS to acquire the entire assets of the Caspian State Energy Company. However, we need a professional CEO who will manage the business on a day-to-day basis. This is where you come in Mr Petrovna.'

Petrovna stayed silent for a moment before replying. 'OK. It's a very interesting proposition and I am delighted you gentlemen have approached me but I have to tell you that I am just an engineer. I have no experience of business and no cash of my own to invest in an enterprise such as this.'

'We understand that Mr Petrovna. Me and the other directors of Caspoil will advise you on the company's commercial policy. Your job is to lend credibility to the company and manage the technical aspects of the business. In return you will of course receive a generous salary but more importantly you will be a part owner of the business. We are proposing that CBS will provide you with an interest free loan sufficient to buy a ten per cent stake in Caspoil'.

'And how much will that be?' asked Petrovna.

'We value the assets at 50m US dollars. This is the consideration we have provisionally agreed with the government of Caspia. The truth of the matter is that the assets are worth little in their present state and there are also outstanding debts. The accountants have agreed that under such circumstances the value of these assets is low. We, I mean CBS, would be prepared to lend you five million Dollars interest free as part of your package, so that you can acquire your stake.'

'And besides myself, who will be the other owners of Caspoil?'

Golitsin sat back in his chair smiling broadly, 'Various people including myself and Modest Gorky here but the majority owner will be a large foreign investor acting on behalf of a charity. Let's just say that President Kornilov holds this charity very close to his heart.'

Petrovna lent forward and stared intently at the non-disclosure agreement desperately trying to appear unfazed at the proposal.

'OK. Let's get this straight. The deal is that you give me a huge loan to buy a stake in a company that is just a fifty million dollar overdraft from an obscure Russian Bank. That company then buys up the entirety of the Caspian state petrochemical infrastructure which I am guessing currently makes a huge loss.'

Golitsin held up his hands in a gesture of surrender. 'Hey, you are getting the hang of this already. Consider this though. If the business were in great shape we couldn't afford to buy it and President Kornilov wouldn't need your help to run it would he? This is how fortunes are made.'

Golitsin had a point. It was a serious opportunity, just not a very salubrious one. And then there was the small matter that the rest of the company would be owned by a man he knew to be a psychotic thug.

It didn't take a detective to work out who was behind the so called charity.

'I need to think about it,' he said.

'No,' Replied Golitsin. 'You must give us your decision now. If you cannot decide this then you cannot run a business. I hope we have not…' Golitsin hesitated,'misjudged you.'

Petrovna paused again as a myriad of thoughts tumbled through his mind: his dreary apartment, the dreary office, the incessant craving. Craving what? Then he knew the answer and nodded his head.

'OK. I am interested in principal but what about my job at the ministry?'

'Don't worry about that,' replied Golitsin. 'Just resign in writing tomorrow. No one will make trouble for you. We have good friends at the ministry. I will start to draw up the various legal documents that you will need to sign. However, you must first travel down to Caspia to meet some very important people down there. President Kornilov takes a very great personal interest in this project. Modest and I will accompany you. We have transport at our disposal. Be ready to leave on Friday morning.'

Modest and Golitsin rose from their chairs, indicating that the meeting was over. 'I am sure you can find your way out,' Modest added.

As Petrovna stepped out into the raw darkness, he wondered what the hell he was letting himself in for.

CHAPTER 4

Present

Tanya always felt a slight thrill at airports. Perhaps it was the expectation of the journey or maybe just the buzz of humanity that emanates from a crowded terminal concourse. She had travelled many times within the United States but had only been abroad once and that was a drunken student jaunt to Cancun. Did that count? She had visited an Aztec pyramid one afternoon, so maybe it did. This was different. This was a business trip and it could make or break her career as a journalist.

The familiar sound of the aircraft engines roaring into full power announced that the flight was about to commence. The plane surged down the runway and soon the endless sprawl of the Chicago-Land suburbs were slipping away beneath her. She craned her neck peering out of the window until the windy city's skyscrapers finally slid out of sight. Now, how was she going to tackle Nicholas Petrovna?

She had built up a bulging dossier on her quarry. The question was how to pursue him further. Unsurprisingly her request for an interview with his New York Office had met with outright refusal. Plan B was to travel to

London and attempt to make contact with known associates in order to get more colour on the story. She had already established that his business history was somewhat unorthodox. Like many of his kind, he seemed to have accumulated his vast wealth virtually overnight without having added any unique dimension at all. Massive fortune, zero value add. How? And as for Petrovna being all buddied up with this odious Kornilov character, the whole thing stank of criminality and collusion. No one gets rich that fast without hurting someone somewhere.

The good news was that there was no shortage of damaging allegations against Caspia Energy Services or CES as it was now called in financial circles. These allegations revolved around accidents, environmental abuse and exploitation of the local populace. Basic stuff for sure but hopefully enough to goad him into making some kind of comment.

Failing that, she could go for one of his associates. When he had started out there where two business partners: Modest Gorky and Yevgeny Golitsin. They must have made fortunes too but weirdly they seemed to have no public profile. Maybe they were running things from the shadows. That could be a line worth pursuing. Meanwhile, there were still plenty of documents to go through. She had managed to access a fat dossier of research and press cuttings but thanks to her hasty departure hadn't finished ploughing through them. The last batch of papers now sat ominously on the seat back table in front of her. She decided to make a start before food arrived. The articles were mainly dry business stuff going over old territory. Mergers and acquisitions, when what she really needed was murders and executions. Weak copy for a journalist and certainly nothing new. Then, one story caught her eye. It had appeared in a Russian newspaper about ten years ago under the title 'Who is the new master of Caspia?' The Russian journalist who had penned it had explored the early life of Alexei Kornilov in far greater depth than anything she had read thus far. He had even interviewed some childhood acquaintances whose names were kept strictly anonymous. The article was lengthy but made for fascinating reading.

It started with Kornilov's childhood. Apparently he had been born a native of Caspia to parents of Russian ethnicity. They lived in Caspov where his father worked in a factory making heavy machinery for the Soviet military. According to the article, little else was known of his early years bar some unflattering anecdotes from classmates. The young Kornilov had been no angel. When he was thirteen, his father had been killed in a grisly industrial accident involving a vat of hot metal. Soon afterwards his mother became an alcoholic and Kornilov was removed to a Soviet orphanage. Two years later, she died too and not long after that Kornilov left to start his compulsory military service where once again, tales of his fearsome temper and menacing behaviour towards fellow conscripts abounded. So far, the whole sorry tale was reading like the script of a Discovery Channel documentary about serial killers. School bullying, torturing animals, beatings in a brutal orphanage. Not the makings of a well-balanced human being, Tanya pondered.

Kornilov had eventually been stationed on a Russian Navy vessel in the Caspian flotilla based at Astrakhan. According to the article, this is where Nicholas Petrovna came into the equation when the two of them first met. It was also where Petrovna had first contact with another crucial business associate, the mysterious Modest Gorky. That was almost the last reference of Petrovna until he cropped up again near the end of the piece, this time as Kornilov's appointee to run the Caspian oil industry. After Petrovna had disappeared back into the obscurity of civilian life, Kornilov had remained in the military, and this is when his ascendancy began in earnest. Once his mandatory service was over he had transferred back to the army. Already a petty officer, he soon graduated to full officer, which had apparently came as a surprise, due to his complete absence of any prior academic ability. However, he had already gained a reputation for physical prowess and a certain fearsome presence that was highly prized in martial circles. He was transferred to special-forces and by 1996 he had been posted to his first command as junior lieutenant leading a platoon in the first Chechen war. Here his trademark reputation for ruthlessness began to gain prominence. The playground bully was getting serious. His success in fighting the Chechen rebels earned him rapid promotion, Captain after a year and Major just two years after that. No sooner had the Chechen war ended, a new but more obscure conflict had erupted back in Caspia and Kornilov, a Caspian of Russian ancestry, was deemed the man to deal with it. So, at the tender age of twenty nine, the not so tender Alexei Kornilov found himself leading the Russian forces in a counter insurgency operation in Caspia. True to form, he did not let his superiors down. His customary mix of cunning and extreme brutality quickly crushed the Caspian rebels. There were countless tales of crimes and atrocities. He had gained a reputation for leading from the front when it came to dispensing merciless savagery. One nameless former soldier under his command described how Kornilov would take great pride in bayonetting prisoners to death in front of his own men. 'These are animals that deserve to be slain like beasts,' he had allegedly said to his troops as he had exhorted them to greater acts of ferocity. And they loved him for it. However ugly this man was, he did seem to command the loyalty of his men and the confidence of his betters.

With the insurgency decisively beaten, a new independent state of Caspia was established as part of the political settlement. Its ruler would be a certain President Bakov, who was in reality nothing more than a Russian placeman in what was in effect a totally compliant puppet regime that was in every sense in the thrall of the Kremlin. Kornilov's reward was to be appointed Colonel commanding the new 'Caspian Defence Force', a position he adopted with relish. It didn't take long for the newly minted President Bakov to upset his Russian masters by attempting to assert independence. Not long afterwards Bakov was killed in a helicopter crash whilst visiting one of Kornilov's military bases. The accident was blamed on poor maintenance, which was of course quite possible. However, the article implied that Kornilov might have had something to do with it. He was certainly the beneficiary of the accident because in the confusion following Bakov's death, Colonel Kornilov miraculously became President Kornilov of Caspia, leader of a government of national unity. A year later the Caspian national oil company Caspoil was privatised under the name of Caspian Energy Services or CES for short. And its first and only Chief Executive was none other than Nicholas Petrovna. The article described him as an astute but highly secretive businessman, a technocrat with a Midas touch who effectively ran the economy of Kornilov's rogue state. But it didn't say how. And as the story ended in 2002 when it was written, it threw no light on the history of either man over the decade that had elapsed since. Tanya made a mental note to contact the journalist who had written the article as soon as she arrived in London. This man, Oleg Borodin, must surely have more recent background that would be useful to her, she thought.

The meal service arrived so she shoved the papers into the seat pocket in front. 'Chicken or fish', the effete steward enquired as an overladen plastic tray was shoved in her face. Chicken sounded like the least bad option so she opted for that and made a token effort to consume the rubbery meat. After the debris was removed and the lights dimmed, she lapsed into as fitful a slumber as her hard narrow economy seat would allow.

Past

The sound of the aircraft engines changing woke Petrovna from his doze, momentarily disoriented by his surroundings. Then he realised he was on a plane. He looked across and saw that Golitsin had also fallen asleep too. After all, it had been a very early start. He had resigned from his job at the ministry the day after their meeting just like they had agreed. He had expected there to be more of a fuss. There wasn't. In the event his boss had responded with an air of casual indifference that had left him feeling strangely deflated.

His explanation that he was leaving to pursue an exciting new business opportunity was neither questioned nor challenged. His superior simply wished him luck and reminded him that he would have to be escorted from the building after he had cleared his office. Security protocols were tighter than ever these days.

It seemed strange after all those years as first a Soviet and then a Russian civil servant, to be so suddenly adrift on a sea of his own initiative. All the old certainties and routines had been cast aside with nothing but opportunity and risk in there place. The enormity of this situation had not fully sunk in yet. Instead he surveyed the lavish interior of the aircraft. His single piece of ugly luggage sat in front of him spoiling the luxurious scene. It contained just a few items of clothing, which were actually most of his meagre wardrobe. As it was, he felt horribly self-conscious sitting in the fancy plane in his very threadbare work suit. He tried to think about something else.

The car had picked him up from his apartment while it was still dark. They had driven to Sheremetyevo Airport but instead of going to the main terminal where the commercial flights departed they headed for a separate building some distance from the others. Here ground agents met him and checked his identification before leading him down a corridor into an aircraft hangar. A small single engine jet aircraft was parked there, which Petrovna had recognised as a 'Yak'. He was no stranger to the Yak, having flown in them on numerous occasions as a paying

passenger on Aeroflot. Being crammed into the grim confines of a soviet domestic flight had always been an ordeal.
The best outcome that could be expected from those hell-
ish trips was arriving in one piece.

The agents had ushered him towards the awaiting
aircraft. When he stepped inside, Modest and Golitsin
were already seated in the finely bedecked cabin and had
made themselves thoroughly at home. In the Soviet days
these planes had been used as small regional airliners but
this model had been refitted as a private jet with all the
trimmings. The décor consisted of heavily varnished dark
wood and thick white carpet that extended half way up the
cabin walls. A dozen cream leather armchairs lined each
side of the plane with a couple of matching sofas towards
the rear.

'How do you like Air Caspia?' Modest joked as
Petrovna had emerged through the cabin door. Petrovna
had to admit it was a serious upgrade from Aeroflot.

The plane was now well into its descent, and as it passed
through the ceiling of thick cloud, the familiar tapestry
of Caspia began to unfurl beyond the cabin window. The
bleak landscapes soon gave way to the stark 1950s apartment blocks that constituted much of the Caspian capital
city. As the aircraft banked steeply for its final approach, it
afforded an impressive view of the refinery and storage depots that Petrovna would soon be running again. A heavy
thud signalled that the journey was about to end.

They disembarked to leaden skies. It was still cold but
not as cold as Moscow. An antiquated Zill limousine that
seemed to have escaped the Brezhnev era was already waiting for them. The car sped off the tarmac and exited to the

airstrip through a side gate, which was already open. No sign of any officials or formalities.

'Now', said Modest. 'We meet the President.'

Petrovna suddenly felt a sharp pang of anxiety. Although he hadn't seen Kornilov since his days as an army conscript the thought of confronting this man still filled him with a strange sense of dread. Bitter memories flooded back. On his very first day on board the ship after training, Kornilov had appeared to smell his vulnerability in the way that dogs seem to smell fear. The motion of the vessel as it left port had made Petrovna seasick almost immediately. Kornilov, had pounced and summoned a gang of his fellow sailors to witness his predicament.

'Are you feeling sick, little boy?' he had jeered. He had then swung a low punch into Petrovna's stomach causing him to double up and vomit. 'Little boy sick,' he had cooed with ironic concern, much to the amusement of the crowd of jeering sailors who had gathered to watch his humiliation. Kornilov had forced him to the ground and then used his boot to grind Petrovna's face in the pool of sick he had just deposited. 'That's right, you clean that all up you filthy scum. You don't mess up this ship. You lick it all up or else you feel my boot in your face.'

Petrovna had made a pathetic attempt to comply with the instruction before Kornilov hauled him upright, laughing as he did so. He remembered the acrid taste of his own vomit, the mocking laughter and the overwhelming feeling of misery that accompanies a situation that cannot be escaped or controlled. In the end, he and Kornilov had reached a strange accommodation. They were both stationed in the engine room. Kornilov had struggled with some of the technical tasks. Petrovna had no such difficulty. This had won him Kornilov's protection of sorts in return for covering up for his inadequacies on duty.

'You help me out, maybe I won't hurt you too much,' as Kornilov had put it at the time. Now, in a manner of speaking, that arrangement was about to be repeated, only this time Kornilov was in a real position of authority, not just a two-bit martinet.

Kornilov's office was situated in what had been the old Soviet ministry. It still looked like the headquarters of a regional bureaucrat that had been hastily upgraded: because it was. Behind a large desk the flag of Caspia filled the space once occupied by the old Soviet hammer and sickle. The new flag was clearly not as large as the old because you could still see the faded outline of the predecessor on the paintwork. The office though large, looked tatty and makeshift with its faded carpet and 1970s fittings. The exception was an obviously brand new desk in the centre of the room. Though hardly lavish, it stuck out a bit. A lot more money had been spent on the Presidential jet than this office.

The man himself was seated at a conference table. He made straight for Petrovna, broke into a warm smile and grasped Petrovna's hand with that steel grip he remembered of old.

'Nicholas my friend, it's so good to see you after all these years. I am delighted you have agreed to come and assist us in this moment of great opportunity.'

'I am very honoured you have requested my assistance at all Mr President' Petrovna replied, not a little taken back by the veneer of politesse. Little had changed in Kornilov's appearance. His close cropped black hair had thinned and he had put on weight but his large thickset frame, flat face and gaunt skull like head were just as Petrovna remembered. The charm however, was not the Kornilov he remembered.

Then, the business of the day began with no further introductions. Kornilov explained that he needed someone he could trust to run the State Oil and Gas industries. He had asked Modest and Golitsin to approach Petrovna because he knew that Petrovna's previous experience in managing them made him extremely well qualified to do this. He also repeated the speech he had first heard in Moscow about how the assets needed to be sold because of Caspia's financial difficulties and that a private company would be better able to invest for the future. So far, it had all seemed surprisingly reasonable, professional almost, much better than Petrovna had been expecting.

'Now, we must formalise this arrangement,' Kornilov announced imperiously.

Golitsin slid a bundle of documents across the conference table along with an ostentatious gold pen. Although Petrovna knew perfectly well what these documents were, he had been afforded no opportunity to read them let alone have them scrutinised by lawyers. They could contain all manner of booby traps but it was too late for misgivings now that he was sitting in a dictator's office. The other three men looked on as Petrovna took several minutes to sign the various legal papers that authorised his authority to run the new business enterprise and borrow the money to take his investment stake. When he had signed the last set of documents Kornilov stood up beaming broadly.

'So gentlemen, now we are in business we must toast our success.' He pointed to a tray with a bottle of vodka and four glasses. Kornilov played mother and filled each to the brim with the chilled spirit.

'Comrades. To wealth and prosperity,' Kornilov intoned. They chinked the glasses and gulped the firewater down. Petrovna downed his in a single motion without flinching, as did the others.

'Now,' Kornilov said, 'you two gentlemen must leave Nicholas and me for a moment for a private discussion.'

Modest and Golitsin banged their glasses down and left without a word. Petrovna and Kornilov were alone.

'So little boy, you are the great engineer. Now I can make you the great businessman too. I like you. I do. That's why I called you here to do this job. Never forget, I remember when you were a snivelling little shit, puking and whining for his mummy on that boat. Now. You do like you are told and I will make you a rich little boy. But always you obey me and only me. Those monkeys Modest and Golitsin they obey me too. Never forget, I am the ruler here now in Caspia. All three of you, you do what I say, always.'

Kornilov paused and lent forward across the table so Petrovna could smell his acrid breath. His eyes were staring and a vein pulsed at the side of his thick neck, just as they always used to. The old Kornilov was still there.

'You fuck with me Petrovna, then I fuck you real bad. You want to fuck someone, you go fuck some pussy down the whorehouse on the docks. You try and fuck me, you get hurt. Do you understand little boy?'

Petrovna nodded. Kornilov sat back in his chair, placid again, the throbbing vein no longer visible.

'That is very good Nicholas. Now we understand each other you can go.'

CHAPTER 5

Past

A few hours later Kornilov rang Petrovna out of the blue at his hotel to suggest that they should celebrate the consummation of their newfound relationship with a trip to one of Caspov's premier nightspots. Petrovna was less than enthusiastic about the proposition.

'It's very kind of you to offer Mr President, but I am not really a party kind of person,' he said hesitantly. Calling Kornilov Mr President still felt totally weird.

'You're coming if I say you're coming,' Kornilov said menacingly. 'Be in the hotel lobby in one hour. I will come in my motorcade to pick you up.' Petrovna hastily freshened up. An hour later he was waiting in the lobby of the Grand Caspian as instructed. The motorcade arrived with a great fanfare half an hour later than billed. It consisted of three SUV's with blacked out windows complete with an escort of motorcycle outriders. The door of the last vehicle swung open and a hand beckoned him inside. Modest and Golitsin were sitting in the back dressed up like overweight Hollywood celebrities complete with ill-fitting designer gear that looked recently purchased. As they pulled away, Modest leant across and said 'Ready to party,' in a stupid voice. It was going to be a long night.

The top nightspot turned out to be a nightclub situated in the basement of the Eurasian Palace hotel. This was a Soviet era 1960s monstrosity that had recently had a splashy makeover. The 'Caspian Nights' lounge bar and disco-tech had become a serious magnet for what passed as 'the beautiful people' in Caspia. Kornilov climbed out of the first vehicle along with a second man Petrovna didn't recognise. He had a scrawny-weasel like appearance that Petrovna didn't much like the look of. The pair of them strode into the hotel surrounded by a haggle of dark suited minders. Petrovna and the others followed in their wake through the lobby and down a thickly carpeted stairwell into the well of the club. This was a large seating area with alcoves round the periphery. These were filled with shiny seated banquettes and wispy Arabic style drapes. Each alcove had a tiny crystal chandelier hanging inside it. A smaller dance floor was situated in the centre of the room with a huge twinkling glitter ball suspended overhead. It was already nearly 10 o'clock so the club was already half full with a small gaggle already dancing to a euro pop soundtrack.

A panic stricken manager intercepted the party and led them over to an unusually large alcove on the far side of the room. 'Please Mr President. Welcome to our VIP area' the club manager said, with a suitably fawning manner as he directed him towards the seating. Kornilov emitted a contemptuous grunt and parked himself in the middle of the main banquette.

'Champagne now,' he barked, then waved the manager away. Everyone sat down awkwardly and waited for the drinks to arrive. The entourage's arrival had attracted some attention from the other revellers who were now casting surreptitious glances in the direction of the presidential party. The champagne arrived and was poured by an ashen faced waiter with a none too steady hand. They started drinking. Kornilov knocked back several glasses of Champagne in quick succession while Petrovna started trying to make some small talk with Modest as best he could above the blaring pop din. For some reason the dance floor had now emptied.

'Who was the other man in Kornilov's car?' Petrovna asked.

'That's Sergei Romanov, the head of the internal security service. He's the guy that will have you killed if you piss off Kornilov. I am not joking' he said a second later.

Suddenly Kornilov was on his feet and striding towards the disc jockey's podium looking every inch the glamorous gangster that he was. He pushed the hapless DJ out of the way and grabbed his microphone. The euro pop anthem ground to a halt.

'What's wrong with you fucking people? Your president comes here for a celebration with important guests and you all stand around talking in corners. This is Capsia. Show us how Caspians like to party. Get on that fucking dance floor now,' he rasped. The room went horribly quiet and no one moved.

'I said now,' he screamed. Then he pulled a revolver out from the pocket of his Armani jacket, took careful aim at the glitter ball and squeezed the trigger. There was an ear-splitting retort as the garish globe exploded, showering the dance floor with crystalline fragments. Then there was screaming as people scattered to the edges of the room. A few people craned their necks to see where the bullet had lodged in the ceiling. The rest just stared at the pistol toting President of Caspia as he surveyed the scene from the DJ's podium. Then he cocked his head back and laughed. A few of the stunned revellers laughed nervously back.

'You see, I even give you fireworks,' he said. He turned to the DJ. 'Now play some tunes you stupid monkey.' The music started and a few hardy souls ventured nervously back to the centre of the room, sweeping aside the shards of shattered glitter ball with their feet. 'That's how you get a party started,' he muttered as he returned to the banquette.

Kornilov sat down next to Petrovna and spread himself out. 'Look at those little rats dance,' he said, waving his hand in the direction of the debris strewn dance floor. The reluctant dancers were the kind of crowd you might expect at a joint like this: youthful twenty somethings. The men were suited and girls short skirted. No one was wearing jeans. 'Look at them all, boys pretending to be men, with their little slut girlfriends. Half of them are only here because their rich daddies paid me to let them off their military service. None of them would have survived their first day in the Chechnya, would they little boy?' he said turning to Petrovna.

'No they wouldn't,' he replied and gulped down some more of the Champagne.

'You realise I can have any one of these women don't you?' he said.

'I am sure you could. Who could resist the charms of the President of Caspia,' Petrovna replied, hoping to lighten the atmosphere.

'Don't fuck with me Petrovna, I am serious,' he snarled. 'If you like, I can let you have one too.'

'Oh, I don't think I will thank you. I am bit tired,' he said.

The DJ was back on the PA system. 'OK, were gonna start cranking it up now. Let's party for the President,' he whooped inanely. The volume soared unpleasantly higher and Kornilov grinned.

'I am going to screw that girl right there,' he said pointing to a statuesque brunette on the fringes of the disco.

Petrovna cleared his throat. 'I think she might be with someone already.' Kornilov grunted dismissively and beckoned a couple of his security guys over. They were soon heading in the woman's direction. Petrovna watched as they accosted Kornoilov's intended date. The security men muscled in and some kind of conversation ensued. Although he was some distance away, the body language said it all. Her dance partner, presumably her boyfriend, was becoming quite agitated judging by his hand gestures. That did him no good at all. Moments later, two men were dragging him out of the room while a third shoved him roughly in the back. Then the girl was marched over to the VIP area where Kornilov rose to his feet to greet her.

He was surprisingly solicitous from what Petrovna could hear of the exchange.

'My dear, you are very beautiful, truly a jewel of Caspia,' he heard him say. Then he kissed her on the wrist, bade her be seated next to him on the banquette and poured her a glass of the Champagne. She wasn't saying much and he could see that each time she picked up her glass, her little hand was shaking. As soon as she had finished, Kornilov downed what was left of his drink and got up to leave. The girl and the rest of the entourage all followed. Everyone stopped dancing for a moment to watch the Presidential group depart. As she left the girl turned and Petrovna caught her gaze. It was a look of wide eyed terror.

Now, only Modest and Petrovna remained in the VIP area.

He turned to Modest. 'I am going to get out of here.'

'Suit yourself,' he said. 'I am going stay here and get totally shit faced.'

'In that case, I will bid you goodnight,' Petrovna said primly. He left through a side exit that went straight back to the street. Once outside, he set about looking for a taxi. Caspov wasn't a good place for a late night walk but he saw what looked like a couple of taxis waiting a bit further down near the main hotel reception. As he was walking towards them he heard a groan. He looked for the source of the noise and saw a man lying in a pool of blood next to a fire exit. It was the ill fated woman's boy friend. The man twitched and groaned again, clearly in need of medical assistance. Petrovna wondered if he should phone for help or at least tell the hotel reception. Then he thought better of it and just carried on walking towards the taxis.

———

The days following the first audience with Kornilov had passed rapidly. The morning after his night out he went straight to the company HQ. He was already more than familiar with the building having toiled there for so many years previously. It felt strange walking into the all too mundane surroundings after a period of absence. It was somehow smaller than he remembered it. The whole outfit smelt of neglect. It probably always had. He passed his old office, which was situated at the end of a long and particularly dreary corridor at the rear of the building. His original desk was still there but the room had been turned into a kind of storage space and most of the floor was now taken up with boxes and files. He continued his journey accompanied by two flunkies. One of them said nothing and seemed wholly superfluous, probably a Kornilov stooge. The other had introduced himself as the senior engineer who explained that he had been drafted in after Petrovna's departure. He didn't look too happy either. Eventually they reached the director's office, which was more sumptuous in so far as anything Soviet ever could be. The desk had been cleared but unlike his old room this office was still functional.

'What happened to my predecessor?' Petrovna said. The horrified look on the engineer's face told him everything he needed to know.

'He had to leave,' the senior engineer replied in a tone indicating that further questions on this subject were inadvisable. Then he started a little speech. 'I just want to say how much I am looking forward to working with an experienced professional like yourself. Your reputation from your time here is very strong.'

Petrovna lifted his hands to cut him short. He seemed like a decent guy but Petrovna wasn't in the mood for sycophancy right now. 'I appreciate your kind words but there is much to do. First, I need you to bring me all the financial accounts for the last three years and a complete record of all the operational documents over the same period.'

'What, all of them? That's a lot of records Sir,' the engineer said.

'Yes. It is a lot of records and I do need all of them. I want to find out exactly what has been going on here. I need them as soon as possible. Please.' He added hurriedly.

Once the men had both gone he set to work. He already had a sheaf of legal and financial documents. He had only skimmed them very briefly and they were barely scratching what was bound to be a very dirty surface. He made a start on the legal papers. These were routine documents covering the formation of the new company Caspoil and its acquisition of the old Caspian State Energy Corporation. The remaining papers concerned his loan from the obscure Siberian Bank and the purchase of his own shares. Finally there were some Caspoil board minutes ratifying his appointment as the new Chief Executive. Petrovna noted that the meeting appointing him had already taken place prior to his formal acceptance.

As he ploughed on he was interrupted only briefly by the return of the senior engineer bearing the first sheaf of the additional documents he had requested. He hovered next to Petrovna's desk expectantly. Closer inspection suggested that the man was probably an ethnic Caspian, which was a rarity in the higher echelons of the old republics. Petrovna made a mental note to be a little more emollient with him in future. He would need every ally he could get from now on. He returned to his studies with renewed vigour.

As the evening wore on the picture became increasingly clear. The legal framework around Caspoil was solid enough as far as he could deduce given that he had no legal training. The financial aspects of the deal were more curious. Although he was no more a financier than he was a lawyer, his background in mathematics and training as an engineer gave him a reasonable grasp of financial concepts. From this he could understand the basic thrust of the financial arrangements and what immediately struck him was that the purchase price of $50m seemed suspiciously low.

The accountants who had prepared the company for sale had depreciated the value of the bulk of the company's fixed assets to zero. In other words they were effectively saying that most of the plant and machinery in the pumping and refining facilities was useless. Although Petrovna had not had the chance to tour his new empire yet, he knew this had to be nonsense. For sure the Soviet kit was ancient and probably in a poor state of repair. It certainly wasn't state of the art. However, it should last for another five maybe even ten years before it was literally useless. He slumped back in his chair resignedly. Whatever this company was really worth, ten per cent of it was nominally his. There were just a couple of provisos. Ten per cent of nothing was still nothing and whatever happened he must remain friends with Kornilov. With that awkward thought in his head he decided to call it a night.

He slept badly in his new bed. Kornilov had laid on a suite at the Hotel Grand Caspian. It was one of those early twentieth century 'grand hotels' but the bed felt like it was from the nineteenth century. Stumbling out of it the next morning, he pulled back the heavy but slightly thread bare curtains to let the early light stream in. He sat back on the bed for a moment wondering what the hell he was going to do next. Suddenly he felt his chest tighten as a tendril of nausea's dread wound its way from the pit of his stomach. He gulped several deep breaths and then dashed to the bathroom where he stood under the freezing shower in the cracked marble bathroom that would once have been elegant. Feeling calmer, he dried off and gathered his composure. Best to keep busy. Get a grip on things straight away, he thought. A tour of all the main facilities, yes that was it. Meet the key people. Maybe he would know some of them from old. It would also give him the opportunity to inspect the state of the physical plant and machinery. He would see for himself just how good a condition it really was in and whether the accountant's assessment was correct. Yes, that was definitely the best way to proceed.

He spent the morning back in the office making the arrangements and then set off to view Caspoil's facilities. As the car weaved its path to the Caspov dock side, he flicked through some more of the papers that the engineer had given him last night. They concerned the company's unexplored oil and gas assets. He had always been aware that the company had rights over the outlying areas of the great 'Shallow Water Guneshli' oil field, but had no idea whether this was of any real commercial value. The field was largely situated in the waters of Azerbaijan but the much smaller end section fell into the domain of Caspia. The papers revealed the results of various seismic studies of the geology of the field that had been carried out some years earlier when Caspov had still been part of the Soviet Union. Although he had been working for the company at the time it had been in far too junior a capacity to have any involvement in that side of things. These studies seemed to suggest that there was indeed a large quantity of oil or at least gas in the area but that it had not been economic to drill. Apparently the cost would have been too high and therefore not worth the risk given the prevailing oil prices back then.

Besides which, the company had lacked the resources to mount a major oil exploration project out at sea. Capital had been scare back then, unless of course, your proposition happened to be a pet project of the Kremlin. Petrovna sighed, yet another problem to be dealt with. Then another thought crossed his mind. He had just received his first copy of the Wall Street Journal that morning and he had read an article about the strongly resurgent gas price. He had never concerned himself with all that finance stuff when he worked at the ministry. Now he had to. The oil price in that morning's paper was probably much higher than when those old Soviet studies had concluded that it wasn't worth drilling any more fields. That really was interesting.

There was a small delegation waiting as he arrived at the first facility, a storage depot. Some faces in the assemblage looked vaguely familiar but none belonged to people he really knew. The site manager stepped forward and formally introduced himself. Petrovna donned a set of drab overalls and hard helmet before proceeding to tour the works. As far as he could see, very little had changed since he had last been there. The basic machinery and equipment were the same as they had always been and were noticeably ageing. Many of the pipes and storage silos bore the scars of patches and repairs. This was pretty much what Petrovna had been expecting to see, very old kit but still functioning. Not worth much to anyone else, let alone an accountant but still fit for purpose. That was good.

The second site was only a few minutes' drive away and promised to be more interesting. This facility was Caspoil's largest refinery. It was where the oil from Caspia's small existing oil reserves were received and then distilled into gasoline, jet fuel and its various other constituent parts. Even though the refinery was aged, it cut a thrilling profile with its soaring towers and teeming jungle of gleaming pipes and tubes.

To the casual observer this profusion of seemingly random metal work might have seemed like an unfathomable monstrosity but to Petrovna its muscular intricacies were a thing of beauty. The manager of this site was not so beautiful. He had a brutish face that looked like it had been flattened with the back of a spade. Another ethnic Caspian, Petrovna observed with a pang of distaste.

'Welcome to our humble facility' the manager intoned whilst folding his arms tightly in front of his chest. 'I think you will see that everything here is in excellent order.'

They took another short tour of the refinery which involved driving up and down between the distillation columns and towers. Like the previous site, the machinery was more than showing its age. Several pipes looked as though they were coming loose and in one case as if it might just drop off. At the far end of the site a gang of workers were attempting some makeshift repairs. They were huddled round a pile of welding equipment discussing something intently. Petrovna made a mental note to find out what, later. His entourage continued until eventually they arrived back at the control centre. This was essentially a concrete bunker. This was situated underneath an ageing stone farmhouse that had obviously been engulfed by the refinery complex. Inside the building, a steep flight of stairs led down to the control room, which was guarded by two sets of sturdy airlock style doors. Once within the confines of the dimly lit room Petrovna reacquainted himself with the once familiar surroundings. Nothing much had changed here either. The rows of control panels studded with gauges and various warning lights were just as they had always been, as were the antiquated computer screens displaying performance data from the refinery. He counted about half a dozen overall clad staff in the room. Most were hunched over the control panels.

In one corner of the room stood a ramshackle exercise bike. It looked distinctly incongruous standing there in a room with all these pieces of technology. The faint aroma of body odour seemed to seep from the very pores of the bunker.

The site manager held court in the centre of it all.

'As you can see Mr Petrovna, we have been operating a highly efficient installation at this plant. We are all professionals here. I don't think you will find it necessary to have any involvement in what we do on a day to day basis. Best you let us experts get on with our jobs,' the manager said.

Petrovna pretended to ignore the reference to experts. In any case, he was by no means entirely satisfied with everything he had just been told.

'Run me through how often you test your safety procedures,' he said.

'Regularly,' the manager snapped back.

'How regularly?'

The manger hesitated momentarily ' A couple of times err…'.

'A month,' Petrovna held out the palms of his hands as if it were a real question.

'Two or three times a year.' The manager was avoiding Petrovna's eye. Petrovna was smelling blood.

'I am not happy with this situation. I would like to see you perform a pressure test safety procedure. Now.'

The manager's shovel flattened face was now black with rage.

'Right now?

'Yes right now. Is there a problem? Is it not safe to even conduct the test?'

'Yes of course it's safe,' he said. Then he shouted some instructions at his subordinates who began the testing procedure. One of them hesitated and pointed at a bank of CCTV monitors. Petrovna could make out some people moving around outside.

'Yes I can see them. Just get on with it,' shovel face shouted. The man shrugged his shoulders and obeyed. Lights on one of the control panels started to flash and an angry warning buzzer blared. More buttons and leavers were punched and yanked until eventually the buzzer fell silent.

'You see,' said the manager smiling thinly, his voice now back in smug mode. 'The procedure is perfectly adequate just as I told you. If the pressure builds in one of the towers the warning sounds and we assess the situation. Then, if necessary, we make a safe controlled discharge of the excess gas to relieve the pressure. This is what my colleague has just done. We have everything under control.'

'Fine. Now I want to see all the safety log books for the past year.'

The manager sighed loudly and skulked off to a tiny office in the corner to fetch them. 'Here you are Sir,' he hissed. 'I think you will find sir, that these are in perfectly good order too Sir. Is there anything else you want to see Sir?'

'Thank you,' replied Petrovna, snapping the logbook shut after only a cursory examination. 'That will be all for the time being,' he said as he headed for the heavy portals that formed the exit.

As he crossed to the other side of the room he felt it in his ears first, a strange popping sensation. Then, there was an almighty thunder crack and he felt himself flung backwards as the two great doors in front of him tried to swing off their hinges. He managed to put out his hands to break the fall. Now, he was on the floor, stunned and gasping for breath from air already thick with smoky dust. He managed to sit up, choking and wheezing as he did so. Then, as his breath and his composure slowly returned he surveyed the hazy control room. The manager and a couple of his colleagues were slowly rising to their feet. Petrovna used the nearest control panel to haul himself up. The panels were now a riot of flashing red and an alarm bell was ringing incessantly. Everybody was coughing but other than that, they all seemed to be OK. The manager leant against the exercise bike panting heavily like a dog.

'What in the name of hell was that?' Petrovna screamed. The manager ignored him and carried on panting.

'There is a major problem,' one of the other men said.

'I can see that. What have you just done?' The manager stopped panting and stood properly upright too.

'We just did the test like you told us. Now there is an explosion and fire,' he deadpanned, glaring at Petrovna. Above them the bank of CCTV screens told their own story. Several had blank screens. Others showed a large part of the refinery now engulfed in a raging inferno. Several bodies were visible, burning vigorously. Petrovna felt a bolus of rage well up inside him.

'Don't you act dumb with me. You did this. This place is not safe and now you have caused an accident. If it wasn't safe to conduct the test you should have said. President Kornilov will be informed of your incompetence.'

The manager blanched. 'No Sir. You can't do this to me. You come here from Moscow and you try and tell us what to do. Then you blame us when this happens.'

'That's enough from you. Enough. Now manage this situation like you are supposed to. There are people dead and burning up there.'

An awkward silence descended as they waited in the bunker until the fire services arrived and got the blaze under control. Given the fires up top, it was safer than venturing out when the risk of secondary explosions persisted. Eventually, when they could see the worst of the flames were quenched, they emerged shaken and chastened into the encroaching darkness.

The evening sky was blackened by a volcanic plume of ebony smoke rising from a still roaring blaze a quarter of a mile in the distance. The gutted towers of the refinery now a disfigured silhouette against the fiery twilight. The stench of hot metal, burnt carbon and charred flesh permeated the atmosphere. The smell of failure, Petrovna thought as he forlornly retreated to his ash dusted vehicle. There was nothing else he could do here. With a heavy heart he allowed himself to be driven away.

CHAPTER 6

Present

Tanya had been in London a week now and she had already figured out that getting an interview with Nicholas Petrovna wasn't going to be easy. She guessed he was never going to just roll over and she was damn right. With her polite interview requests rejected it was time to aim below the belt. Dig up some filth. Everyone's got a skeleton somewhere. All she had to do was find his and threaten him with a hatchet job if he wouldn't talk. Then after he had cooperated, she would simply dish the dirt on him anyway. Bastards like him didn't deserve fair play.

Her enquiries began in London's Russian community. These soon revealed the existence of an uber expensive town house in Mayfair. Not a surprise. No address yet either but he was bound to show his face at some point she thought. Meanwhile she had visited various upscale bars and restaurants that Russia's wealthy expatriates were known to frequent. This involved chatting to the bar staff in the hope that they had served Petrovna or anyone who knew of him. This approach had proved to be as fruitless as it was expensive. Fending off the repeated approaches from men who seemed to think that any beautiful woman drinking alone must be a prostitute had also proved tedious. She had even tried flirting with some of the more handsome barmen and then leaving her business card with them, so that they could contact her if they got wind of any useful information. This succeeded in garnering numerous romantic proposals but absolutely no useful information. She packed that in pretty sharpish when the suggestions became indecent. Slowly her budget and her patience began to wear thin. She couldn't stay in London forever at her company's expense. She needed a break and fast.

Then it came. She had just finished breakfast and was replying to some emails in her room when the mobile rang. The caller ID was blocked. She took it anyway. When she answered, the voice at the end of the line had a thick Russian accent. 'Is that Tanya?' it said.

'Who is this? Where did you get this number?' she said.

'You have been putting your name around. I am the person you have been looking for,' the voice said.

'What do you mean?' she said guardedly, thinking he could be just another creep.

'I hear you are asking about Petrovna.'

'Yes, yes. Do you know him?' she said, her voice inflecting a bit more than she would have preferred.

'Yes I know him. Used to know him. What is it that you want?'

'I am a journalist. I am trying to write an article about him. He is very secretive. I just want to talk to people who can give me information about his background and history, that kind of thing. Could you help?'

'Oh yes. I can tell you some things. Lots of things, but we must take great care. There could be danger for both of us if certain people discovered we had been talking. When you play with men like Petrovna you play with fire. You do know that don't you?'

Tanya's pulse quickened. 'Who are you and how do we meet?' she said.

'Be outside the entrance of Goodge Street tube station at midday. I will be in a grey Volvo. Just get in. You can call me Peter. Just Peter.' The line went dead.

Two hours later, Tanya was standing outside the tube station as instructed. Dressed in boot cut jeans and a red sweater she looked inconspicuous to the passing pedestrians on Tottenham Court Road. This is dangerous, fucking dangerous, she thought. This Peter guy could be anybody. He could be some pervert or a nutter. Getting into his car to go god knows where was extremely risky. Nonetheless, it was a risk she was going to take. She stared intently at the traffic waiting for the Volvo to appear. Midday came and went. She checked the time on her phone nervously. Five past. Still no sign but the lunchtime traffic was heavy. Seven minutes past. Maybe the whole thing was a wind up. Then, a Volvo sidled up. The lock on the passenger door clicked open.

She opened the door and stuck her head in first. 'Peter?' she said. He nodded and pointed to the empty passenger seat. She hesitated for a moment. It was risky, stupidly risky. Then she got in. Neither spoke as they drove north along the edge of Regents Park towards St John's Wood. She noticed that every minute or so he glanced at his rear view mirror. Soon, the white stuccoed villas changed to red brick Victorian mansion blocks. They parked and walked the last hundred yards to a small terraced house down a side street. It had a tiny security camera positioned above the front door.

He led her into a compact sitting room that oozed the rancid scent of neglect and cigarettes. She sat down and took in her surroundings. With its pockmarked wallpaper and stained carpet, the room looked as stale as it smelt. There was a whole load of Russian memorabilia littered about the place. Miniature icons, military medals, photographs and ornaments hung from the walls.

Peter himself was in no better shape than his house. It was hard to age him exactly. She put him in his late fifties but he could have been much younger. His paunch belly and a ruddy complexion confirmed he drank way too much. Most striking of all was the patch over his right eye.

'Would you like some tea' he said politely. His left eye lingered on her a little longer than was strictly necessary.

She accepted and a few minutes later he reappeared with a pot and two cups along with some cakes. The cakes looked as though they had been hanging around longer than the sofa so she decided to give those a miss and instead produced a small tape recorder from her handbag. Peter shook his head.

'No recordings. I told you we have to be careful' he said. She reluctantly put the device away and watched his hand shake as he poured the tea.

'What shall I call you? Do you have a second name?' she said.

'Just call me Peter. That's what I call myself now. No second names.' Peter's English was laboured and she wondered whether they should switch to Russian but then thought better of it. Her fluency maybe wasn't quite what she had claimed back home. This would be hard work.

'Now' said Tanya. 'What can you tell me about Nicholas Petrovna?'

'Ah, Nicholas, little boy Nicholas. That's what we used to call him. We first met during our military service. Everyone had to do that in the Soviet Union. He was a typical conscript. Not as young as the others but still soft and naïve as hell. His types were like lambs to the slaughter during basic training. It wasn't just the military discipline. All the young guys got the hell knocked out of them. I was a natural soldier but even I found it tough. Someone like Nicholas was just a prime victim for the likes of Kornilov.' He paused momentarily and looked at Tanya. 'I suppose you know all about Kornilov?'

'Only a bit. I would love to know more,' she said.

'Well, Kornilov was a young non-commissioned officer in the navy. Nicholas and I were both stationed on his boat. Kornilov smelt weakness like a dog smells fear. To begin with it was pitiful to watch. He denigrated and terrorised Nicholas during his every waking hour. Then something strange happened. There seemed to be some kind of accommodation between the two of them. I never understood it really. Nicholas was clever, very clever. We could all see that. Maybe Kornilov found that interesting in some way or just useful. From then on he became a kind of protector, although Nicholas was still frightened of him and did his bidding. It was weird but these things happen.'

'So were you and Nicholas actually friends then?'

'Yes, of sorts. Not close ones though. I lost touch with him for a long while after he left the military. Then we met again when the Caspoil venture started. It was Kornilov's idea getting him involved in the project. Kornilov desperately needed a technocrat he could trust to run that oil business he was about to seize. He needed someone who knew exactly what he was doing but who would also be completely compliant, someone who was totally competent but not a threat. Nicholas was the perfect combination of technical brilliance and subservience. My job was to contact him and set the whole thing up along with another guy, Golitsin. He was the original moneyman, a lawyer by training. So that was how Caspoil, CES, whatever you want to call it started. I helped found a multi-national company and look at me now.'

His voice rose in pitch, betraying more than a hint of self-pity. He lifted himself out of his chair and reached across for a bottle of vodka on the adjacent shelf. He tipped some into his teacup and took a swig. The shot of vodka seemed to have a calming effect.

'To begin with everything went brilliantly. I could hardly believe my luck. One minute I am a burnt out intelligence officer at the end of his career. The next thing I know, Kornilov has seized power in Caspia and is offering me the deal of a lifetime. I am not going to shit you that any of us thought it was clean. Coups never are. Not in the Soviet Union and especially not if they involve men like Kornilov. We all knew he must have engineered his predecessor's death. Not difficult when Russian aircraft are involved. But who were we to play saints? So the three of us play along with the plan. Kornilov sells off all the Caspian State oil assets to himself using a bogus charity as a front. Then Nicholas, Golitsin and me, run CES for him. Nicholas is the respectable front man, Golitsin does the finance and I do the messy stuff that makes it work. We all make a shit load of money and secretly Kornilov makes even more.'

'But how exactly did you make so much money? I mean Caspoil was just a run down state gas company, with busted Soviet kit. So how does that become a multi billion dollar business?'

'Quite easily. Especially if you buy it off a corrupt government for far less than it was really worth. We paid $50 million for it. For sure the kit was busted but it was worth a lot more than that. And actually, Petrovna did a good job. As I said, we got him involved because he was a qualified engineer who knew the business. We just wanted him to run the operations and do what he was told. Kornilov told us he was shy and would make no trouble and he was right. Of course, things got off to a bad start with the accident but once he got over that, he also turned out to be a great businessman. The Ramberger deal was just the beginning.'

'You mean Ramberger as in the US multinational?' she said.

'Of course. Who else?' Peter snapped.' 'That deal totally re-valued CES financially and gave him the credibility and the firepower to do more acquisitions. So he did.

Local at first, mainly small oil companies in Azerbaijan and Georgia but then he started to do more stuff in the United States. Not just oil either. Property too. And his timing was brilliant. He just seemed to have the knack of always buying the right business at the right price.'

'OK. So what you are saying is that Petrovna turned out to be a great businessman but actually the whole thing started as an accounting fraud?'

Peter looked pained. 'Yes. That is correct. We robbed the Caspian people. I am not proud. Not proud at all. But it is all gone now anyway.'

'Tell me more about that accident' Tanya said. ` I am really focused on investigating the track record of CES on environmental and ethical issues but I am like struggling to get beyond the corporate propaganda. I know there was a massive fatal accident at a CES refinery just after Petrovna took over but I can't find many details. I have seen a couple of single paragraph articles in Russian newspapers but that's it. I want to get to the bottom of what happened and whose fault it was. Was Petrovna personally negligent? Have there been other safety incidents? That kind of thing.'

'There's not a great deal I can tell you as I wasn't there myself. Nicholas had only been in charge a few days. He was visiting the various sites including the main waterfront refinery just outside Caspov. They were conducting some kind of test when the explosion happened. Nicholas told me they messed up the test and released a cloud of gas into the air instead of just simulating it. I think a welder's spark ignited the gas triggering a huge explosion. It destroyed half the refinery. Killed about a dozen people. Most of them were just vaporised by the explosion right where they stood. Others survived but were so badly burned they died later. It was a bad business. Nicholas was unhurt but we all thought he was finished. We feared Kornilov might kill him for screwing up. That's what he is like. But he didn't. I guess he must have had a soft spot for Petrovna. Anyway, the whole business was hushed up pretty well. One local newspaper was going to print a big article but the editor soon changed his mind after Kornilov sent a few of his men round to have a little talk with him. Nothing ever appeared. I guess Kornilov's emissaries must have been very persuasive. After that, things just got better and better. The price of gas started to soar. Nicholas started a drilling program in the offshore field. We found huge new reserves out there, oil and gas. Much bigger than we had hoped. And the best bit was, the higher oil prices went the richer we all got. We didn't have to do a goddamn thing. All we had to do was sit back and watch the value of CES go through the roof. First it was a few hundred million Dollars, then a billion then ten billion. We all had decent stakes back then. Of course, Kornilov had the controlling interest, then Nicholas had the second largest but Golitsin and I had enough to make great fortunes. Then like all thieves, we quarrelled over the spoils and that's when I had my little disagreement with Kornilov.'

'Is that how you got that' said Tanya, pointing rudely towards the eye patch. He nodded.

'I can't tell you exactly what happened. If I did, they will know it is me that has been talking to you. That would be bad news for the both of us.'

'Who exactly are they?' she said.

'People think that because the Cold War is over there are no agents left anymore. That's not true. Kornilov has people in London and Moscow. They even do the Kremlin's dirty work when an arm's length operation is needed. If they find out I have been talking to a journalist they might send a mercader for me and you.'

'What is a mercader?' Tanya blurted. Peter looked at her as though she was an idiot.

'You have haven't done a story quite like this before have you?'

She blushed.

'A mercador is an assassin.'

'Why are you telling me all this then, if it's dangerous?'

'I am telling you, miss, because I want someone to know the truth about Kornilov and Nicholas and what they did to me. What they took from me. I used to be rich like them. And now. Well just look and see for yourself.' He held out his hands in an expansive gesture and then pointed at his disfigured face.

'Kornilov is just a gangster and Petrovna is no better than his whore. Now I must sit here in this dump, cowering like a mongrel dog, drinking this cheap poison,' he said pointing to the half empty bottle.

'And what can you tell me about Kornilov?' said Tanya.

'Not so much. I never got as close to him as Nicholas. You don't get close to someone like Kornilov. I know he was an ethnic Russian born in Caspia. He came from a very humble family. I think both his parents were dead. I don't remember him ever speaking about them. The military was his family. We all thought he would rise through the ranks but we would never have guessed he would become a political figure. He was brutal and frightening but too crude to ever go right to the top, so we thought. We were wrong,' he said wistfully.

Tanya racked her brain for more questions but could think of none of any substance.

'Is there anything else you could tell me or anyone else I should be talking to?' she said.

'No. I have told you more than enough. Remember, Nicholas owes everything to Kornilov and wherever Kornilov goes, he leaves blood and pain. If you look hard enough you will find it. Just beware, Miss, that Kornilov doesn't find out that you are looking. And if you ever print your story, you keep my name out of it.'

He lapsed into a sullen silence and stared at his china cup. Tanya sensed that the interview was at an end and announced that she would see herself out. No way was she getting back into his car after all that vodka.

She managed to find her way back to the hotel without too much trouble. She now had quite a bit on Petrovna, but it suddenly occurred to her that she had never got round to looking up the journalist who had written the Kornilov article from the flight over. She shuffled through her papers until she found it. The article had been in a paper called the Moscow Sentinel. She had no idea whether he would still be working there after so many years, so she decided to Google his name first. Oleg Borodin only threw up a few search results and they were all unrelated articles he had written for other Russian journals. Then she noticed one small article that was not written by him but about him. It was titled JOURNALIST STABBED TO DEATH IN RANDOM ATTACK. It had appeared in August 2002, just a few months after the original Kornilov piece had been published. Apparently, Borodin had been killed by knife wielding robbers on a Moscow street. Some money was missing. No one had been arrested. For the first time in her life, Tanya felt a tiny twinge of fear.

CHAPTER 7

Past

He knew the call would come at some point. It was just a matter of when. After he had left the refinery, he spent the rest of the evening in the office making frantic phone calls to various officials in an effort to contain the crisis. The emergency services in Caspia were as run down as one of his oil plants so it had taken a while to coordinate a proper response to the disaster. Even though the first fire crew to arrive had subdued the primary blaze, it was still a dangerous situation.

Eventually, when he had concluded that he could do no more, Petrovna retreated to his hotel to wait for the fateful summons. The fear had come again just like he knew it would. That vice like sensation that engulfs the brain like a kind of sickness that cannot just be vomited away. He paced up and down his faded chambers incessantly until exhaustion got the better of him.

After only an hour or so of the strangest dreams the phone finally rang. Petrovna awoke instantly and snatched the receiver off the hook knocking the bedside lamp to the floor in the process. It was almost a relief when he heard the distinctive gravel snarl at the other end of the line.

'I give you a chance little boy. I give you the only break you have ever had and then after three days. Three fucking days you fuck up. You fucking idiot. Fucking piece of shit. Give me one reason I shouldn't send someone round to blow your tiny fucking brains out right now?'

'I can fix this,' he stammered. 'The refinery was a death trap. The manager was a completely incompetent. He had no idea what he was doing. I was going to sack him anyway but he managed to totally screw up first.'

'So you are blaming the manager' Kornilov sneered.

'Well yes,' said Petrovna. 'But I know exactly how to fix all this. There is some insurance. I can put all this right, I just need more time. I'm sorry. Give me another chance. Please.' There was an agonising silence.

'You sort this out right now. There is no need to sack the manager, I will have him dealt with. Understand this. If you fuck up like this again, I will cut your fucking balls off and feed them to my dogs'

Then he hung up. Any pang of sympathy for the refinery manager who was about to be 'dealt with' was more than tempered by the knowledge that it could have been him.

———

Kornilov himself had enjoyed making that phone call. Inflicting human misery had always been a pleasurable pastime of his. It had almost been worth having the misadventure at the refinery just so that he could have fun tormenting his old victim again. After all, Caspoil's equipment was a load of old junk. Replacing it at some foreign insurance syndicate's expense was no bad thing. As to the men who had died - who cared? Men's deaths had never bothered him before so why should they trouble him now? Besides which, the evening was still young and his playing with Petrovna had only been the aperitif. The entree was yet to come.

Kornilov rang for his car before reaching into his presidential desk drawer. He extracted two items: some aftershave, which he applied rather primly and a small wooden box that he slid into his trouser pocket.

When he arrived at his security HQ, he went straight to the soundproof basement chamber where the guards stood to attention on his arrival.

'Has this piece of shit said anything yet' Kornilov asked a man in military fatigues who looked to be in charge.

'No President. Nothing we didn't know already. His whole outfit were amateurs. They didn't even have a lookout posted. We could have killed the lot of them in no time but we knew you would want us to take this one alive. We warmed him up a bit first though,' he said, grinning.

The unfortunate man in question was stripped to the waist and tied to a steel framed chair that was bolted to the floor. His left eye was already badly swollen and his broken nose had bled profusely down his chest. Kornilov walked up and pretended to survey the man like an artist.

'I see you have been trying to make friends with people round here. Looks like you managed to piss them off instead. You look, shall we say, a bit shit. You should take more care of yourself.'

The rebel commander glared at Kornilov and spat out a bloody globule in his general direction. Kornilov looked at the spit and shook his head sadly.

'I am not even going to waste time trying to pretend we want any information off you. We have already got enough to clean away the rest of your scum. No, I just wanted to come down here to see you myself. Spend some quality time. Get some feedback,' he continued, saying the feedback bit in a fake American accent. The man cracked an awkward smile.

Kornilov let out a peel of raucous laughter. The captive rebel and the guards joined in nervously.

'So you think this is funny yeah?'

The man went silent again.

'You think its funny plotting to kill me? Yeah, really fucking funny. You know, you and I could have been part-ners. Friends even. But instead you try and overthrow my government. Real nice.'

Then Kornilov reached into his pocket, removed the small wooden case and casually flicked it open as one might a box of cuff links. He revealed the knuckle duster and slow-ly toyed with it in his hand so the insurgent could see it.

'So what was your fucking problem? Don't you like taking orders off a Russian? Or was it just that you don't like taking orders off me? Which was it?' The vein on the side of his neck was pumping frantically as he consciously worked his rage into a crescendo.

The man still said nothing.

'Oh, you going to be silent hero now are you. First you laugh at me then you go all quite. Let's see if you think this is funny.'

He slid the knuckleduster into position and shoved his metal clad hand right up against his victims face. The man flinched back with fear. Then Kornilov withdrew his hand.

'Not such a big hero now then,' he said.

The man exhaled.

'Do you really think I am going to waste my time beating the living crap out of you? Me? The President of the Republic of Caspia? I pay people to do that sort of thing for me,' he said, waving towards his henchmen.

The man let out another nervous laugh.

Kornilov nodded inanely and laughed too. Then he suddenly stopped.

'But this is different. This is for fun.'

The knuckle duster tore through the air and caught the man square on his already broken nose. Then the screaming started as blow after blow shredded the skin off his face until it was quite unrecognisable as that of a human being.

CHAPTER 8

Past

In the months after the accident Petrovna had busied himself ensuring that there was no repeat of that day's events in any of the other facilities. Kornilov had been right about the insurance. One of the few things the last manager of Caspoil had got right was taking a policy in Moscow that was underwritten by Lloyds of London. It was the first time he had heard of this institution but he was very glad the expensive policy was in place. The cash pay-out would help rebuild and repair some of the old kit, which quite apart from being dangerous was also extremely inefficient.

Meanwhile, the price of gas had been steadily rising. This created an opportunity. The oil field in the Caspian Sea that had not been worth drilling suddenly was, and just as importantly, other companies were starting to take an interest in CES.

Golitsin rang Petrovna one day sounding excited.

'Hey. Good news I am hearing that a US company wants to do a joint venture with us on the new Caspian field. It's not official yet but you should definitely look at it when they approach you.'

'Who is it exactly?'

'It's Ramberger. I suppose you have heard of them?'

'Yes, yes. Of course I have heard of them. They're massive' Petrovna snapped.

'OK, good. Look, they want to get involved with Russia. The details are all subject to negotiation but they basically want to give us a load of US dollars to invest in the Caspian field in return for a stake in the joint venture. CES and Ramberger share the profits,' Golitsin said.

'Why have they come to us though? If they want to get involved in Russia then why don't they go to one of the big Russian companies?'

'They have come to us Nicholas because they know we are an easy lay. Let's face it we need external capital if we want to develop that Caspian field properly. We need their money and they know it. Anyway, Caspia is warmer than Siberia.'

A few weeks later Petrovna found himself in Ramberger's headquarters flanked by Golitsin and a retinue of lawyers. They had insisted that he come to Houston in person to sign the final joint-venture contract. He had readily agreed. Never having left the old Soviet Union before, he was curious to see what America was really like. He had once watched some old video recordings of Dallas that had been dubbed into Russian and wondered if Texas would be like that in real life.

When he had arrived at the Ramberger Tower, he wasn't disappointed. Their offices were situated in one of Houston's tallest skyscrapers. He had been whisked straight to the company's boardroom at the very top of the building. He had tried not to look too impressed by the view or the sumptuous leather swivel chairs round the table. The CEO of Ramberger was about the size of a walrus. Petrovna now knew why the leather chairs were as big as they were. It was to accommodate the fat Americans who sat in them. Until quite recently it had been rare to see anyone that large in Russia. It seemed that the old Soviet propaganda had been right about fat capitalists.

It had taken weeks to thrash out the final deal. The precise terms the fat Texan was offering were a quarter of a billion dollars in cash for half of any revenues from the new field in the Shallow Water Caspian block. This valued just the new block at half a billion dollars.

After the last document was signed the Ramberger CEO said 'So, Mr Petrovna, what does it feel like to be a capitalist now?'

Once the interpreter had translated he replied 'it's just like being a communist but with more money.'

This amused the Texans greatly.

'I think he's blowing smoke up our arses' the CEO replied to general jubilation of his fellow executives.

As they were flying home Golitsin turned to Petrovna and said 'You do realise that the money Ramberger is paying us for just half the revenues of the offshore implies that CES as a whole must be worth at least one billion US dollars. That means your stake alone is worth a hundred million dollars and myself and Modest's fifty million apiece. As for Kornilov's action through the charity, he's gotta love us now.'

Petrovna responded with his customary silence. Golitsin's observation sounded unreal. Since he had taken over Caspoil he had been so wrapped up sorting out the accident and trying to turn the company round that he had given no thought to his own financial interest.

'Hey. Modest has just bought a dacha right outside Moscow. He's having a party this weekend, a house warming I suppose. I am going myself. Why don't you come up and join us? We can all celebrate the deal and you can get yourself out of Caspov for a change,' Golitsin said.

Generally speaking, Petrovna was not a fan of parties. He had always found them tedious hard work. Mindless small talk with strangers and drunken bores were not his idea of a good time. However, he decided on this occasion to make an exception. He had business in St Petersburg on Monday morning anyway. There was no harm in going back to Moscow a couple of days early. Golitsin might be right. Maybe it would be fun. After all, there was always a first time for everything.

He regretted his decision almost immediately on arrival at Modest's new residence. The dacha was about twenty miles north of Moscow and it had taken a good hour to drive there from Petrovna's old apartment that he still used. The long slog through the Saturday evening traffic more or less guaranteed his bad mood by journey's end. Traffic never used to be a problem in Moscow, but it was becoming one now. The price of progress he thought. When he did finally arrive, he had to admit that the dacha looked genuinely impressive. He had guessed that it wouldn't be the little wooden holiday house like the one he had spent summers in as a child. He wasn't expecting anything on this scale though. It was more akin to an old Tsarist palace at Tsarskoye Selo than a traditional dacha. The place was effectively a huge mansion built in the style of the nineteenth century. Faux classical trimmings included as standard. The frontage was decorated to resemble a Greek temple complete with Doric columns. The rest of it was more traditional. Elaborately painted window frames were complimented by onion shaped domes atop each end of the building, just to give it that authentic Russian look. These were painted bright blue, which added to the general air of ostentatious vulgarity that the building was emanating. A bit like its new owner in some respects, Petrovna thought.

As he got out of his car, it was very clear that the party was already in full swing. The reception lobby was already packed with a curious collection of people, none of whom Petrovna recognised. A uniformed server was holding a tray of champagne for the convenience of new arrivals. He grabbed a glass and started to fight his way through the throng in search of Modest, Golitsin or anyone else he knew. As he headed in the general direction of some loud rock music, he was already trying to formulate an exit strategy from this ghastly jamboree. His instincts about the awfulness of the party were already being vindicated. He passed through several lavishly appointed rooms before locating Modest in a kind of games room. There was a drinks bar at one end, a large billiard table in the centre and various well-padded red sofas around the edge. Modest was reclined like a roman emperor on one of the sofas. There were two very young women perched at either end, one of which was busy feeding him some champagne. They both dripped with expensive looking designer gear. Modest sat up and rudely pushed the girl aside when he caught sight of Petrovna.

'Nicholas,' he exclaimed, holding out his arms and grinning from ear to ear. 'How good of you to join us. Goltisin told me he had invited you but I didn't think you would turn up.' Both the girls burst into giggles for no apparent reason.

Petrovna mumbled something about not wanting to appear anti-social. Modest was obviously preoccupied with the girls so he decided to try and circulate. He tried chatting to a few people. It really was hard work. Most guests were a bit drunk already. The men all seemed to be in business of some description. The women just seemed to be pointless but very expensively dressed.

After half an hour of banal tipsy conversation the idea of the early exit strategy became more and more attractive. He decided to look for Golitsin. He found him in the conservatory at the back of the dacha. It had looked like it had been added on as an appendage and contained as its centrepiece, a sunken pool area. The piped music had been turned up loud and the pool contained several women in a state of undress splashing about in the water. A couple of the girls were indulging in a slightly contrived Sapphic display. A group of male admirers had gathered at the poolside as the water nymphs kissed and fondled one another's glistening breasts. As the pawing escalated to kissing, cheers of approval emanated from the onlookers who could not conceal their delight at the free show unfolding before their eyes.

Golitsin waved Petrovna over to join him on the other side of the pool. Like Modest, he also appeared to be in the not so early stages of inebriation.

'How do you like the party?' he said. 'Modest's got a pretty impressive place here hasn't he? Fit for a Tsar, no less. You need to get a place like this yourself. I am, so you can definitely afford it after that Ramberger deal you just pulled off. Can't have you skulking around that old apartment of yours. It's bad for the corporate image.'

Petrovna started to say that he hadn't had time to think about that sort of stuff when two of the girls emerged from the pool and appeared at Golitsin's side. They were both dripping with water that left their soaking underwear clinging to their bodies in an eye-catching fashion. Even Petrovna felt the first prickle of lust. Golitsin shamelessly ogled the alluring sight and put his arm round both women's wet shoulders. They both managed big white smiles.

'This' he said directing his gaze to Petrovna, 'is one of the richest men in Russia.' The girls cooed admiringly while Petrovna looked straight ahead. Then Modest appeared as well, right on cue with his own female entourage.

'Hey. I see you are a hit with these lovely ladies' he said as he pointed his fingers at Petrovna whilst making a pistol firing gesture. The two pool girls abandoned Golitsin and draped themselves over Petrovna instead. He tried to remain impassive as he felt the damp from their dripping limbs seep through the fabric of his jacket.

Then, out of his own gaggle of groupies, Modest ushered forward a very tall brunette in towering heels.

'Svetlana. This is the guy I was telling you about. He's a real serious player.' Golitsin nodded earnestly as if to endorse Modest's comment. 'A few of us are going to have a little private party amongst ourselves. I would hate for you two to miss out. Why don't you give him a tour of the upstairs rooms? He's a bit quiet but I am sure you will help him come out of his shell,' Modest said.

The pool girls let go of the rigid Petrovna. Svetlana attached herself to him in their place.

Modest slapped him on the back. 'Relax,' he said. 'You are making everyone nervous.' Then he leant into Petrovna's ear. 'Don't worry, all the girls have already been paid for.'

Svetlana led Petrovna away, still clinging to his arm, her varnished talons biting a little deeper than he would have liked. She escorted him back into the main building and up the sweeping staircase to the upper level where a long corridor stretched into the two wings of the dacha. Various doors adjoined it. They proceeded down one of the wings trying each door in sequence. Petrovna could see that many of the rooms were as yet unfurnished. There was still a hint of damp paint in the air. Most of the other rooms were already occupied by couples who were 'partying in private'. Eventually, they found a room that was furnished but unoccupied. Svetlana practically pushed him inside and closed the door behind her. The room was elegantly decorated. However, the windows were not as yet curtained. There was a large unmade bed in the centre and two Louis XIV style chairs still wrapped in sealed plastic.

'You really are shy aren't you,' she said, pulling him down to sit next to her. She reached into her designer hand bag and produced a dainty little hand mirror and a small metal case, which she proceeded to open. It contained a miniature steel tube, a kind of metal ruler and some pellet size pieces of screwed up paper. Petrovna watched mesmerised as her delicate fingers with their painted nails unscrewed a little paper pouch and emptied its white powder contents onto the mirror's surface. He had heard about this sort of thing on news reports about the decadent West but this was the first time he had encountered it in the flesh. She meticulously arranged the substance in a thin line on the glass and then drew the mirror close to her nose. Closing one nostril with a finger she snorted the powder up the steel tube into the second nostril in a swift deft movement. When she started to reach for a second pouch Petrovna grabbed her hand and shook his head.

'No problem baby,' she simpered. 'Just lie back and let me relax you.' Petrovna felt his trousers being unzipped. At that moment the door swung open revealing another couple in a clinch. The man grunted an apology and retreated, closing the door behind him. Svetlana's hand was now caressing his member in a gentle stroking motion.

He sat tense as he began to feel himself slowly harden within her grasp. She paused to remove her top and then her bra, exposing her small but beautifully proportioned breasts. The sight of them held him transfixed as she began tearing open a condom packet with her teeth. It took her a minute because she kept pausing to push her cascading hair back behind her neck. Then, he felt himself being sucked between her shiny pouting lips. Moments later he was succumbing to the pleasure of her warm wet mouth.

Then it was all over and she was zipping him up. A business card was being offered.

'You like that, you call me again. I can see you in private next time,' she said. Petrovna politely took the card then secreted it hastily into his jacket pocket.

'Thank you,' he said lamely. 'I must go.' He rushed out of the room without looking back and headed down the corridor towards the stairs. He noticed all the doors were now shut and a backlog of would be occupants had formed on the stairs. He attracted a few odd looks as he barged his way out of the bacchanalia. Once outside he stopped for a moment to gulp down the cool night air before returning to his car.

Later, back at the sanity of his apartment, he turned on the television to distract himself from the evening's events. It was the news. There was little of interest to report other than that a new head of the 'Federal Security Bureau' intelligence agency had been appointed. Some guy he had never heard of called Putin. Presumably he was an old KGB apparatchik. He wondered if Modest had ever had dealings with him. Soon the news was boring him so he got up, turned the set off and shuffled into the bedroom. The smell of damp was getting worse. Perhaps Golitsin had a point about the apartment after all.

CHAPTER 9

Present

It hadn't been difficult for Tanya to find her way home after her meeting with Peter. It was a mystery to her why he had bothered with the petty subterfuge of driving round the neighbourhood in the first place. She presumed it was just force of habit. One thing was for sure; he was certainly frightened of someone.

The good news was that there was now sufficient material to start writing a serious piece of critical journalism. Precisely the kind of article, in fact, that would put the shit up someone as secretive as Petrovna. These guys loathed publicity about their business activities, especially if it was revealing uncomfortable truths.

It was getting dark as she set to work on her laptop. Her hotel room wasn't very large and had a magnificent view of a back yard. She drew the curtains, threw herself on the bed and started to type. It proved easy enough to get the basic story down about the opportunistic engineer who exploits his contacts to build a business empire. Then she had the story about the accident at the refinery and how the deaths were hushed up. She sat up and read back through the article. It was alright but maybe wasn't quite enough. It just wasn't the great scandal she had sold them in that New York board room. She needed more and to be certain of bouncing Petrovna into an interview she needed a much bigger smoking gun, but what?

Then she started to think about all the questions she should have asked the mysterious Peter but hadn't. She sat there and let him tell her what he wanted her to know without really quizzing him properly. He got off lightly. Sure, he had claimed that was all he could tell her but he was bound to know more. She kicked herself for not pushing him a lot harder while she had the chance. She really needed another go at him. That could be difficult. She didn't have his number.

However, all was not lost. She did know where he lived and it hadn't escaped her notice how he had been looking at her. How difficult could it be to use that to extract far more detailed information out of a drink sodden lech like him? And if all else failed she could resort to threats. He seemed pretty hyper about secrecy. That could be another useful lever. She resolved to give him a day to stew while she worked on the other leads. Then she would pay him another visit.

She decided that a trip to the hotel gym might help her formulate new questions. She had been on the treadmill for a good ten minutes when her phone rang. She caught it in time. It was a caller-withheld number again. That looked promising.

'Yes' she gasped, still slightly out of breath from the treadmill.

'Who is that?' said a voice she didn't recognise.

'This number has been called by you,' they said. Tanya hesitated for a moment while she caught her breath.

'I am sorry, who is this? I don't know what you mean.' The other voice spoke slowly and deliberately.

'I am Detective Sergeant Paul Ingles from the Metropolitan Police. There has been a serious incident involving the individual who owns this phone. We need to speak with you very urgently. You may be a witness to a crime. Please identify who you are and where you are so that myself and another officer can come and talk to you.'

Tanya wondered whether she should just kill the call right away. It could be anyone on the other end of the line. Maybe Petrovna, or worse, Kornilov had realised that she was on their case and had decided to send someone round to have a 'chat' with her too. Then she decided that it was probably OK. The man sounded English and if they really were police, it should be obvious when they came to the hotel.

'OK,' she said, ' I am staying at the Penta in West Kensington but I am going to need to see some ID when you get here.' Ingles assured her that he would bring some and told her to stay in her room until he arrived.

———

Past

Kornilov angrily threw the pile of papers aside. He had tried to read them but found the detail overwhelming. Detail wasn't his strong point. He saw himself as a leader and a man of action not a pen pusher. Pretending to be a head of state was surprisingly hard work. Making decisions and getting, or in his case, forcing people to do what he wanted was the easy part. Appearing credible in public and dealing with diplomats and the like was much harder. It was one thing to intimidate a subordinate into carrying out his instructions but it was another thing entirely to make a foreign ambassador bend to his will. Tact and persuasion were required. Skills that Kornilov found challenging. He could lay on the charm for a few minutes, beyond that it was a strain.

Ever since he had seized power the gnawing ache of insecurity had been growing more insistent. Every rumour, every murmur of the mildest criticism suddenly assumed the status of mortal threat. Now he was hearing that some of his own guys were ripping him off. Kornilov had no issues with corruption as such. In fact he was a great personal advocate of it. What he didn't like was the idea of his lieutenants going behind his back to do deals that he was not cut in on. In his opinion, once they felt at liberty to do that, it was a short leap to betraying him personally. Corruption was one thing but betrayal was another matter entirely.

The papers he had been looking through concerned all the contracts that had been struck in the past year between foreign companies and the government of Caspia. Unsurprisingly, most of them related to the oil industry and a few were with the government itself. These were mostly for defence and armaments. As far as he could make out, there was no problem with those.

The foreign defence companies had dealt with him more or less directly and he had already received very generous 'extra contractual payments' from those companies that were already safely ensconced in his Swiss bank accounts. That side of things was all in good order. Oil contracts were a different matter. Various agreements were being struck all the time so it would be much easier for someone to cut him out of the equation and enrich themselves instead. If there was any problem at all, it was going to be with Petrovna's outfit. He had hoped the papers would clear things up but instead they had simply made his head spin. He picked up his phone and called for his head of security.

The man appeared after twenty minutes or so, the time it took to trek over from his security HQ a short distance away. He was a weasel faced individual about the same age as Kornilov but with a slighter build. His one distinguishing feature was not physical though. He was perhaps the only man in Kornilov's entourage who was even more sadistic than he was. Crucially, he lacked Kornilov's raw charisma. Although it seemed counter intuitive to have appointed a head of intelligence who was, not to put too fine a point on it, not too intelligent, in a situation like this it made perfect sense. Kornilov already had an animal instinct of where the threats lay and he knew only too well how to eliminate them. Indeed he enjoyed that aspect of his position almost more than any other, but he needed someone to do the grunt work for him. Sergei Romanov, his head of security, was easily cruel enough to instil fear in others but in Kornilov's opinion not quite cunning enough to pose a threat to his own supremacy. Kornilov cut straight to the point.

'Some fucker's robbing me,' he said.

'What do you mean? Has something been stolen?'

'No. Someone's skimming cash on contracts without my permission. Taking commission and arrangement fees without cutting me in. I don't know who it is but I have narrowed it down to Petrovna's lot. I want you to start a surveillance operation on all the CES directors. I want this stamped out. You understand?'

The security chief nodded his weasel head. 'Does that include Petrovna too?'

'Yes. Especially Petrovna. Bug them and have them all followed. Here and in Moscow. Especially Moscow. If those fuckers are freelancing then that's where they will doing it.'

As Romanov opened the office door to leave, Kornilov called after him. 'Sergei, my friend. I am surprised that you didn't inform me about this problem yourself. Do not fail me on this. You wouldn't want me thinking you have been involved would you?'

'I will find them, don't you worry,' he said as a chill ran through him. He needed results on this. Fast results. A sacrificial lamb might be required.

CHAPTER 10

Past

Petrovna hadn't felt too good the morning after the party. It wasn't a hangover because he had barely drunk anything at all. The events of the evening culminating in the incident with the girl had left him with a sour aftertaste at the back of his palate. This vague sense of uncleanliness had lingered for the rest of the day no matter how hard he tried to efface it from his mind. However, it was slowly beginning to dawn upon him that his situation had changed or at the very least his financial situation.

Petrovna was no fool. In fact he had already developed a very keen sense of business intuition. As a gifted mathematician he understood the arithmetic of the Ramberger deal and how it impacted the CES valuation. He also realised that given the ownership structure and the success of the business as a whole he must be making some really serious money. It's just that what with all the wheeling and dealing and the usual nonsense with Kornilov, he hadn't got round to counting how much exactly.

In the following days he set about rectifying this knowledge gap. First he visited a lawyer, then an accountant.

Then, he started to get some answers that seemed almost fantastical but perfectly plausible.

The accountant was far more excited about the situation than he was. Petrovna had sent him some selected papers about CES and Caspoil in advance of the meeting. When he arrived at the accountant's Moscow office the moneyman burst into the reception area and shook Petrovna's hand effusively as if he were an old acquaintance. Petrovna retrieved his poor hand and returned a watery smile. He gave the man some more background and repeated what the lawyer had told him the previous day about the legal situation regarding the CES stake. The lean faced accountant had lent forward earnestly to give his verdict.

'Well Mr Petrovna, your true financial position is very much dependent on what CES is worth. That is not my area of expertise but having reviewed all the information I would say that based on current oil prices and the value Ramberger paid for the joint venture, your stake in CES should be worth at least one hundred million dollars. In any event you are a rich man Sir. A very rich man,' he said, as if to make certain that Petrovna had taken the point on board.

'These situations are always complicated. Your lawyer has already explained that your ownership is sound in Russian law but with all the assets in...' He had paused as a pained expression had spread across his face, like a doctor about to break some bad news to a patient, '...an unstable political area like Caspia. That makes it more problematic. If you wanted to realise the whole stake now, you would need to sell or float the company on the stock market. That's a job for a banker or a corporate financier not an accountant like me. I can help you with your two main problems. Your first is Caspia. The second is that you are asset rich, cash poor. Your salary is decent but you only have a modest balance at the bank and no other equity investments outside of CES. No government bonds, no property, no equities. In fact you have nothing outside of Caspia at all, let alone Russia.'

He paused again as if for even more dramatic effect. 'What you need to do is monetise some of your stake without selling it and you need to diversify your interests outside of Russia. I know people in London, Zurich and New York who can help you with that.' he said, ending on a slightly triumphant note, presumably pleased that he had not only diagnosed the disease but also offered the cure.

'One thing you could do right away though is to use your authority to pay a dividend to all the shareholders including yourself. That would give you some cash. Once they can see some cash flow, there are plenty of banks that would lend you more cash against your CES stake. Then you can diversify outside Russia. It's easy. Just use your authority. I can help you with the details.'

And so it was that Petrovna made the beautiful discovery that wealth begets more wealth. Like entering a chamber with many adjoining doors, the emergence of riches leads to the proffering of yet more riches or in this case, offers to lend money that would not have otherwise been forthcoming. When he had no money, no one would have been willing to lend him a single rouble but now he had at least ten maybe even hundreds of millions of dollars to his name, suddenly everyone would apparently be keen to lend him a whole lot more. That seemed perverse. On the other hand, the idea of laying hands on some hard cash suddenly seemed very appealing. The whole set up with Kornilov left him with a feeling of deep unease. That little arrangement could turn sour at any time. Diversifying his business interests and acquiring some foreign properties he could use as a bolthole if things got ugly. Actually, it made good sense. The kind of cash the accountant had been talking about could easily buy him apartments in New York and London whilst leaving him enough for a serious pad in Moscow. As he returned to his shabby old Moscow apartment, his mind was already pondering more handsome abodes.

———

Present

The story had already made the rolling news channels by the time Tanya had got back to her hotel. They weren't giving many details. They just said that a man of eastern European origin had been shot dead at the door of his home and that police were considering various theories and appealing for witnesses. There was some boring footage of police officers standing outside Peter's house while a crowding of ghouls gawped from behind a flimsy yellow crime scene cordon. The film report did not give the victim's name.

The meeting with police had turned out to be surprisingly mundane. She had waited nervously in her room for the police to arrive, carefully checking the spy-hole on the door before removing the safety chain and opening it.

There were two officers, a woman, who was uniformed and a man who was not. That was still no guarantee of her safety. Abductions by people impersonating police or military were not unheard of. Once inside, the plainclothes officer introduced himself as Sergeant Ingles and presented his warrant card just for good measure. Tanya's room was not huge. The Penta wasn't the Ritz and the budget sure as hell didn't stretch to a suite. Tanya sat in the room's only easy chair. 'Take a seat I suppose' she said pointing to an office chair wedged under a tiny writing desk with a tea and coffee tray on top. He wheeled it out and sat down, the uniformed WPC hovered awkwardly in the far corner.

Ingles produced a notebook and started to write something without looking up. 'Thank you for agreeing to see us at short notice Ms Georgievna. I daresay this has all come as a bit of a surprise to you.'

'Totally' she said. 'It's all kind of scary. Can you explain what is going on here?'

'Yes of course. Your phone number was discovered on the mobile of a man who was shot dead yesterday so I am going to be asking you some questions about how and why you were talking to him, what you know about him and what if anything you know about his death.'

'OK. But am I a suspect here? Do I need a lawyer?'

'No. At this point you are just a witness. You are not being interviewed under caution. That's why we are talking to you here. We just want to hear what you know in case it is relevant. Let's start with how you know Modest Gorky.'

'Modest Gorky' Tanya exclaimed. 'Is that the person I was talking to? He just called himself Peter, no surname.'

'Correct. Modest Gorky was found shot dead outside his home and your mobile number was on his phone. Maybe you should start from the beginning. I know you are a journalist. We need to know everything you know.'

'Well yes, you are right. I am a journalist working for several IMC media publications based in Chicago. I recently arrived in London to investigate a story about a Russian businessman named Nicholas Petrovna. I have been trying to interview known associates of his. A man called Peter called me and said he was prepared to talk so I arranged to meet him. He picked me up in his car and took me to an address somewhere in North London. He was like, really secretive about it, but I think it was actually near your Regent's Park. We had a long conversation about Nicholas Petrovna and his business dealings. It was interesting but he didn't say anything that helpful to my main story. I tried to call him back to arrange another meeting. Then you called back instead and the next thing I know the killing is all over the news channels.'

'So let's get this straight. You didn't know this Peter guy was Modest Gorky?' Ingles said.

'No, I had no idea. I know of Modest Gorky because he was one of Nicholas Petrovna's early business partners. I didn't realise that Peter was he, and if I had, I would have asked him a whole lot more questions. I guess it's too late now,' she said with a sigh.

'Fine. Obvious question. Do you have any idea who would want to kill Modest Gorky?'

'Not exactly. He seemed really scared though, even when he was talking to me. Scared and angry. No disrespect officer, but he was hiding from an oppressive regime with known gangster connections. He told me he had lost his eye after some kind of business dispute. He didn't want to give me details so I guess he was tortured or something. I have no idea who shot him but its feels like he had a lot of enemies who might have wanted him silenced.'

Ingles nodded. 'Yes. We will be investigating that line of enquiry and also the Russian mafia angle. Is there anything else you can tell me?'

'No. I can't think of anything. I am just like totally stunned by this whole thing you know.'

'Yes. I am sure you are' he said looking almost cheerful. He spent a while longer going through some details about dates and times. When he was through he stood up to leave. 'If you do think of anything else, anything at all, however trivial, then please contact us immediately.'

The WPC headed for the door and Ingles followed. Then he stopped on the threshold, looked back and said 'We are grateful for your assistance Madam, but if you are continuing your own investigations, please be very careful how you proceed. A man is dead. These are dangerous people involved. You need to consider your own safety and whether it might be better to return to Chicago. That might be sensible, just let us know first so we can keep in touch. We may need to speak to you again. It's important we know where to find you. Please give that some thought. If you do feel threatened at any point, call us straight away.'

'We will see ourselves out,' the lady officer chipped in as they left.

She mulled these words after the hotel door had clicked shut. She knew she hadn't been quite as forthcoming as she could have been. Obviously she suspected that this was something to do with Kornilov but the truth of the matter was that she didn't have the slightest piece of hard evidence to support this. Furthermore, coming up with a madcap theory that the police would then begin to investigate could actually cut right across her own investigation. No, she thought, it was better to say nothing beyond the facts she had already provided them with. If they believed she was just some naive American journalist who had bumbled into a Russian mafia killing then that suited her purposes just fine. It was disappointing that she had not managed to elicit more information out of the interview. However, she did at least now have Peter's real name which would give her an extra angle to confront Petrovna with. No way was she going back to Chicago now.

CHAPTER 11

Past

Petrovna had a bad feeling about the dinner from the very outset. The Republic of Caspia was not exactly renowned for its pomp and circumstance but even a two bit Head of State like Kornilov had to engage in occasional diplomatic niceties. These usually took the form of visitations by representatives from Moscow and the odd dignitary from neighbouring countries. On other occasions there might be delegations of foreign businessmen hoping to get a piece of the action. Caspia was far too small to warrant a full ambassador from most countries. However, they would often send a trade attaché or a chargé d'affaires to accompany the executives instead.

It was on such an occasion as this that Petrovna found himself seated round a formal dining table in the new Presidential compound. The room resembled a function suite in a five star hotel. It was plush but entirely formulaic. You could be anywhere. At the head of the table sat Kornilov sporting a Savile Row suit he had had made up especially for these occasions. He also wore a Presidential sash styled in the colours of the Caspian National flag: black and green. Petrovna thought it made him look vaguely comical but had absolutely no intention whatsoever of telling him that.

The other guests were mainly American businessmen who might be interested in investing in the country. Kornilov had greeted them warmly on their arrival taking the trouble to shake each one by the hand and welcome them to Caspia. They were being chaperoned by a US trade attaché who had been sent down from Moscow especially for that purpose. Petrovna was seated next to him. So far so good he thought. He had the ear of the main man and Kornilov seemed to be on his best behaviour. He was almost invariably drafted in on these occasions to play the role of business supremo, and seeing as the puppet finance minister spoke no English, unofficial economic spokesman. His own English had come on nicely since the Ramberger deal and he was now quite proficient. Kornilov spoke only very limited English, not that he had much small talk anyway so Petrovna usually ended up holding the evening together socially even though he was hardly the gregarious type. Nonetheless, the President still loved to preside with an interpreter at anything formal.

Petrovna glanced around the table looking for Modest and Golitsin. They usually got invited to this sort of event too. Tonight for whatever reason there was no sign of either of them. He suspected that they had made an excuse so that they could stay in Moscow and party. Those two seemed to specialise in having a good time recently and who could blame them.

This dinner was different in that it had been instigated at Petrovna's suggestion. He was regretting that already. Several of the Yanks were noticeably wincing at

Kornilov's atrocious table manners. He had a nasty habit of shovelling food into his mouth as if he were still in a Russian army canteen. His infrequent contributions to the general discussion were often made with a mouth full of food. It wasn't a pretty sight for anyone. The conversation, such as there was, hinged around what a wonderful new opportunity the Caspian oil industry presented and how those assembled would love to be involved with the project. That had always been the object of having the dinner in the first place. By the time the main course had arrived, the whole exercise was beginning to feel worse than pointless. Kornilov's behaviour wasn't soothing anyone's nerves, quite the opposite in fact and as the evening wore on Petrovna found it harder and harder to keep the conversation going. Even the American trade attaché was proving to be an effort. Petrovna was mindful that these men were often intelligence operatives so he needed to be on his guard. Even seemingly innocent questions could be a CIA fishing exercise and the last thing he wanted to do was say anything indiscreet within earshot of Kornilov.

Then, Kornilov's masque of charm suddenly started slipping. The body language wasn't good, he was draining his wine glass with indecent frequency and Petrovna noticed him taking deep breaths while clenching and unclenching his fists as they rested on the tablecloth. Every now and again he would sit bolt upright in his seat for no apparent reason. Petrovna had seen the jerky body movements before. They were bad news, and to make matters worse, the guests were starting to notice them too.

Petrovna decided it would be a good time to give his usual speech about the wonderful prospects for the Caspian oil industry. The President obviously wasn't going to say anything and the evening desperately needed to move on fast before Kornilov got really weird. But no sooner had he risen to speak, when without warning, Kornilov rose abruptly from his own chair and made a rude hand signal to the effect that Petrovna should sit back down. Kornilov spoke very slowly in Russian. The interpreter started to translate.

'Petrovna here was going to bore you all shitless about the Caspian oil industry' he said in Russian with a noticeably drunken slur. A couple of the businessmen tittered politely. The deadpan translation just made things worse.

'But he didn't build the modern Caspia. The city you saw when you drove here from your hotel, Caspov. I built that. Nicholas here.' He pointed dismissively at Petrovna down the table. 'Nicholas Petrovna. Little boy we used to call him in the navy. When I first met this man he was a conscript on my ship. A snivelling little creep. Couldn't even keep his food down. Threw up all over my deck on his first day at sea. I told him to get down on his knees and lick up his own vomit. And do you know what he did when I told him to eat his own puke?'

By now, the Americans were concentrating intently on their napkins. Anywhere was preferable to looking at Petrovna or worse, catching Kornilov's evil eye.

'He got down and ate his own puke. Nicholas Petrovna, the great businessman, ate his own puke because I told him to. Now, I am a reasonable man, so I let him run the country's oil business. He's good at it now because I gave him that chance. Now he is rich because of me and if even he can make a fortune, then so can you. So I say to you, invest in Caspia. I can make you rich too. But none of you forget, when you invest in Caspia, you are always dealing with me.'

He sat down to a glacial silence. The American attache tried to style the moment out by starting some applause that drew only half hearted support. Kornilov just stared down the table until the polite clapping died away. Then, to everyone's relief, the deserts arrived, creating a very welcome distraction. When the last plates where cleared Kornilov rose again from his seat, this time signalling that the ghastly dinner was drawing to a conclusion. After the President of Caspia had exited the room, Petrovna was left with the job of thanking the various guests for attending. An agonising task for all concerned thanks to Kornilov's little anecdote. The US attaché hung back and was the last to depart. As Petrovna shook hands with him at the door, the man stepped closer and said.

'I see you have been making some investments in the United States recently and an apartment in Manhattan too. That's real nice. If ever you want to have a chat about anything in confidence, you know where to find me in Moscow.' Then, as he turned to leave, he added as an afterthought 'Oh, and please do be discreet. We wouldn't want you getting into trouble with the boss would we.'

The man left to join the rest of the entourage in the reception area where they were about to be escorted out of the compound by security. Petrovna lingered in the official dining room while he waited for his own car. Then he heard the door click open. Kornilov had reappeared. The silly Presidential sash had gone, as had his Saville Row jacket.

'I need to have a meeting with you about Caspoil' he announced brusquely.

'When?' said Petrovna. 'We don't have a board meeting until next month but I am sure I could arrange something for next week if you want me too.'

'No' said Kornilov. 'The meeting is tonight. You, me, Golitsin and Modest. We need to discuss a problem with Caspoil. We will go to meet them now.'

Kornilov nodded his head towards the door. Petrovna's car was waiting for him at the entrance to the building. Kornilov climbed into his own vehicle and drove away. Petrovna's car did likewise before he could give any instructions to his driver. He lent forward and tapped him on his shoulder. It was not his usual man.

'Where are we going?'

'You will see in a moment,' the driver replied after what seemed like a very long silence. Petrovna suddenly felt that nasty sinking sensation. He noticed that they were not heading in the direction of Caspoil's offices. Soon they were pulling up outside the headquarters of the security service. The sinking sensation got a lot worse.

Kornilov was already waiting for him at the entrance of the building. Petrovna meekly followed him inside. They took the elevator down to the lowest floor and walked down a long Spartan corridor. When they reached the end of it they entered a room that was nothing like a corporate meeting room. It was large and almost empty. There was no normal furniture and just a concrete floor. The room was not empty of people though. Modest and Golitsin were there, seated on two chairs in the centre of the chamber looking ashen faced. Both were smartly dressed in lounge suits like they had been expecting to go someplace else. They were encircled by half a dozen of Kornilov's usual heavies.

The room was filled with a very odd smell, a bit like burning kerosene or similar. The sound of something cooking emanated from behind an old fashioned medical screen in the far corner of the room. It wasn't really a cooking type smell though. It reminded Petrovna of something but he was struggling to place it. The closest his recollection could get was one of the metallurgy labs at university but that made no sense either. The whole scene made no sense. Kornilov closed the door with a sharp clank and started to talk while pacing round the room. He often did this when he was agitated.

'I invited you three to help me run this country because I trusted you. I allowed you to help me run Caspoil because I trusted you. I allowed you three to get rich, very rich, because I trusted you.

Now I find that I can't trust some of you.' Despite his physical agitation, his delivery was calm, clipped, and almost matter of fact.

Modest stared ahead blankly while Golitsin just stared at his shiny loafers. Both men were sitting in their seats in a very awkward fashion. Then Petrovna realised that their hands were cuffed behind their backs.

'I trusted you and made you rich and now I discover I am betrayed. Fucking betrayed.'

Kornilov had been speaking quietly but now his pitch was rising to a shout. He nodded in the direction of Sergei Romanov, the security chief, who produced a small tape recorder from his pocket. Romanov pressed a button and they all listened. It was a poor quality recording of what sounded like a telephone conversation between Modest and Golitsin.

They were discussing a business deal of sorts. This involved a large Russian oil company who were hoping to build a pipeline from Caspia to Russia. The suggestion was that some kind of arrangement fee was to be paid to a company owned by Modest and Golitsin in return for helping them secure the contract. Petrovna had never heard of their company or the Russian counterparts. Then they made the mistake.

'That shit for brains oaf Kornilov is never going to find out, he's too busy acting the Tsar to notice. What is it to him if we do some little extra business on the side. As for his little puppy dog Petrovna, who cares if he notices.'

All the while the tape was playing Kornilov had been fiddling with something in his pocket. Petrovna caught the sight of a glistening metal band threaded between his knuckles.

'So you think I am a shit for brains oaf do you? You rob me. You insult me. Well, this shit for brains oaf has been bugging all your calls.'

Modest started to try and say something. The first words had barely left his mouth when Kornilov's metal bound fist struck him hard on the side of his face. A series of blows followed. One of the ridges of the knuckleduster caught his right eye causing a thin line of spray to squirt out. Modest's head slumped forward senseless with the damaged eyeball bulging from its socket.

Now his attention turned to Golitsin who was surveying with horror the fate that had just befallen his friend.

'This is how I punish scum who betray me. Him, I just scar, but you. You cooked this whole thing up. For you I have something different to cure your greed. If the cash I gave you was not enough then I will give you some gold as well.'

Two of the heavies moved towards the screen at the far corner of the room and wheeled out a large trolley type contraption from behind it. This had a heavy duty gas burner on top. The hissing jet of powerful flame was heating a crucible above it.

Golitsin stared in disbelieve as the heavy item was pushed up alongside his chair. 'Do it,' Kornilov said.

Two men grabbed Golitsin by each shoulder whilst a third wrenched back his head. Kornilov strolled nonchalantly over to the trolley and picked up what looked like a large pair of oven gloves. He made a point of pulling them onto his hands very deliberately. Then he picked up another object from the trolley, a metal funnel. Golitsin started to scream.

'No, no, in the name of god don't do this. I can pay the money back, all of it.'

His frantic protestations were cut short as Kornilov rammed the funnel into Golitsin's mouth, right down to the back of his throat. A fourth thug, also gloved, held the funnel in place as the victim gagged and thrashed. Petrovna stood transfixed as Kornilov grasped the crucible in both gloved hands and lifted it towards the rim of the funnel. Modest groaned as he regained consciousness just in time to witness his friend's nemesis.

'You like gold so much, you can eat some, you fucking cheating scum.'

With that he slowly tipped the crucible until the stream of molten metal began to pour down the funnel into Golitsin's throat. For a moment nothing seemed to happen, then Golitsin's body convulsed as if some surging electric current was racking it. He started to emit a high pitched screeching sound but this guttered out after a second as the boiling liquid gold burnt through the tender fibres of his throat. The heavies fought to hold the convulsing man and the funnel in place as Kornilov decanted the last of its contents into his victim. Then after no more than a few seconds, Golitsin slumped forward lifeless. As his head lolled to one side a tiny trickle of molten fluid flowed from his mouth and down the side of his chin sending more wisps of smoke into the air as it burnt a path down his face.

Kornilov stepped back looking pleased with himself while the heavies removed the funnel. Modest was just groaning as blood and fluid wept from his eviscerated eye. The room was now filled with the foul stench of burnt human flesh. Petrovna felt a wave of nausea engulf him and had to breath hard to resist the urge to wretch. Fearful of fainting, he stepped backwards to lean against the nearest wall.

'That is what happens to people who betray me,' Kornilov announced. Then pointing to Modest he added 'I will let you live as an example to others. Get this piece of shit out of my country. If any of you ever speak of this, you will end up like him,' he said, pointing at Golitsin's scalded carcass. 'And get as much of that gold out of his mouth as you can. That shit's expensive. I don't want it wasted on that scum.'

No further clarification was necessary as Golitsin was released from his chair and dragged out of the room by two guards. The men circled and prodded the corpse, wondering how the hell they were meant to extract the fast cooling metal from its mouth and throat.

Kornilov suddenly broke into a broad grin and slapped Petrovna on the back as though they had just been watching a sports match or similar entertainment. 'Hey there little boy, how you holding up? Not pretty I know. I knew you would never betray me like those scum but I wanted you to see what happens to people who do. Just so we understand each other real good. Right?'

Petrovna nodded. Then Kornilov's mood seemed to drop an octave. He perched himself on the edge of the table.

'Have you ever seen a man burned before? It's not pretty is it?' he said.

'No I have not,' Petrovna replied.

'It smells foul doesn't it? The smell of burnt human flesh. Imagine the pain he must have suffered in his final moments. Can you imagine it Petrovna, can you?'

'No I can't. It must have been appalling, but he betrayed you.'

'That's right. He betrayed me. That's why he had to suffer. I poured it down his throat to kill him quickly. I could have tipped it over his body and let him die slowly.'

'You were very merciful,' Petrovna said in a very thin voice.

'Yes. I was. I could have let him suffer just like my father did when he died. Did I ever tell you how my father died?'

Petrovna shook his head.

'He was scolded by boiling fluid at the factory where he worked. That's how he died, very slowly, after spending days in agony. My mother took me to the hospital to visit him. I will never forget that sickly smell, the smell of his burnt flesh. Now I smell it again, in this very room. But this time, the little fucker deserved it.'

Then Kornilov's mood seemed to lighten again.

'Hey little boy. What doesn't kill you makes you stronger. Let's get out of here. You've got work to do. I want you to take up Golitsin's old position on the board of the National Bank of Caspia. You can do that can't you?'

'Of course,' he replied.

In his heart of hearts Petrovna had always known Kornilov was deranged at least, maybe worse. He heard all the tales and witnessed his rages, sometimes on the receiving end. He had even read the usual guff about human rights in the London press; corruption, arrest and torture of dissidents. Usually in The Guardian. It went with the territory. Now, as he was driven home, he could no longer deceive himself about the truth.

CHAPTER 12

Present

Petrovna stared at his reflection in the mirror even more intently than usual that morning. He didn't know why in particular. It wasn't as if he was usually vain. This morning though, he had been seized by a mood of introspection. He had celebrated his forty fifth birthday a few days' earlier, if you could call that a cause for celebration. The passage of time was one of the few things that even his wealth could not control.

In truth, he did not look bad for his age. He still had most of his dark brown hair, even if it had thinned somewhat and his slight frame was still in reasonable shape save the beginnings of a paunch round the waist. The few crow's feet lines emerging from beside his eyes weren't visible from a distance. He might not be able to stop himself getting old but he could take some comfort from the fact that at least it wasn't too obvious to the casual observer.

He straightened his silk tie in the mirror. He didn't normally bother with ties. Never one to be troubled with fashion he normally just wore one of his dark tailored suits with an open collar. He had a dozen of these suits. They were all the same, that kept things simple and avoided wasting time thinking about what to wear. But today was different and he needed to look business like. He was doing something he hated and tried to avoid whenever possible: being interviewed by a journalist. It was a young American woman from a newspaper in the United States. Apparently it was from some Chicago publication. How on earth she had managed to track him down to London was an irritating mystery to him. She had made several requests for interviews in the past, all of which had been flatly rebuffed in line with his policy of blanket refusal. However, she had been annoyingly persistent and had just faxed through to his London office a draft of an article she was proposing to publish about himself and CES. It was not flattering, not flattering at all.

She had somehow latched onto the accident at the refinery and inflated it into something sinister before going onto make the usual kind of allegations about environmental damage. The article also probed some painful detail about his relationship with Kornilov in the early days. Most worrying of all, the piece contained a reference to the fact that about ten years ago two of Petrovna's business partners had suddenly just disappeared more or less without trace. Mention of that topic in a press article could bring down a whole load of bad shit.

Petrovna had taken some hasty advice from his team. The meeting had been convened in a hurry on a Friday afternoon in his London office. The PR girl looked hot and tired. His in-house lawyer had just looked bored. Everyone had obviously been looking forward to starting their weekends and having to actually do some work was most unwelcome.

The lawyer started. 'Well I think we can all take it as read that there is nothing of any serious substance in any of these allegations other than the incident at the refinery which was very a long time ago. Everything else is, as far as I can see, pure unsupported conjecture. We can always sue if she says anything more specific but I am not sure that's a tactic we want to pursue unless we really need to. I thing we all know how unpredictable the libel laws are and at this stage it's more a case of innuendo rather than a clear defamation.'

'Ya, I would just like to second that,' said the PR girl looking up from her Blackberry. 'This is typical of the sort of ill-informed fishing expedition you get from a young journalist on the make. At the moment the article is just potentially annoying as much as anything, but I don't think we want to antagonise her with legal threats. We could just issue a standard press release rebutting the accusations but my thinking is that it might be worth you actually agreeing to give her the interview. At the end of the day, there is nothing in the article that we can't talk our way out of in terms of the environmental human rights twaddle, is there?'

She and the lawyer both looked expectantly across the table to Petrovna. He shook his head. 'No. You are right. There's nothing,' he said.

'And there's nothing about this issue of some of your former business partners disappearing that we should be worried about either?' the lawyer said.

Petrovna looked momentarily pained. 'No there isn't. People come and go all the time in Caspia for their own reasons. That's how things worked in Russia back then.

I am not my brother's keeper for god sake,' he spluttered betraying uncharacteristic exasperation.

'Fine,' said the lawyer. 'But giving an interview is always a bit risky, you never know where it's going to go. Are you sure you are comfortable with this Mr Petrovna? You don't have to do it if you aren't comfortable.'

'No, of course I am not comfortable with it. You all know how much I hate publicity. It's just that I sense this girl isn't going to let the thing go. If I ignore her, she will claim I am evasive. It's far better if I just meet her and get the whole damn thing over with. I have done nothing wrong after all. Just get on and arrange this please.'

The PR nodded primly. 'In that case I will call her back and arrange an interview. Obviously I will be preparing a briefing pack with the standard rebuttals, key messages and as much background on her as I can lay my hands on. Would you like me to sit in with you just in case?'

'I don't think that will be necessary,' Petrovna replied rather curtly.

It was a relief for all parties when the meeting broke up. Petrovna took some comfort from the fact that the annoying PR girl's weekend would by ruined by having to prepare the pre meeting briefing. Still, everyone was allowed some pleasure.

The briefing document eventually arrived late on Sunday evening. It was largely boilerplate stuff. The rebuttals about the refinery explosion and the environmental abuses were standard fare. He had dealt with it all before on numerous occasions. Then there was a load of nonsense about sustainability and diversity straight out of the corporate playbook. Petrovna smiled as he read those 'key messages'.

Every company worth its salt had to spout this crap these days. No one really believes in it, but it kept the corporate social responsibility mafia at bay. Annoying, to actually have to pay someone to come up with that sort of drivel though. His smile faded at the thought of paying a salary for constructing sentences about focus and positivity.

The section about the journalist herself was far more interesting. He knew she was young. Twenty seven, to be precise. Pretty good pedigree too, Harvard, Masters, IMC trainee on the Chicago Mail with a big story under her belt already. Presumably with a name like Tatiana Georgievna she had some Russian ancestry too. There was a poor quality mug shot that had obviously been pasted into the report off the net. Despite the bad photography the beauty of this woman was very apparent. Petrovna speculated that she might have utilised these charms to further her career on more than one occasion. Probably a pushy bitch he thought. Most of the female journalists he had dealt with in the past had been.

He had agreed to meet her in the afternoon at his London offices. These were not a particularly large affair. It was just a couple of floors in a Georgian town house in Mayfair, with a skeleton crew of secretarial staff. Although it was small scale it was perfectly good for holding corporate meetings when he was in London. Also, crucially, it gave the right impression. CES's foundations in

Caspia were still regarded as being a little exotic by some. Corporate nerves needed to be soothed and reassured. A plush office in the heart of one of London's most prestigious areas helped achieve this. It was also convenient for reaching Petrovna's own private residence a short distance away in Belgravia.

Petrovna planned to play it cool. Big oil boss in a big fancy office. Hopefully she would be overawed by the whole set up and simply lose her nerve. His private office was a minimalist affair despite the grandeur of the building in which it resided. The handsomely proportionated room was furnished simply. The centrepiece was a large glass topped desk on which sat just a telephone and a sleek PC. On one side of the room there was a separate conference table with some suitably uncomfortable looking chairs. The room was in fact more or less a replica of his office back in Caspia. His office in Moscow was the same. Petrovna liked it that way. You always know where you are with uniformity, he often said.

There was a tap on the door. It was his secretary. 'She is here. Shall I offer her coffee or just bring her straight through?' she said.

'No. Just show her straight through please, I don't want to prolong this with niceties.'

Petrovna was seated behind his desk when she entered. He instinctively got up from his chair as she did so and offered her his hand in a formal greeting. She took his oddly cold grasp and they both sat down, mentally sizing each other up across the expanse of barren glass. The fuzzy web shot in his briefing pack had not done this girl justice at all he thought. She was formally dressed in an elegant cream jacket, plain blouse and classic pencil skirt. He felt his eyes gravitating down to her long legs that terminated in some expensive looking heels. Her hair was tied up in a top bunch. This nicely accentuated the impact of her high cheek boned symmetrical face. She was obviously of some Slavic origin but her features were heavily tempered by some other element that made them all the more subtly gorgeous. He could see by the way she carried herself that she knew she was beautiful and had no qualms about using it.

'You are a very persistent woman Miss Georgievna, I don't think anyone else has gone to this much trouble before just to speak to me. I fear you will be a little disappointed though. Now shall we continue in English or do you want to switch to Russian?'

'I think your English is better than my Russian, so let's carry on as we are,' she replied.

'Do you mind if I record us?' she said, brandishing a small device from her little clutch bag.

'No problem, I think it's better for both of us,' he said. She activated the device and the interview commenced.

'Well first, I would like to thank you for agreeing to meet me. I may be persistent but if you don't mind me saying so, you are a very elusive man to pin down. You are also a bit of a mystery. Very few people as rich as you have such a low profile. Hopefully today will give you the opportunity to answer some of the questions people have been asking and give your side of the story.'

For a moment his spirits lifted, the concept of telling his side of the story did sound promising. She continued.

'I would like to start by asking you about the explosion that occurred at Caspoil's main oil refinery just after you first took over as chief executive of CES in 2000. As far as I can make out, this was a very serious accident in which a number of your employees were burned to death. However, there was almost no publicity or press coverage at the time. I also understand that you were present at the site when the accident occurred. To a journalist like me, that sounds like a cover up. Perhaps you would like to explain what really happened on that day?'

Petrovna sighed and flashed a resigned smile. This was all in the briefing pack. 'I see you have done your homework,' he said, trying not to sound too patronising. 'You are absolutely right about the accident. It was exceptionally tragic and yes, I was there when it happened. As a matter of fact, I was reviewing the safety procedures when the incident occurred during a routine test. There were a number of casualties, about a dozen from memory. Anyone who was on site and outside at the time of the explosion would have been killed instantly by the blast. The incident was very poorly reported at the time because no one was interested in what happens in a little country like Caspia that no one has heard of, or cares about. It is very sad that people take this attitude. Most Americans don't care about anything that happens outside of the United States. I can assure you that there was no cover up,' he said.

'But Mr Petrovna, this is not the only safety incident that has occurred on a Caspoil site is it? You are quite right. I have been doing some homework, as you put it, and accidents seem to be very commonplace occurrences at CES owned facilities. Is it not the case that you are presiding over a company with habitually low standards of safety and security for employees and the public alike?'

In spite of her line of questioning, her voice was proving strangely hypnotic, almost music like and Petrovna was really enjoying listening to it. She had an American accent but it was softened into something more pleasing in much the same way as the Slavic features in her lovely face. Stay on message he thought. You have met women like this before. You know she's hostile, concentrate.

'You have to realise Miss Georgievna, that by the time of the Soviet Union's collapse, most of its infrastructure was in a very lamentable state of repair. As you will be aware from your very diligent research, I am an industrial engineer by training and spent many years in the energy business, much of it in Caspia. I can tell you that the situation I inherited at Caspoil was very far from satisfactory. I had a lot of what you would no doubt call legacy issues to deal with and one of those was safety. Ever since that first accident, my absolute priority has been to improve safety on all our sites for all our employees and that's something I am very proud of.'

'You say first accident, so there have been other accidents since then. Can you tell me about those.'

'Tatiana' he said, leaning forward. 'You have to appreciate that any heavy industry, especially the extraction and processing of oil, is an inherently risky enterprise. Some accidents are inevitable. Look at the track record of some of your own companies in the USA and in the Gulf of Mexico. I think you will find that they have had some little incidents as well. As I explained we had a lot of legacy issues and we at CES have worked very hard to put them right.'

'Okay, Nicholas, and please, call me Tanya. Let's talk about your track record on the environment and corporate social responsibility. It doesn't look a whole lot better than your safety record. Pollution, environmental damage and very low wages. It's not much to be proud of is it?'

He liked the way he had switched to first names. It was giving the whole conversation a pleasantly personal edge. He imagined her calling his name in slightly different circumstances and then reluctantly wrenched his mind back to the briefing pack response.

'CES is totally committed to sustainable policies with respect to the environment and the communities where we operate. Again, we had a lot of issues to deal with when we first inherited that old Soviet infrastructure, cultural as well as engineering issues. It takes longer to change attitudes than it does to change equipment but that's our goal and we have been making real progress in the last ten years. That is also something I am very proud of,' he said feeling vaguely pleased with his shtick so far. Maybe that PR guy who wrote the diversity stuff had his uses after all.

'Let's move onto a much broader issue. Many people see a so-called oligarch like you and they say "what did you do to get so rich". I mean, don't take this personally but one minute you are some Soviet engineer who no one has ever heard of, the next thing we know you are worth billions of dollars and running a company that controls half the oil and gas production in the Caspian sea. Just how did that happen so quickly without you having apparently done anything special to deserve it? It's not as though you invented something like Bill Gates or set up a business from scratch is it?'

She smiled sweetly and sat back in her chair expectantly. Petrovna smiled back weakly as he considered his answer. Again, her question was not wholly unexpected. It's just that he hadn't expected it to be posed in so stark a fashion. It was a very pretty smile though. Somehow nothing she said could entirely detract from the pleasing cadence of her voice that became more entrancing with every passing moment in her presence.

'I can understand people saying that. I don't think we have time to go through every step in my career, which I expect you are already familiar with anyway. For sure I didn't invent anything but I had skills that other people needed. In life you have to be prepared to make the most of opportunities when they come. An opportunity presented itself because of these skills and the people I know. I took that opportunity when it came. You can say that I was lucky to be at the right place at the right time. Maybe you are right, but I recognised that opportunity when it presented itself and not everyone does. In business seeing opportunities is just as big a skill as creating new ones. Remember, the guy who invented Coca Cola never made any money out of it, it's the guy who saw the opportunity and bought the rights from him that did that,' He said with a flourish.

'Ah yes, the people you know, the people you know,' she said savouring the phrase every time she repeated it.

'Let's talk about some of these people you know. How about your old friend President Kornilov of Caspia? Looks like you weren't the only person who was at the right place at the right time. How exactly does a navy conscript turned army colonel suddenly become head of state of a small ex-Soviet republic? I guess it helps when your predecessor conveniently dies in a helicopter crash. You meet this guy when you are both conscripts, then he just gives you half his country's heavy industry to run, plus a huge stake in the privatisation. I wish the people I know were as generous as the people you know. What can you tell me about your relationship with President Kornilov?'

Petrovna clasped his hands tightly together. 'Well, I think you have already described it. It's not for me to comment on someone else's career. The politics in that part of the world are very different to the West. Ten, fifteen years ago the situation was very chaotic. People look for stability and firm leadership. I think President Kornilov has provided that leadership and I might add, the country is very much the better for it. Obviously, as I am responsible for running the most important sector of the economy in Caspia, I have a close professional working relationship with him. Since Caspia became autonomous it has enjoyed huge economic growth under the Kornilov Presidency. It is very easy for you in the West to mock but he has replaced conflict and chaos with stability and prosperity.'

He was particularly pleased with the last line and watched her intently as she scribbled down a few notes on her jotted pad. Hopefully the stability quote would make it into the piece. Kornilov would like that. Then his mind wandered back to her. She had long elegant fingers, like a pianists but very feminine. He waited for her to look back up so that he could fleetingly catch her blue eyes.

'But he doesn't have a very good human rights record does he? Not everyone has been as lucky to make his acquaintance as you have been. A lot of people have disappeared in Caspia since your man Kornilov took over. Like two of your former business partners for example. When CES was first, privatised, your friend Modest Gorky and his associate Yevgeny Golitsin were both major stakeholders and sat on the board with you. Then five years later they are both gone from the company records and no one has heard of either of them since. How do you feel about operating in a country with such a poor human rights record? Oh, and what did happen to your former business partners?'

This was always going to come up, he thought. Stay cool. After this he could steer the conversation onto something more convivial.

'My two former business partners were only involved with the business during the initial privatisation process. Once CES was established as a standalone business their contribution was no longer necessary so they resigned from the board and realised their stakes. Regrettably I have been too busy to keep up with them since.'

'So you have no idea at all about what they are up to now? None whatsoever? Really? Well allow me to help you out with that. God only knows what happened to Golitsin but Modest Gorky was living in London until last week. Then someone blew his brains out for some reason. Maybe they didn't like the fact he was talking to me. And speaking of legacy issues, how exactly did he come to lose one of his eyes?'

Petrovna went quite pale as he felt his heart sink. This wasn't in the briefing.

'I am afraid I don't know anything about that' he said, his voice suddenly diminished. 'And I am also afraid I am going to have to call this meeting to a halt. I have another meeting due to start in a few minutes and I really can't keep them waiting. I am very sorry. If you leave your card I can always contact you if I have anything to add.'

'But...' She started to talk again but he held up his hand and shook his head.

'As I said Tanya, I am very sorry. We were about finished anyway. Please allow me to show you out.' He stood up and moved towards the door avoiding her gaze. She sighed, shook her head and then reluctantly rose from her seat to do his bidding.

CHAPTER 13

'And she got all of this down on some kind of digital recorder?' the lawyer said in a rather deliberate fashion.

'Yes, that's what I told you. I dealt with all that environment nonsense pretty well and I don't think I said anything scandalous. It was just awkward, especially the bit about Modest. We knew that was going to come up. I have only just got into town and hadn't realised he was dead. It caught me off balance that's all,' Petrovna said.

'You were absolutely right to cut the thing when you did. The police are investigating that man's death. You don't want to be associated with a murder inquiry in any shape or form.'

'Yes, that's what I thought at the time but I don't like leaving stuff hanging in the air. Unfinished business isn't my style and it can't look good terminating an interview like that in practically mid-sentence. She's bound to say I looked like I had got something to hide isn't she?'

The PR girl nodded her head sadly.

'Look. She's just a young girl on the make,' Petrovna snapped 'This is CES. We are a multinational company. We can surely handle a rookie journalist, right?'

'I have thought about that and I may have something,' the lawyer said. 'I did some serious digging on her after our last meeting, made a few calls to a few people I know. She might not be so clean herself. You know that small refiner you bought in Texas last year?' Petrovna nodded.

'You remember you were in a bidding war with that private equity fund that got pretty nasty. Well guess who put up most of the risk capital for that fund?'

Petrovna looked blank for a moment and then a smile of recognition slowly invaded his face.

'Hank Stewart?'

'Yes. Hank Stewart no less and I am sure you will re-call that Hank Stewart is also the majority shareholder in IMC Group, who of course own the Chicago Mail and Global Affairs Magazine. I doubt it is a coincidence that Ms Georgievna's employer is owned by a business rival with a deep grudge. Do you?'

Petrovna nodded, grimly, trying to disguise his irrita-tion that he had not spotted this himself earlier. 'OK. This could at least give us some leverage over her but how do we stop her printing something now? I sense she really feels that she has tasted blood.'

'We can try leaning on someone further up the food chain but that won't work if the whole thing really has been authorised by Stewart from the outset. There's no real rea-son why they should back off now and we have no legal grounds to stop them publishing as the situation stands,' the lawyer added.

'You know what?' said Petrovna 'I think I should meet her again.' The lawyer and the PR woman grimaced in unison at the suggestion.

'Very bad idea. Forgive me, but I think it was a mistake meeting her the first time,' the lawyer said.

'No, hear me out. I think the girl is genuine. She probably doesn't even realise that she's being used in someone else's vendetta, assuming that is what has happened. If I agree to meet her again and tell her that none of this is really about Caspia at all, I might be able to take some of the heat out of the whole thing.'

The lawyer cleared his throat. 'Are you sure that is a wise idea? Given what happened last time I am not convinced it's prudent for you to have any more contact with her. The whole scenario is just too unpredictable.'

'Of course I am sure,' Petrovna snarled. 'I pay you to give me legal advice not question my judgment.'

―――

Kornilov studied the photographs intently and cracked one of his cruel thin smiles. They has been taken in haste so were hardly works of art but they served their purpose of confirming that his instructions had been carried out to his satisfaction. They showed the man's body slumped against the doorframe where he had fallen. There was no doubt who the man was or that he was dead. The eye patch and gaping head wound left by the assassin's single skilful gunshot told that story well enough. The dark spatter of detritus on the wall behind told the rest.

Kornilov thought letting Modest off with merely a permanent mutilation had seemed like a sophisticated move at the time. Kill one off in a suitably inventive fashion and let the other survive as a warning to others. It had sent out a pretty strong message that the President of Caspia was not a man to piss about with. However, memories fade with the passage of time and now it was necessary to send out new messages. Messages like the authority of Alexis Kornilov didn't stop at the Caspian border. It stretched to Russia as well. And London. With friends in Russia at the highest level, as long as he did their bidding, he could operate there more or less with impunity.

Occasionally he had to do them a little favour in return. Sometimes it was an arms-length operation. Other times, something a little too messy to be carried out directly. Kornilov's emissaries specialised in messy. They had grown good at it. Notorious at it even, and now their expertise was increasingly in demand further afield. Want someone dead in London or Paris? Kornilov's bad guys were the men for the job.

Slaying Modest had served two very useful purposes apart from shutting him up: first it demonstrated that his agents were now capable of operating effectively outside Russia, including London. With so many wealthy and politically active Russians residing there, London was now the prime venue for this sort of thing. Secondly, it reminded anyone who needed reminding that if you crossed Kornilov, you would never be safe again. If he wanted to, he would find you and he would send people to arrange your nemesis wherever you hid.

Modest had got bold. Or maybe his drink-addled brain had simply stifled his fear. He had contacted a journalist. Now he was dead with a bullet in his skull and his brains sprayed over his porch. That was the kind of corporate message Kornilov had wanted to send out and he had.

'Good,' he told Romanov. 'That stupid fucker's brain was probably half pickled anyway. Our operative made a clean getaway, right?'

'Yes' Romanov said smugly. 'Got him with the first shot. Took the snaps and rode off on the motorbike. Smooth. No witnesses. Hah. They were probably all cowering behind their English net curtains. He was out of the country in a matter of hours. It was a pretty clean job. No blow back.'

'And this girl he was talking to. What of her?'

'She only met him once. She is an American with a Caspian father. We don't fully understand her motivation yet. We do know that she is pursuing the story on behalf of Global Affairs magazine. She is bound to know something about us from her conversation with our departed friend. What we don't know is, what exactly did he tell her? Do you want me to have her dealt with too?'

'No. Not yet. That would be clumsy. Let's see who else she is talking to and why. Has she contacted Petrovna?'

'Oh yes. She saw him yesterday at his office. She was there about half an hour and then left alone.'

'Good. Keep a close eye on both of them. I want to know how often they meet and where they are going. See if you can get them bugged

CHAPTER 14

Tanya got back to her hotel early evening and collapsed onto the bed feeling tired and exasperated. The interview had actually gone as well as could reasonably be expected. She had finally met her quarry, asked the right questions and got some useful answers on tape. Better still, he'd definitely seemed rattled when she raised the subject of Modest's death. True, he had cut the interview short just as she was getting him on the ropes. Then again that was probably always going to happen. No one in their right mind would continue giving an interview in which they were likely to incriminate themselves. Objectively the day had gone well. Somehow though it also felt anticlimactic. Sure, it was worthwhile journalistic material. But smoking gun? Not really.

She lay on top of the bed thinking for a while. Where was this story going? Was there really a big scandal? The answers he had given her sounded suspiciously like pre-prepared corporate spin. However, they made sense in themselves and would be difficult to disprove. She really needed more to write the sort of career making article that she had first envisaged.

She switched on the TV. On came the usual stuff that was barely worth watching, so she settled on BBC world news. The stories whirled round and round with the funky program theme interspersed between them. Credit crisis, Islamic terrorism, European summit then back to credit crisis again. There were no new stories so the reportage just went on a loop with only the presenters occasionally changing.

After a while she lapsed into a kind of news trance. When she snapped out of it, the sky had darkened outside and she felt the first gnawings of hunger. She didn't fancy going out again and there was nothing appealing on the overpriced room menu, so she helped herself to a beer and a very expensive bag of potato chips instead. Suddenly, an overwhelming sense of exhaustion descended and she decided to call it a night, even though it wasn't especially late. Then she slept like the dead.

The ring tone on her mobile woke her with a start. It was watery daylight outside. She reached across to the bedside cabinet and grabbed the phone. The number on display was not familiar. 'Hello,' she said, sounding groggy and feeling it too. The voice at the other end was familiar though it took her a few seconds to place it in her semi comatose state.

'Good morning Miss Georgievna. I hope this isn't too early for you. This is Nicholas Petrovna speaking.'

'Oh,' she croaked, still feeling disoriented.

'I wanted to speak with you again after yesterday. I felt maybe I hadn't expressed myself very clearly when we met. When you told me Modest Gorky was dead, I was just stunned. Way too shocked to continue our conversation. Hope I didn't offend you. I wondered if I could make amends by taking you to dinner this evening. If you leave your recording device at home I can give you much more background information off the record.'

Tanya hesitated as she considered her options. She hadn't been expecting this at all. On reflection though, the choice was hardly difficult. She just didn't have enough material as things stood. Meeting him again gave her another chance, even if it was technically 'off the record'. There were always a means of getting around that issue if she needed to.

'OK, Mr Petrovna. You have got yourself a deal. Where shall I meet you?'

'You can meet me at the restaurant at seven thirty. I will text you the venue later. Remember. This will be strictly off the record.'

She spent the rest of the morning considering her tactics for the evening. She needed to coax him into saying something more incriminating. One thing was bothering her though. Why had he offered himself up in double jeopardy? It seemed a risky tactic on his part given he now knew the line of questioning she would be pursuing. He must have some point he wanted to try and get across to her but what?

About lunchtime she got an email from her boss in Chicago asking her to call him back, which she duly did. She had an inkling of what he wanted and was right. Although she had been keeping him up to date with developments by email his responses were betraying a growing tone of impatience.

'Just how are you doing down there? It's been over two weeks now. How did you get on with him yesterday?'

'Pretty good thanks. I managed to get him seriously rattled. He didn't like some of my questions at all, which is great.'

'Yea, that is great Tanya but have you really nailed this story? Remember we want to publish a damaging exposé of this guy with plenty of lurid details about corrupt business practices, links to the oppressive regime in Caspia. We want sick kids, pollution, hookers, all that shit but we need hard evidence. Remember, this guy is a billionaire. He can afford to sue if we can't prove it. Have we got evidence Tanya?'

She hesitated. 'Sure, I have got evidence but this story is only just opening up. I need to develop it further so the whole thing really sticks.'

'This Petrovna guy, he's real smart. He ducked and dodged like a boxer in the interview. If we run the story on what we have got now he and his fancy lawyers will just talk their way out of it. I feel if I can just pursue some leads a little bit further, I can totally nail him to the fence.'

'OK Tanya. I am hear you. Use your judgement but remember the meter is ticking. We need results here fast. Look, I gotta take another call now. Keep me posted and hey, be careful. You say some Ruski got whacked? That is some serious shit Tanya. You watch your step, you get me?'

'Sure thing,' she said before ending the call. For some reason even she couldn't quite process, she had not mentioned the fact that she was meeting Petrovna for a second time. Somehow it didn't seem relevant. He might have even gotten the wrong idea about how she was pursuing this. It just seemed easier to leave that detail out for the time being. She could always tell him all about it later when the context would be more evident.

For now though she was preoccupied with the altogether more pressing issue of what she was going to wear this evening. She assumed he would be taking her somewhere upscale so it would be crucial for strictly professional purposes that she looked hot as hell. She opened her wardrobe to review her options. They were limited. She had packed as many trouser suits as her baggage allowance permitted but somehow they didn't feel right for the occasion. She couldn't wear the skirt she had interviewed him in yesterday twice either. It was just the excuse she had been looking for to visit some of London's famous fashion emporiums. It was really important that tonight went well. That must surely justify some retail therapy.

An hour later she found herself walking down Bond Street. It was quite busy despite the veil of light drizzle. Most of her fellow shoppers seemed to be Middle Eastern or Asian. Many of them were carrying bags of extravagant purchases, which Tanya eyed enviously. She entered a large corner store that had fancy stuff in the window with prices to match. An hour later she emerged with a load of serious couture kit because she deserved it. She caught herself wondering if he would approve of her choice of evening wear but slapped the thought down quickly.

Her phone beeped to indicate the arrival of a text. She pulled it out, grateful for the distraction. Meet me at the main restaurant at The Connaught Hotel at 7.30 as agreed, it said. A black cab appeared from a side street. As she trundled back to the hotel, her thoughts once again returned to how she was going to tackle Petrovna over dinner.

Petrovna's reaction had made it clear that it was the subject of Modest's death that had caused him the most anxiety. That subject needed additional albeit careful probing. Anything too up front and he might just walk out of the restaurant. That would be no good at all. A more subtle approach would be required.

CHAPTER 15

It was just starting to get dark as the first of the cars approached the clearing in the woods. There were six vehicles in total. All SUV's with blacked out windows. There was a gap of a few minutes between each car as they all slowed at the same spot before furtively turning off the main road down a narrow track. As the last of the evening sunshine faded and died their headlights speared through the cold air. The piercing beams illuminated a path through the dense pine trees lending it a tunnel like appearance. Eventually, the last of the vehicles reached their destination and the occupants clambered out, stealthily closing their vehicle doors behind them as if they were somehow fearful of disturbing any dwellers in the sombre forest surrounds. In the centre of the clearing was a modest wooden dacha. A glimmer of light emanated from behind the closed wooden shutters as the shadowy visitors filed though the entrance.

Inside was sparsely furnished with just a pine table and chairs. In one corner of the room was an old fashioned stove. This had been lit and was doing its best to provide some meagre warmth against the rapidly chilling night air. Sergei Romanov was seated at the head of the table destined to play host to the covert gathering. Though possibly not a meeting of minds it was certainly a meeting of potentially aligned vested interests. The other participants took their places with much shuffling and clearing of tobacco-scorched throats. Everybody looked awkward. Romanov opened the proceedings.

'You all know why we are here and you all know the consequences if anyone finds out about us.'

The remark was greeted with silent nods and more clearing of throats. Someone lit a cigarette. The hiss of the match igniting seemed unusually loud.

'You have come here tonight because you know that any one of you could be the next one to go. You don't have to have said or done anything. If Kornilov just so much as thinks it, that's enough to get any one of us killed. No questions asked. There are six of us here tonight. If we had met like this a year ago there might have been eight or nine. The question is, do we just wait another year until there are only three or four of us, or do we try and do something now?'

His words hung pregnant in the smoke filled air. There was an agonising pause then the man to Romanov's left spoke up. He was thick set, nearly bald and wore the uniform of a General in the Caspian Army.

'For sure, we are probably all fucked if we do nothing but what can we actually do? My men are all fiercely loyal to Kornilov. They take orders from me because I am their commander but they love him because they see him as one of their own. They would never raise their hand against him. You know that Sergei Romanov.'

'I do know that Vladimir Kerenski, I understand it well. That is why we have travelled half way to Finland to sit in this god-forsaken hut. We have come here to work out how we can kill him before he kills us, one by one, after one of his paranoid vodka rages. When Kornilov wants someone liquidated he comes to me. I can't use my own agents on Kornilov for the same reason you can't use your men. If we want him assassinated we are talking about outside help here, unless one of you is volunteering to do it yourself?' Romanov paused for dramatic effect. 'I am guessing not. Felix, what would the reaction be from Moscow if Kornilov were to meet with an accident?'

Felix Antonov was one of the few non-military men in the room. Petrovna aside, there wasn't much call for professionals in the Kornilov government but even a regime like Caspia's needed one or two technocrats to give it some credibility in the outside world. In this case, Antonov was Caspia's Foreign Minister and generally regarded as the acceptable face of the regime or as some might call him, its apologist.

'Well. The position at present is that Kornilov has the full support of the Kremlin and will continue to do so as long as he does exactly what they tell him. However, lately there has been a feeling that some of the more lurid reports about what goes on in Caspia have become an embarrassment. It hasn't helped that your guys have started to get careless of late. That journalist your operatives did in St Petersburg last year was really messy. It was in all the papers. Stirred a shit storm. The

Kremlin doesn't like shit storms. It attracts unwelcome attention.'

Romanov shot Antonov an evil look. 'My agents are professionals. You can't always kill people without leaving a mark. Forget the diplomatic shit. If we managed to kill Kornilov, would the Kremlin intervene or would they let us play out?'

'I think they would wait and see what replaced him. They don't really care who runs Caspia as long as whoever it is, is compliant to their wishes.'

'OK. So Moscow would probably run with a regime change. We just need to think how we do this. I can't use my agents and Vlad can't use his troops because they are all fanatically loyal to Kornilov. We could use foreign mercenaries though.'

'Yes, but how does that work and where do we get the money?' one of the other uniformed men said. A murmur of agreement rippled round the table.

'Nicholas Petrovna, that's how'. Romanov pulled out a cigarette and lit it, leaning back on his chair and took a long heavy draw. The others looked down the table at him expectantly. He hesitated a moment longer, took a second long draw and then exhaled the smoke before continuing.

'We persuade Petrovna to back an armed coup against Kornilov. We tell him some bullshit about it all being about human rights and that he has to be the figure head of a new democratic regime.'

A peel of laughter echoed round the table. Sergei held up his hand to calm the mirth and continued. 'We get him to pay for the mercenaries. We tell him he is going to lead this new liberal regime. Petrovna arrives with the mercenaries who kill Kornilov.'

'But then what are you going to do about Petrovna? He's going to think he's running the show' Antonov enquired.

Romanov smiled broadly as he rose from his seat and walked round the table behind the backs of the men he was addressing. 'That's easy. We just kill the bastard. All the troops loyal to Kornilov will back us because we claim we are the counter-revolution avenging Kornilov's murder. We get Petrovna to pay for our coup. He kills Kornilov for us. Then we stitch him up, kill him and seize power ourselves.'

There was another pause. The General broke the silence. 'That could actually work,' he said. Antonov nodded in agreement. Soon the rest of the men in the room were thumping the table and cheering loudly in approval of the plan's ruthless logic.

'But Sergei Romanov, with Kornilov and Petrovna both dead, which of us is actually going to assume the presidency in their place?'

The room went very quiet again as everyone turned to stare at the questioner at the head of the table next to Romanov's empty chair. It was true that none of the assembled had until this point viewed the security chief as anything other than Kornilov's ruthless hatchet man, tasked with carrying out his vilest instructions. They certainly hadn't rated him as a great political operator let alone a successor to Kornilov. Yet, it was he who was now assuming the mask of command complete with its cold sneer.

'My friends' he answered. 'It is only I that has shown the courage to stand before you and say the things that had to be said. It is I that arranged this meeting in this place and took the risk of flying you all discreetly to Moscow. I have also told you how we must proceed. I am the one that has grasped the initiative and shown true leadership. Given that I have done all of this, I think it inevitable that I should lead the new regime in Caspia.'

No one challenged his assertion. He continued his walk round the table until he was standing directly behind the man who had queried his pre-eminence.

'I hope your loyalty is not in question Vladimir Kerenski,' he said, emphasising the syllables of the name very deliberately as he planted his hands firmly on the questioner's shoulders. The atmosphere thickened with tension as all eyes were fixed on the General in anticipation of his response. If anyone in the room was going to challenge Sergei Romanov's authority it would be General Kerenski, the only man in the room with the wherewithal to do so. Kerenski looked directly ahead. His rival's hands were effectively pinning him to his seat.

'Very well Sergei Romanov, seeing as you are assuming the risk of this enterprise, it is only just that you command my loyalty.' Sergei laughed and slapped the general on the back as if to congratulate a friend on some joke.

Everyone else breathed a collective sigh of relief. It was bad enough dealing with Kornilov's erratic behaviour without having a dispute with his sinister deputy.

'So are we all agreed on this plan?' Romanov said.

They all nodded.

'I will proceed but we must be wary. I will contact Petrovna and start to make the other arrangements. Don't talk about this. Don't discuss it with others. Never try to contact me about it, not ever. Remember, my agents have already bugged all your phones and probably my own. I will contact you individually in the utmost secrecy to tell you how the plan proceeds. If Kornilov hears a word of this we are all dead men for sure. Good luck to you all comrades.'

A few minutes later the door of the dacha swung open as the plotters exited to their motor vehicles. Soon the headlights were once again illuminating a path through the pine trees as their newly emboldened occupants departed. The light in the hut was extinguished and the last car faded into the night as the scene of the conspiracy and the forest that concealed it were once again engulfed by darkness.

CHAPTER 16

Petrovna felt apprehensive as his car approached the restaurant. He wasn't sure why. It was hardly the most dangerous meeting he had been obliged to handle. Compared to dealing with Kornilov and his henchman or even hostile business advisories this was little more than a mildly taxing social engagement. All he had to do was turn on a bit of charm with the girl and perhaps make her aware of a few other relevant pieces of information. That would surely be sufficient to draw her journalistic sting. However, despite all of these perfectly logical considerations, he still felt a vague sense of trepidation gnawing away at him. The fact it was irrational only fuelled his unease.

The car was turning into Grosvenor Square. The rain was getting heavier. He was glad he had not decided to walk, even though his office was only a short distance away. He glanced again at his watch, a Patek Philippe, that he only bothered to wear for formal occasions. It was seven fifteen. Perfect. He always preferred to be the first to arrive.

'I will be approximately two hours but I will send you a text when I am ready,' he told his driver at the hotel's entrance. A porter opened the door of the car and Petrovna strode purposefully inside. He had thought of getting a quick drink first then decided against the idea on account that the bar looked uncomfortably busy and the music surprisingly loud. The place was packed with the usual Mayfair crowd of well-heeled American tourist types and men in suits but no ties. Instead he headed straight for the table.

The main dining room was reassuringly old school with sumptuous chairs and oak panelled walls. It was calm, elegant and ever so slightly intimidating. This was not an accident, it was precisely why he had selected it. He wanted an atmosphere that would dampen heated debate and inhibit the use of note pads or other obvious recording devices. Of course, this would be no defence against covert recording but that was a risk he would just have to take.

He was about to order a vodka and tonic when she arrived. She was wearing a sheer black dress that came down just low enough to be decent but just high enough to afford a full view of her extravagant legs. She was also wearing some patent black stilettos. It was very obvious that a special effort had been made, a successful one at that. The overall effect was quite exquisite. He stood up to shake her hand, rather stiffly.

A waiter quickly materialised and offered them some champagne.

'Are madam and monsieur celebrating this evening?' he asked.

'Not exactly,' Petrovna replied. 'But we will take two glasses of champagne anyway.' He turned to Tanya.

'I am assuming you like champagne?'

'I certainly do' she said. 'I don't get to drink it as often as I like. I am sure you do though.'

'Not really, I think it's one of those things that are overrated. I am making an exception for you this evening. I suggest we both have the tasting menu by the way. It's supposed to be very good and there will be plenty of time to discuss what we want to discuss between courses.'

'OK,' she replied. Petrovna signalled to the waiter and instructed him accordingly. The man reappeared almost immediately with two dishes of amuse bouche. These consisted of a tiny thimble containing a kind of foaming broth.

'Chefs signature lobster bisque taster,' the waiter said.

Petrovna pushed his thimble away un-tasted while Tanya gulped hers down in a single swift move.

'What's the matter?' she said. 'Don't you like lobster or are you Jewish or something?'

'I am not Jewish as such but I do have a bit of ancestry. Being religious in Russia used to be a bad career move so I was brought up a good Soviet atheist. Shellfish was hardly a staple when I was growing up anyway so I prefer not to eat it. So, are you religious yourself?'

'No. No one has ever practised in my family either. I was taken to a Russian Orthodox church a few times when I was a child but that was all.'

Tanya waited for the waiter to clear the thimbles and then it started. 'So Mr Petrovna, you have invited me to this wonderfully expensive restaurant so that I can give you a hard time about your business practices. Now, why would you want to do that?' she said, smiling sweetly as she picked up her linen napkin and unfurled it in a very dainty fashion.

'Well, I fear I might have left you with a false impression last time we met. I felt that some of my comments could have been misinterpreted if taken out of context. I wanted the opportunity to put the record straight in a less formal setting.'

'I would hardly call this a less formal setting. I guess I don't' get to eat out as often as you do,' she said, tossing her head and gesturing at the sumptuous surrounds. 'Why don't you start by telling me about why your company isn't dangerous to work for. It seems awfully accident prone to me. The accident at the Caspov refinery wasn't the last was it?'

Petrovna winced inwardly and hoped the first of the tasting dishes would arrive soon. His intimidating venue strategy wasn't having anything like the subduing effect on her that he had anticipated. He fumbled mentally for the carefully crafted first response he had rehearsed with his lawyer.

'Heavy industry is a risky business in whichever country you operate in Ms Georgievna. As I tried to explain last time, in the former Soviet Union all the equipment is very old and not always safe.

Accidents used to happen all the time. It takes years and enormous amounts of money to replace all that equipment. In the Soviet Union, human life was cheap too, so it takes even longer to change attitudes. The accident at Caspoil took place within days of me taking over the company. I have been working on raising standards ever since.

It's been a long journey but I really do feel we have been making some progress.'

The first of the plates arrived. It was a single poached quail's egg mounted on beef Carpaccio. Petrovna dug in, grateful for the diversion. Tanya prodded her small egg suspiciously at first and then after her first mouthful, attacked the dish with greater gusto.

'That was very good and I see you have been studying American business speak but you went through all that stuff the last time we met. I hope you are not going to just repeat yourself or else this could be a rather boring conversation for both of us. Now let me guess, next you are going to tell me that Caspoil is committed to equality and diversity.'

Shit, he thought.

'You must know Tanya, that American companies have industrial accidents and environmental disasters too. It happens in the USA and it happens overseas. Take India, your US company Union Carbide killed many innocent people. The funny thing is, no one cares about that so much because they were all impoverished Indians and not rich Americans. Why are you so interested in my company when there are plenty of scandals closer to home?'

'Do we have accidents in America? Sure we do. But the reason I am interested in your company is because unlike Union Carbide or Exxon it's effectively owned by a dictator with one of the worst human rights records in the world, who by the way rumour has it, enjoys killing people in a variety of interesting ways. Was your friend Modest one of them? What do you think?'

'You don't believe in taking the subtle approach do you?' he said. He thought he saw the trace of a blush, just for a moment.

The waiter arrived to clear the plates. Petrovna hesitated until he was back out of earshot before continuing. 'Look, I really wanted to set the record straight on that. Modest was an old friend but I hadn't seen him for many years. I was stunned when you told me he was dead. I didn't know what to say, that's why I terminated the interview. I have no idea at all who killed him or why and I certainly wouldn't want to speculate about it. After all it is now a police enquiry.'

'So you can't tell me anything about what happened to him or your other business partner who disappeared then?'

'No, I am afraid I can't. I can't tell you what I don't know now can I?' She looked disappointed at the reply. The waiter reappeared with the next course, another small cup of foaming soup – this time with a rich beef and truffle flavour.

Petrovna lifted his cup, then stopped and looked at Tanya.

'You do realise that you are being used don't you?'

She put her cup of expensive broth down and looked at him quizzically.

'No. What do you mean?'

'Hank Stewart. That name must mean something to you. He is your ultimate boss after all. He owns your company in fact. He and I had a business dispute a few years back. It was in the press if you want the details. It looks to me like he took it all rather personally and is getting you to do some of his dirty work for him. Let's face it, you are obviously being gamed. I mean, did you really think your journal would go to all the trouble and expense of flying you out to London just to mount a fishing expedition about the safety record of a foreign company? Do you think people in Chicago care, let alone Alabama? I mean come on, really?'

With that comment her beautiful eyes narrowed and seemed to glow like deep blue gems. She pushed the soup cup aside and leant forward.

'OK Mr Petrovna, you can come up with your funny conspiracy theories but this story didn't come from Hank Stewart, it came from me. I discovered it and researched it. I even found out about you. Maybe Hank Stewart does like the story but the story is real because it comes from my heart. You can try and spin it to yourself that you are the victim if it makes you feel better. The fact remains, I care about what people like you and Kornilov are doing to the people of Caspia and no amount of PR or fancy restaurant meals are going to alter that. Oh and by the way, I believe you have a Senator from Alabama on the board of your US oil service division, so actually readers in Alabama might be interested in what you'r up to after all.'

'Actually, he is a former Senator,' Petrovna mumbled.

The nasty sinking feeling was back again but even though she was visibly angry, there was something about the flush of temper that inflamed his desire. He had felt it when they first met and now he felt it again. It was not merely her physical beauty that was captivating him but something in her nature that was awakening long forgotten feelings of passion with a hefty helping of lust thrown in.

'So you think I am just some silly American girl who is being used by her boss to settle a petty business score. Is that what you think of me? Is that why you invited me here Mr Petrovna? Do you really think this will make me drop the story?'

Suddenly the restaurant seemed unpleasantly hot and what little appetite he had was gone.

'No I don't. I can see that you are genuine. I just thought you should know the context that's all. I am sorry if I have offended you.'

'Well you are right about something then,' she said, putting the soup cup down firmly. 'So why did you really invite me here this evening?'

Petrovna's mouth turned dry as he struggled to find a combination of words that were not emotionally incontinent.

'I asked to see you because, I thought perhaps if I saw you again and I explained then maybe you would understand.'

'Understand what?'

'That I am not the kind of person you seem to think I am. It's just that in politics and business you have to deal with bad people whether you like it or not. It's just complicated.'

Tanya let slip a peel of giggles that drew glances from the occupants of nearby tables. She quickly clutched her napkin to her mouth. Petrovna shrank back into his chair as his hollow face stared intently at the soup cup.

'My god,' she said. 'You are actually serious.' The waiter reappeared to remove the cups. Petrovna continued.

'I never usually talk to journalists but I made an exception in your case because I thought you might be different. I thought that if I could make you understand what it is really like to be in my position then perhaps you might not take quite such an aggressive approach.'

'Oh I see. You want me to be sympathetic. It's kind of hard to feel sorry for someone as rich as you when they are involved with someone like Kornilov.'

'I understand that I promise you. But you have to understand that sometimes you have to take the chances life gives you and in Soviet Russia they were not very many. I took my chances in Caspia with Kornilov because it was the only one I had. I was only an engineer. It was just a job. I never had any inkling I would make a fortune. I never planned it, it just happened. It was a consequence. As for Kornilov, he disgusts me. Always has. But I can't change him. If he even knew I was talking to you about him like this he would probably snuff me out too. Just like poor Modest.'

Now Petrovna leant forward and fixed her straight in the eye for the first time that evening. 'I am trusting you Tanya. If you print this, I am a dead man,' he said.

'Ah, so you are a poor little rich boy? I am sorry. I thought this was supposed to be an off the record discussion not a therapy session.'

'So did I but believe me, I am serious. When you possess wealth on the scale of mine, money ceases to be part of your life at all. The cash is just numbers on a piece of paper. The trappings are like trinkets. They don't feel real. They are not what really matters'

'Uh huh. Really?' she said looking as unconvinced as she sounded.

The fish course arrived. They spent a few moments eating in silence, both of them grateful for the interlude in the conversation. Petrovna struggled to swallow the tender morsels of sea bream, which were turning to dust in his mouth. He was forced to take a gulp of water to take them down, like they were some foul tasting pill. Eventually she finished her dish and surveyed him quizzically across the table.

'Maybe you are a tortured soul Mr Petrovna. That still doesn't alter the fact that I have a story to write.'

'I am not asking you to abandon your story, I am just asking to hear my side of it. I will tell you what. What if I were to take you on a fact finding trip to Caspia to see all the progress we are making in rebuilding the country? We could visit my main headquarters in Moscow first. It's much bigger than London. Then I can take you down to Caspia itself to show you some of the new equipment we have installed. I think you will be impressed. If at the end of it you still think I am the bad guy, then at least when you publish the story you can say it was balanced.'

The fish plates disappeared and yet another course arrived. This time, a single medallion of beef drizzled in a rich sauce with a suitably elaborate description. Petrovna didn't really want it and was now regretting just about everything about his choice of venue.

'That's a very interesting invitation,' she said tentatively. 'But won't it be difficult to arrange with flights and visas?'

'Not at all. We could leave in a day or so. I have my own plane and I can sort out a visa in no time at all. I just need to make a few phone calls to some people I know.'

'Some people you know'. She grinned and shook her head. 'I will need to think about your offer. Can I give you an answer tomorrow?'

'For sure you can,' he said.

Miniature sweets arrived, finally signalling that Petrovna's ordeal was near its end. He managed to eat his in a few gulps, his appetite strangely rejuvenated.

'So. Shall we definitely speak tomorrow?'

'Yes,' she said.

He pushed his plate aside and demanded the bill.

CHAPTER 17

Petrovna suffered another one of his fitful nights. Tanya had declined his offer of a lift so they had solicitously bid each other good night and gone their separate ways. He was left with the overwhelming feeling of having somehow underplayed his hand. It was most unlikely that she would be persuaded to desist from publishing a damaging article. By the same token, neither had he advanced the romantic agenda whose existence he was only now bringing himself to acknowledge. That night, his slumber was invaded by sweaty feverish dreams about her. Finally, at dawn he abandoned any further attempts at sleep and made himself a cup of coffee in the kitchenette on the upper floor of his house. Despite the early hour, he found himself reaching for his mobile every few minutes to see if there were any messages from her. He didn't usually bother to check his phone very often at all. Suddenly, at eight thirty, it rang. He snatched at the receiver.

'Good morning little boy. Guess where I am?' It wasn't Tanya.

'Good morning President'. Petrovna said. 'This is a great pleasure Sir. Where are you?'

'I am in London, near you, at the Landmark Hotel. I am on my way to New York for a meeting at the United Nations. I have decided to pay you a visit. I knew you would be pleased. We don't see each other so much in Caspia these days.'

'Well actually I do have quite a busy day myself but...'. Kornilov cut him off.

'Hey little boy. You are not avoiding me are you? That would be very unfriendly wouldn't it?'

'No, No. Of course not,' Petrovna stammered.

'Well then. You come to my hotel at midday sharp and we will have lunch, like old times. Then you can introduce me to that guy who looks after all your money in London.'

'I am not quite sure what you mean,' Petrovna said guardedly.

'Don't you fuck with me little boy. You have a stock-broker, private banker or whatever you call him. You give him your spare money to invest in the stock market. I want you to get me in front of him this afternoon. I want to invest some money too. You can act as interpreter.'

'Well look, I will do my best but he's very busy and it's very short notice. I am not sure whether it will be possible to get you in this afternoon.'

'Look you little shit. I am not asking you, I am telling you. You tell your fancy stockbroker The President of Caspia is coming to see him this afternoon and you tell me when you have done it. You understand?' The line went dead. He looked at his watch. The UK stock market had been open for over half an hour. This was going to be a pain, but he started dialling and a minute later he was put through.

'I know it's short notice, but if you could just see him for twenty minutes to explain what you do, anything else can be dealt with by the lawyers afterwards,' he said.

'No problem at all Nicholas. I am sure we can make time for a head of state, even if they are, to use your words, a bit of a character,' the financier had replied in his distinctive cut glass accent causing Petrovna to mentally sigh with relief.

———

Tanya's conversation with her boss was going really badly.

'What do you mean, a fact finding visit? You are supposed to be exposing this son of a bitch not helping him do his corporate PR. What in the name of god has got into you Tanya?'

'I do want to expose him. This was my story remember. I am winning his trust. The closer I get to him the more he reveals about himself. He was really talking freely over dinner.'

'Sounds like you're getting a bit too close to me and oh, let me guess, he will be paying for all the expenses on the trip?'

'What's that meant to mean?' she said tartly.

'It means that you are a young inexperienced reporter and he is a billionaire with powerful connections. It means he is probably gaming you. That's what it means.'

'Oh, if we are talking about gaming people, how about the fact that our CEO has been in a business dispute with Petrovna and no one thought to mention this minor detail before I started to investigate the story? Not my idea of full disclosure,' she said.

'You listen to me Tanya, you are a very promising reporter but you are in way above your pay grade here. You are not to go to Caspia with this man. You are not insured to visit dangerous locations. I want you to wrap up this story best you can in London, then I want you back here, in this office, in Chicago, with your finished copy by Monday afternoon. If you are not here, consider yourself fired. You understand?'

'Sure,' she said. The call ended leaving her more than slightly shaken. So this was it, she thought. Decision time.

She rang Petrovna next. His phone was on answer mode so she left a message instead.

CHAPTER 18

Lunch with Kornilov had been grim. Petrovna's appetite was in no better a state than it had been the previous evening, faced as he was with the distinctly un-enticing prospect of having to chaperone Kornilov to the investment meeting afterwards. It was hard to envisage any scenarios that weren't going to be just plain awkward. On his way to the lunch he had managed to grab a copy of the London Evening Standard to read in his car on the way to the meeting. It was only a short journey but long enough to catch the headlines. It was boring stuff about the impending Olympics so he flicked through the pages inside. Then his eye caught on a headline that made his heart sink. 'HARDLINE CASPIAN RULER VISITS LONDON' The article went on to describe Kornilov and his stewardship of the Republic of Caspia in a most unflattering light. It contained all the standard fare about human rights abuses and links with Russia. Nothing he hadn't read before. But then it got worse. At the bottom of the piece it said 'see editorial.' He flicked to the comment pages and there it was, under the title 'UNSAVOURY VISITORS'.

'London prides itself on being a cosmopolitan global city, but must it really pay host to corrupt politicians and dictators like President Alexei Kornilov of Caspia? This so called head of state may be the effective ruler of his country. He might even have diplomatic immunity but must we really welcome with such open arms a man whose reputation is little better than a gangster, a cut price Pinochet from the Caspian who should arguably be standing trial at the Hague, not living it up at the luxury Landmark Hotel. The presence of this man in London and of his secretive business sidekick, the billionaire oligarch Nicholas Petrovna, does London no credit.'

As Petrovna's car drew up outside the lobby he prayed that Kornilov had not seen the offending newspaper. Tanya was bound to but he would just have to deal with that. The man himself was already waiting for him in the hotel's Winter Garden restaurant. This was a palm tree fringed affair, set out open plan in a cavernous, atrium style lobby. He had seated himself at a corner table, flanked by his thick-necked bodyguards on two adjacent tables. It was hardly subtle and the scene was already beginning to attract surreptitious glances from fellow early diners. It didn't help matters that he had decided to wear a badly fitting tweed jacket and garish kerchief. Presumably this was some attempt to look English that hadn't quite worked.

Kornilov caught sight of Petrovna and beckoned him over to join them at the table's empty seat. They both ordered expensive beef burgers and bottled beer. Kornilov insisted on ordering some vintage champagne as an afterthought.

'So this is the kind of place you hang out when you are avoiding me is it?'

'I guess so,' said Petrovna attempting a strained smile.

'Don't think I don't know how much money I have allowed you to make, little boy. Remember, I know everything about you. You would have nothing if it weren't for me. You would still be a little engineer pushing paper in your little Moscow office, still living in your mummy's little old apartment. Just you remember that.' He crammed the last piece of burger into his mouth and then continued talking. The contents of his mouth made for unappetising viewing.

'I want to find out how you are doing all your clever investments. Your stockbroker man must be good. A yid like you would never trust his money to someone who wasn't. You can give the name of that banker you use in Geneva too while you are about it.'

Petrovna ignored the comments and glanced at his watch. 'We should probably go in a minute.'

'Yes we should,' Kornilov said, wiping his mouth with his napkin and tossing it casually to the floor.

'Put the lunch on my room and have them bring the car round the front,' he barked at the nearest guard.

As they approached the lobby doors one of Kornilov's bodyguards sidled over to them looking distinctly concerned.

'There is a problem President. There is a crowd of people waiting outside the door. They are waving placards and shouting. There are police and a television film crew. I think they might want to make trouble for you Sir.'

'Well tell the police to get rid of them you monkey,' Kornilov sneered. The man looked reluctant, Petrovna doubted his English was that great, but he went outside again. Petrovna watched through the glass as the man attempted to converse with the two constables controlling a small but very noisy mob of protesters. There was some gesticulation and shaking of heads before the man slunk back inside looking sheepish.

'I ask police to get rid of them but they say it is not illegal in this country so they can do nothing. Maybe we leave through a side door,' the man said avoiding Kornilov's eye.

'Useless monkey.' Then he turned to Petrovna.'You, go and see what he is on about.' Petrovna walked back to the revolving doors and peered outside again. He counted about twenty protesters in total. Most of them were obviously students but a few of them looked like they might be Caspian. There was indeed a BBC film crew with reporter. The two police officers stood beside them in their yellow vests looking mildly amused by the whole thing. The placards read, 'KILLER KORNILOV' and 'HUMAN RIGHTS NOT OIL'. Then someone caught sight of Petrovna watching and the chanting started.

'KORNILOV AND PETROVNA, HUMAN RIGHTS FOR ALL IN CAPSIA.'

Petrovna cracked a smile. At least it rhymed. He returned to the presidential party. 'I am afraid we really do need to move the cars round the side. It is a demonstration. The BBC are there and things could be difficult.'

'No,' Kornilov interjected. 'Do you think I am scared of these scum? They can go to hell. I will not leave from the back like some servant. Let us go to the cars now.'

With that he strode towards the revolving doors with the others trailing in his wake.

As soon as they emerged on the steps outside it all kicked off. Kornilov's guards formed a human barrier as the President headed for his SUV. The demonstrators jeered and blew whistles with added gusto as the party emerged through the hotel doors. Kornilov was bundled into the vehicle straight away but for a moment Petrovna was exposed. Suddenly he found a microphone being thrust in his face.

'Are you happy to be associated with an oppressive regime like Caspia Mr Petrovna?' the BBC man shouted above the demonstrators' din. Before he could say a word, a Kornilov guard had his gloved hand over the camera lens and another was roughly shoving the reporter away with his palms. 'Is this how you treat journalists?' was the last thing Petrovna heard before he himself was unceremoniously bundled inside the SUV. The vehicle lurched out into the traffic on the Marylebone Road leaving the melee behind it.

Meanwhile, inside the SUV, the tell tale vein in Kornilov's neck was throbbing with rage. 'Fucking traitor scum,' he yelled, slamming his right fist into the uphol-stery of the seat in front. 'Some of them were Caspian. I want Romanov's boys to hunt those cunts down and make them pay. Fucking scum.'

Then he went silent for the rest of the journey to Francis Cooper Asset Management. It only took a few minutes in the light traffic. Their office was situated in Mayfair in a handsome Georgian town house off Berkeley Square. They soon found themselves being offered coffee in a fine period room adorned with a large print of Constable's Hay Wain. Beside it, numerous specimens of obscure or worthless government securities hung in picture frames like the financial equivalent of the stuffed heads of slain animals. These wall mounted decorations were in fact old Tsarist bonds that were now of little more than historical interest.

Petrovna wondered if Kornilov would notice them. He suspected that even if he did the irony of what they represented would be well and truly lost on him. Hopefully he had at least calmed down after the fracas with the demonstrators.

James Francis Cooper strode into the room and shook a slightly surprised Kornilov by the hand.

'President Kornilov, it's absolutely wonderful to finally meet you. Nicholas has told me so much about you. It's not every day I have the privilege of entertaining a head of state in my office.'

Petrovna repeated the pleasantry in Russian. Kornilov looked pleased. Francis Cooper was a serious player of the old school and was no stranger to flattery. He actually looked like you would expect a stockbroker to look. Tall, with a finely tailored pinstripe suit clinging to his slight build. Although his demeanour was superficially bookish, he still retained the vague whiff of arrogance that only old money exudes.

Kornilov gave a strange little courtesy, something he often did at very formal diplomatic occasions. It looked a bit odd but at least he was back in polite mode. 'So' Kornilov began. 'Nicholas here says you are an expert on stock markets. I have money I want to invest. What would you do for me if I gave you some of my money?'

Francis Cooper waited intently for Petrovna's translation and then gave his usual measured response.

'Well Sir, our philosophy here is that investment is not just about making money it's also about not losing too much in the process. We describe our approach here as getting an enhanced return whilst ensuring the preservation of capital.'

Kornilov looked blank but Francis Cooper pressed ahead.

'What we would do is find out not just how much you have to invest but how much you want to preserve and what your investment objectives are. We specialise in both equities and bonds. We can also look at hedge funds for you if you are interested in that area. I am a great personal believer in a holistic diversified strategy. After all, however safe an investment may seem, you should never put all your eggs in one basket or else look what could happen,' he said, making an expansive hand gesture towards the worthless Tsarist bonds on the walls.

'Of course, I am sure the sovereign bonds of the government of Caspia are as safe as houses,' Cooper Francis said innocently.

Petrovna struggled to translate the financial terminology and Cooper Francis's smooth politesse as best he could, which was not easy.

Kornilov did not laugh at the reference to Caspia's own financial status.

'So what do I do if I want to invest with you?' Kornilov said.

'It would probably be easier if we deal with your accountants and lawyers but in essence we would discuss your detailed requirements with them and then make arrangements for the transfer of assets to our custodian. Then of course we have to go through the rather tedious process of formally establishing your identity and how you came by your assets.'

'What?' snarled Kornilov.

'I know, I know. It's an absolute bore. We need to see a passport, an energy bill and maybe some evidence of the source of your income. It's a legal requirement by the UK regulator to prevent the laundering of money. I am afraid even politicians like yourself are not exempt. In fact we have to be extra careful with politicians these days. It's all very silly of course.'

Petrovna guessed this would not play well even as he attempted to tactfully translate it. He was right. Kornilov went red in the face and the throbbing vein was back in action.

'Fuck them, fuck them I say,' he shouted, using his favourite English word as he banged his fist on the table causing the coffee cups to rattle.

Francis Cooper looked pained. 'Well that's certainly one way of putting it Mr President,' he said primly. Another awkward silence descended.

Petrovna turned to Kornilov and asked him if he had any more questions.

Kornilov, who had now calmed down, mumbled something in Russian and shook his head.

'I think we can leave it here. Perhaps you can write to the President care of my office with details how he might proceed if he wanted to invest with you,' Petrovna said.

'Absolutely Mr President. It's been such a pleasure to meet you,' said Francis Cooper angelically while manoeuvring himself towards the door.

Petrovna finished the pleasantries and joined the party descending the marbled staircase to the front door. When Kornilov finally told him that his presence was no longer required he walked quickly back to the relative safety of his own office, anxiously checking his phone for any messages from Tanya as he did so. There were indeed several messages and one was from Tanya but there was also a message from Sergei Romanov requesting a meeting. He sighed. That was unlikely to be a pleasure.

CHAPTER 19

The message from Tanya was that she would accept his invitation. She had left a voice mail rather than a text that Petrovna fancied sounded strained on the answer phone. Maybe it was just concealed excitement or at least that's what he hoped. He texted her back suggesting a departure date in a couple of days' time and immediately set about making travel arrangements for her. In Caspia, whatever he said ultimately happened, so flying her in and out wasn't going to be an issue. Then there was the other element of his agenda. Caspia was a dump, that meant that if he really wanted to make a good impression he needed to take her to Moscow first, where more impressive entertainments could be provided. For sure, he could wine her and dine her in London but he had no further pretext. In Moscow he had an excuse and the novelty factor would be far greater. He put in a call to his tame contacts at the interior sections of the Kremlin. A visa would have to be issued at very short notice, maybe tomorrow. Was that a problem? Apparently not if you know the right people and treat them in the manner they have come to expect.

Dealing with Sergei Romanov was much more problematic. Petrovna struggled to think of any legitimate subject the man could possibly want to discuss and it would not be a social call, that's for sure. It took him a while to get through and when he did, the man was strangely reticent. Petrovna was always very much aware that at any given time his phone calls could be tapped. He assumed though that Kornilov's spy master would at least make sure that any calls to himself were erased but who could say. Romanov mumbled something about administrative matters that need to be discussed. He had been putting it off but now it had become quite urgent. Could they meet in Moscow next week when he was passing through? Petrovna reluctantly agreed. He didn't really want any distractions from his agenda with Tanya. Even so it was probably best to get Sergei out of the way rather than be pestered by him. Whilst Kornilov had to be appeased at all times, his security boss still needed to be humoured given that it would be unwise to make an enemy of him. With that settled, his thoughts returned to how he might entertain Tanya on their fact finding mission.

Three days later he found himself at London City airport awaiting her arrival at the VIP lounge. She arrived looking flustered with way too much baggage for what would only be five day trip. They shook hands rather stiffly then he talked her through the formalities.

'Don't worry, I have arranged all your travel documentation' he said. 'All you have to do is stay with me and not lose your passport.'

She laughed nervously and followed him downstairs to the departure area. They got into a car and were driven out to the waiting aircraft. It was one of the Gulfstream range, a vast improvement on that old converted Yak Petrovna had flown in when Golitsin and Modest had taken him down to meet Kornilov for the first time. Vulgar though it had been, it had still impressed him back then. He hoped the G5 would have the same effect on Tanya now.

He watched her reactions carefully as he ushered her into the painfully stylish cabin. Everything was ergonomic and smelt of opulence. He thought he detected a brief flicker of awe on her face as she surveyed the interior or was it just his fancy? His previous attempts to impress and intimidate her had produced very mixed results. This could be a war of attrition.

'This is nice,' she said, nodding her head in approval when her survey of the cabin interior was complete.

'It's a feature of my existence,' Petrovna relied nonchalantly.

'It normally takes nearly five hours to fly to Moscow. Today it should take only four. This plane is very fast and it can cruise at much higher altitude than a normal jet,' Petrovna commented as they buckled their seat belts.

'Wow. That's amazing. I am guessing this is not carbon neutral.'

'CES has a comprehensive environmental sustainability policy,' he started to explain.

'Please.' She held up her hand to interrupt him. 'I was joking about the carbon.' They lapsed into silence as the plane taxied onto the runway for take-off. They conversed little on the flight. Petrovna pretended to work on some papers whilst Tanya switched on her iPod and stared out of the window. As they approached Moscow, he dared to offer her some champagne from the fridge at the front of the cabin. She politely declined.

When they landed, another car took them straight to the hotel. Then with Tanya safely parked at the Ritz Carlton Hotel, it was time to deal with Sergei Romanov who had insisted that they meet in a new lounge style bar just off Arbat St. Petrovna took an instant dislike to the venue the moment he stepped inside. The main bar was situated in an old bank hall and had styled itself as "Derjinskis", with a huge blown up photograph of the founding father of Soviet espionage suspended from a vast wall at the far end. The bar itself was right in the centre of the room and surrounded by a scattering of tables which were bathed in the remains of the natural light from windows high above. A DJ was spinning lounge tunes at the far end of the seating area beneath Derjinskie's glowering gaze. It was still early so the room was only just beginning to fill with a young trashy crowd. The joint had an austere 1950s retro look and the circumference was lined with self styled 'interrogation cells'. These were semi enclosed booths containing a small metal table, just two hard chairs and the kind of swivel desk lamp you could shine in someone's face. Each was named after a former NKVD or KGB boss complete with a matching photograph of these notorious spies. Romanov had already made himself at home in the 'Yagoda' booth. Petrovna recalled that the career of Stalin's spymaster had not ended happily and hoped it was not an omen. Once again, he found himself pondering what the purpose of this meeting could be. In any event he needed to be careful, Sergei Romanov was not a pleasant man.

He sat down on an unforgiving chair and was forced to lean forward uncomfortably so that he could actually hear what the other man was saying. The lounge music DJ was literally pumping up the volume.

'I hope you like my choice of venue', Romanov said with an annoying smirk on his face. 'I think you will agree, there is no risk of anyone hearing our conversation.'

Petrovna nodded in agreement as he scanned the drinks list. He lent in even closer. 'How can I help you Sergei?'

'Actually, it's more a question of how I can help you my friend.'

He paused as the waiter arrived to take their drinks order. Petrovna winced at the prices. He could buy the whole damn brewery in the blink of eye but objected to paying this much for a tasteless lager. Instead, he decided to double down on an 'Enemy of the People' cocktail. Romanov ordered an 'Extraordinary Rendition'.

'You know what. I like you Nicholas, you are a decent man in a shitty place. For sure, none of us are saints but we do the best we can with the hand fate dealt us.'Petrovna kept on nodded tentatively.

'We make the most of our cards and you have done better than most with yours. We have all made fortunes but with the exception of our dear President, none of us has made as much as you have. You know what they say though, all good things must come to an end.' He paused as the waiter reappeared with the cocktails. 'I summoned you here in confidence to warn you Nicholas Petrovna, that I fear your good fortune may indeed soon be at an end.'

Petrovna felt an all too familiar needle of fear and hurriedly took as sip of his cocktail. As he suspected, it tasted foul. He grimaced visibly.

'What's the matter? Don't you like enemies of the people?' Romanov sneered, looking pleased with himself.

A conversation like this had always been a possibility. He had rehearsed it in his mind many times over. In practice, this forethought did little to diminish the chill of it now that it was actually occurring.

'What exactly do you mean by that?' he said guardedly.

'I think you know perfectly well what I mean unless you are a total fool and an imbecile. You have profited from supping with the devil, just like the rest of us but one day the devil always takes his dues.'

Petrovna emitted one of his watery smiles. 'You are talking in riddles Sergei Romanov. I appreciate your concern for my welfare but I am not one for riddles.'

'What I am saying Nicholas, is that Kornilov has tolerated you all these years and allowed you to prosper because he needed you. Hell, I think he even finds you funny, certainly not a threat. But now I have to tell you that I sense you are losing your novelty. He is already having your calls tapped and your movements followed. You do know that don't you?'

'I didn't but I am not surprised. I have always assumed that it would end up that way,' Petrovna said, trying to sound nonchalant.

'You shrug your shoulders like you don't care but the truth is this could end very badly for you and your young American friend. Yes, we know all about her too and her secret investigations. You remember what happened to your two business partners when they had a falling out with our mutual master. They were just the beginning. You know this. Being his friend is no guarantee of safety. Actually it could get you killed. Believe me I know because I usually end up making the arrangements. And if I am asked to make arrangements for you, then I will.'

'So what are you saying, that I am next on the list?'

'Not yet but you could be at any moment and so could I. For all I know Kornilov is instructing my deputy to have me arrested as we speak. He would do if he knew I was talking to you here. I deliberately waited for him to be away in New York with most of my subordinates so that I could slip up here and meet you without being tracked.'

'OK, thanks for the tip-off but just exactly what is it that you want from me Sergei? You never do anything as an act of charity.'

A brief smile cracked across the spy's cruel face. 'You have grown cynical in your old age Nicholas Petrovna. Seeing as you ask, myself and a number of others are of the opinion that maybe rather than waiting to be picked off one by one it would be safer for all of us if our dear leader met with a little accident just like his predecessor.'

Petrovna suddenly laughed. 'Now, let me guess, I pay for you to arrange a little private regime change. You become President in his place and you get to swipe Kornilov's stake in CES.'

Now Romanov joined in the laughter, nodding inanely as he did so. Then he stopped laughing and lent across the table in the booth until his face was level with Petrovna's.

'Yes, that is exactly what I am proposing,' he said, locking Petrovna in an icy stare.

'And how do I know you are not taping this conversation that you can play it to Kornilov, get me whacked and swipe my stake instead?' said Petrovna.

'You don't. That's just a risk you are going to have to take, though I don't think the conversation on the tape would be very audible do you?'

He was right; the lounge music was now so oppressively loud Petrovna could barely hear himself think. He lent forward across the table again to make himself heard without shouting.

'I don't think I could get involved with anything like that Sergei.'

'I thought you might say that. But can you afford not to be? Maybe nothing happens, or maybe Kornilov just seizes all your assets in Caspia without bothering to kill you first. But hey, don't come crying to me for help if your brains are spattered on the floor of one my cells. Oh, and you know what, maybe I just do this thing anyway and guess what, I will remember who my friends were.'

Romanov rose to leave, carefully negotiating his way out of cramped booth.

'You know where to find me if you want to talk. I presume you can afford to get the tab' he said before leaving Petrovna to his own devices.

Later that evening Petrovna had the altogether pleasanter task of escorting Tanya to the Bolshoi. He thought it would be a suitably congenial way of breaking the ice a little further without getting into any difficult conversational territory. He had managed to get two tickets for

The Queen of Spades, an opera by Tchaikovsky that happened to be a favourite of his. He had been taken to see it once as a teenager. At the time he had hated its seemingly impenetrable score. Later in life he had revisited out of curiosity and had grown to love the piece. The story of an obsessive gambler corrupted by his own greed had always had a strange resonance for him. Admittedly, a ballet like *Swan Lake* would have been more suitable but it wasn't in the current repertoire.

Tanya was waiting for him in the lobby at the allotted time. She was wearing a figure hugging black dress that afforded ample views of her long legs, again. He hoped this was deliberate? He imagined that being an American she had only seen the interior of an opera house on a movie screen. She no doubt thought everyone wore ball gowns and tiaras. Although she hadn't gone quite that far, the outfit and the jewellery was definitely overkill. He resolved to say nothing on the subject.

'Ready to go,' he said. She nodded and looked him up and down, betraying perhaps a flicker of disappointment at his lounge suit attire but maybe that was just his paranoia. His car was already waiting at the front of the lobby. They both got in and sat in silence for a minute or so as the car scythed its way through the thick Moscow traffic. She broke the silence.

'This is really great. This is my first time at the opera. We have one in Chicago. My boss entertains corporate clients there occasionally but I have never been myself. I am really looking forward to seeing inside the Bolshoi. I remember my father talking about it. He told me that only the big party bosses ever got to go there.'

'Yes. It is a very large auditorium. It is also a very famous and historic building renowned for its performances of Russian ballet. There is an opera company here too. It was also used for Communist party meetings just like your father said. Stalin had a box there reserved for his personal use and he often came.'

The car was arriving up outside now. He opened the car door helped her out of the vehicle solicitously. She followed him into the vast pillared edifice through the various palatial stairways and antechambers to their box.

'Was this Stalin's box?' she said.

'I don't know which one was his so I suppose it could be,' he replied. She gazed around taking in the expanse of the extraordinarily ornate auditorium.

'Can I take a photograph on my phone?'

'It's not really the done thing here. You definitely need to make sure it's switched off before the music starts'.

'I can see other people taking photographs.'

'That's because they are ignorant peasants.'

She shot him a look. 'You are starting to sound like Stalin.'

Her familiarity pleased him.

The lights started to dim as the conductor entered the orchestra pit. Petrovna sat back in his seat savouring the exquisite opening chords of the prelude. The sinuous opening theme had never sounded so mournful yet his heart soared at the prospect of what was to follow.

At the end of the first act, he applauded enthusiastically. He looked across to Tanya who was stifling a yawn as best she could.

'What do you think?' he said.

'I think you need to tell me what is going on.'

'OK. Let's get some champagne first then I will explain the plot to you. It's not that complicated really.'

They stood in the corner of a pillared foyer clutching their flutes of Cava, as the curious mixture of the Moscow smart crowd and wealthy tourists milled around them. Looking at the slightly blingy throng, Petrovna wondered whether he had been a little harsh in his earlier assessment that she was overdressed.

'It's set in St Petersburg, Russia, during the era of Catherine the Great and is based on a story by Pushkin, one of our most esteemed writers,' he said.

'Go on,' she said smiling.

'An impoverished young army officer called Herman visits a gambling house every night without ever placing a bet. One day he sees a beautiful young girl called Liza in the park. He learns that she is already engaged to a wealthy aristocrat, Prince Yeletsky. He also learns that her ageing guardian the Countess possesses a secret combination of cards that will always win. Later, he attempts to seduce Liza in her room. Although his first attempt has failed she finds him alluring. At a masked ball he tries again and this time she gives him a key so that he can visit her later. He takes the key but it is not her room he goes to. Instead he goes to the chambers of the aged countess. He pleads with her to reveal the secret of the cards to him. When she refuses, he threatens her with a gun that causes her to literally die of fright. He flees the scene. Back at his barracks he writes to Liza begging forgiveness and asks her to meet him by the canal at midnight so they can elope together. Suddenly, the countess's ghost appears and reveals that three cards are certain to win if played, three, seven, ace. The apparition holds up the cards for Herman to see. When he arrives at the canal at midnight Liza is already waiting. She tells him that she has jilted her fiancé Yeletsky so they can elope. He replies that he has the secret of the cards and must go to the gaming house first. He departs. Liza realises she has been used and drowns herself in the canal. At the gaming house Harman plays the first two cards and wins and as the countess predicted. Herman boasts about his winnings and dares the others to play again against the huge amount of money he is now wagering. No one will play against him until the jilted Yeletsky arrives. He hears the boasting and agrees to meet Herman's massive bet. They play and Herman declares himself the victor with his ace. However, Yeletsky points to the card and says "no, that is a queen of spades." Herman has lost everything. He looks up and sees the ghost of the countess hovering above him, she is laughing and taunting him with the bogus card combination. Distraught, Herman turns his gun on himself and dies.'

'Wow, it's a real good story. I thought you said it wasn't too complicated. I would not have a clue what was happening if you hadn't explained,' she said.

Petrovna's explanation had taken so long that the interval was almost over. They both drained their flutes hurriedly and returned to the box. The curtain rose and once again Tchaikovsky's sinuous melodies slowly emerged like silhouettes out of the darkness. As Yeletsky sang his great aria, Ya las lubyu, 'I love you beyond measure but your coldness troubles me,' he looked across to Tanya and pondered that the ill fated prince's predicament could in some sense be similar to his own.

On their way back to the hotel, he asked Tanya if she was hungry.

'A little, it's getting kind of late though,' she said.

'We could have a light snack and a drink. Nothing heavy. It might be better for us both if we are not seen dining together in the lobby. It is quite a public place, much more so than the opera. I will tell you what. I have got a dining table in my suite. We can eat there if you like.'

She hesitated for what seemed like an eternity before answering.

'OK,' She said, tentatively. They swept through the marble lobby briskly and took the lift straight up to the Ritz Carlton's grandest suite where he unlocked the double doors and entered. She paused on the threshold for just a moment, though to Petrovna it seemed longer, then she followed him inside.

'Make yourself at home while I order us some supper,' he said, pointing towards a sofa in the main section of the suite.

Petrovna made a short phone call in Russian while Tanya waited. The hotel was built in the classical style though it has all the opulence and accoutrements of an Arab palace. This suite was a bit different in that it was decked out like an English drawing room with a large king size bed at one end. Next to it was a wood panelled study that led into the dining room.

Petrovna turned round after he had finished the call and noted with satisfaction that she was admiring the stunning view of Red Square in all its illuminated glory.

'Don't worry. They won't be long with the supper,' he said and sat down in an easy chair opposite her. 'So, you like the view then?'

'Yes, it's amazing. I heard lots of stories about Moscow when I was a child but they weren't good ones. I never realised it was this impressive. I always think of it as communist style blocks of concrete social housing. I didn't know you had all these grand boulevards and churches.'

'Most people don't. If you think this is impressive, you should see St Petersburg. That's really grand. The palaces there are really something. Crumbling but beautiful and the whole city is criss-crossed by a web of canals, a bit like Venice.'

They spent a few minutes admiring the view while Petrovna gave a commentary on various floodlit landmarks. A buzz at the door announced the arrival of a morning-suited butler bearing a trolley with elegant food and yet another bottle of champagne. He wheeled it through to the dining room and started to lay things out.

'Shall we go through?' Petrovna said as the butler sidled into the corridor. The dining table was set out with the champagne, a large tray of caviar and some small pancakes.

'Oh, more champagne,' she said rolling her eyes.

'It's traditional to have champagne with caviar and blinis. There's some sour cream as well if you want. Before the revolution, Russian aristocrats used to eat caviar for breakfast.'

'I guess not much has changed then,' she said as she gulped some down. It was a much better variety than the substitute they had been drinking at the Bolshoi.

'So' she said, 'what's it really like being a communist, I mean why did people put up with all that poverty and oppression for so long. Why didn't people just, like, rebel, when they discovered how much better off everyone was in the West?'

'Well Tanya, it wasn't as simple as that. Most people in Russia have always been impoverished and Russia has always been an autocracy. Remember, the Tsars were total autocrats, and most people were starving. That's why the revolution happened in the first place. To begin with, most people were better off under the communists. They continued to believe this for many years even though standards of living were way below those in the West. They believed it because that's what the Russian media repeatedly told them. Hardly anyone travelled outside Russia so there were very few people to contradict the propaganda.'

'But don't Russians value freedom and democracy like people do in America? In the USA, freedom of speech and liberty are enshrined in our constitution,' she said, as her voice was growing increasingly loud and excitable.

'They do. But again, you must remember that communism was democratic. You could vote for deputies. It's just that they were all communist because that's the system we had decided to adopt at the time of the revolution, rather than capitalism. Not everyone was badly off and when communism ended, quite a lot of people ended up worse off. I was one of the lucky ones.'

'So, let's get this straight. It was a democracy because you could vote for anyone you like as long as they are communist?' she said and then, without warning burst into another one of her girlish giggles.

'I can't believe we are discussing revolutionary communism over caviar,' she added.

'Then perhaps we can talk about something else,' he replied.

'Like what?'

He took a deep breath.

'Like why has a beautiful young journalist like you agreed to drink champagne with someone she is supposed to be investigating?'

She pursed her lips for a moment and spoke a little bit slowly. The champagne was finally doing its job.

'Maybe I think you are interesting, so I decided to give you a chance to put your case. Anyway, why did you invite me here and go to all this expense to impress me when you could have just crushed me with your lawyers?'

'Perhaps I find you interesting too Tanya. Perhaps, I saw something in you that I rarely see in others. Honesty, tenacity, maybe some naivety but above all, passion and not the passion my HR people go on about. I saw it when you first tried to interview me at my office. Then I saw it again in the restaurant when I told you Hank Stewart was gaming you. And now, I must tell you, that you have awakened a passion in me,' he said rather stiffly.

'OK, Nicholas. Now we are having a real conversation,' she said looking over at him intently.

'Yes we are,' he said. Then he moved over to the sofa, sat down next to her and reached for her hand. She took it willingly and felt her grasp tighten around his. He turned to look at her then she started to lean forward. A moment later their lips connected and her tongue slipped into his mouth. He felt himself becoming aroused as she pulled him closer and continued to explore his mouth with her tongue. He pulled away. 'Let's go to bed,' he said.

He led her to the other end of the room where the bed was and started to undress and then halted, transfixed, as he watched her do likewise. The black evening dress was already off. The bra came next in a single graceful movement revealing her pert, perfectly hung cleavage. Petrovna observed that her nipples were already stiff. She rested one foot after the other on the side of the bed as she slowly peeled down her black stockings revealing those long slender legs and delicately painted toes. He breathed hard to keep his composure whilst completing his own undress.

Now she was lying on top of the bed looking strangely vulnerable.

She looked at him and nodded. He required no further bidding as he caressed her lithe form. He kissed her again on the lips before moving down the side of her neck and then all the way down her chest to her lower rib cage. She closed her eyes and moaned as he reached between her legs with his right hand searching for the source of her pleasure. His fingers easily sank into her wetness causing her to moan again, utterly responsive to his lightest touch. Then, he completed the sweetest of tasks.

———

He awoke with a start, as he often did when he was in a strange place. It took a few seconds to get his bearings but after a moment the surrounds of the lavishly appointed hotel suite became familiar. He looked at the girl sleeping next to him and was instantly filled with a feeling of disgust. She had given him great head the night before. That wasn't an invitation for her to stay the night in Kornilov's book. Not when the meter is ticking. He shook her hard.

'Hey you. Why are you still here?'

The girl looked at Kornilov through squinty eyes. The agency had warned that he was a difficult client. They had said that he was a very senior diplomat who required the utmost discretion. They had also told her that he had certain tastes that she might find unpalatable. The phrase 'rough sex' had been used which was one hell of an understatement. The tip would be excellent but the warning had not prepared her for what had followed. Caesar's Club clients always paid top whack but sometimes a small fortune just isn't enough.

'I mean, get the fuck out of here now,' he said. Then without warning, he lashed out, belting her across the side of the face. It wasn't a heavy blow by Kornilov's standards but it was sufficient to elicit a scream from the poor girl. She vaulted out of bed, snatched her clothes off the floor and fled to the suite's adjoining chamber. This barely raised an eyebrow from Kornilov's security guard who had been dozing on the sofa in the sitting room. He'd seen it all before. This woman didn't seem too badly bruised compared to the whores he used in Caspia. Kornilov had obviously let her off lightly because they were in America.

Kornilov lumbered over to the window and ripped apart the heavy curtains to admire the view over Central Park, which looked very pleasant in the morning sunshine. A procession of joggers paraded past the ponds and the empty ice rink below his window. He scanned them with an air of indifference. Little ants going about their little lives. His mood was bad. He had taken rooms at the Plaza because it was convenient for the UN and because he had heard that the American President stayed there. The trouble was, everyone else visiting the UN had the same idea, consequently he had only been allocated a relatively small junior suite. Apparently some of the other UN attendees were more important than the Caspian head of state. The reality was that Caspia's status under international law was tenuous at best. As a barely autonomous Soviet spin out, they were allowed to have a representative at UN meetings. In practice, his invitation was little more than a courtesy that entitled his to watch from the sidelines. Even Palestine had more UN bragging rights than Caspia. This was a concept Kornilov found hard to stomach. Nonetheless, he still liked to attend these meetings in person. If nothing else it gave him an excuse to visit New York and shop on Fifth Avenue. The Caspian retail experience was a bit limited by contrast.

He rang and ordered some breakfast before getting on the phone to Romanov. He had tried calling him yesterday. Romanov's secretary had claimed he was out. His mobile had been turned off as well. Kornilov hated that. He liked his subordinates to be contactable at all times. Romanov wasn't there this morning either. It would be late afternoon in Caspia by now. Where the hell was he?

Sergei Romanov did eventually return Kornilov's calls later in the morning. Kornilov had just returned from his Fifth Avenue sortie laden with a variety of designer clothes and other luxuries that were not so freely available on his home turf.

'Where the fuck were you Romanov? I have been trying to get hold of you for days,' he said.

'I am sorry President. I had some business problems I needed to sort out. It took me out of circulation for a day.'

'Never do that again. I want you contactable twenty four seven, especially if I am abroad. Now, what's the latest on Petrovna and the stupid journalist girl he's trying to screw?'

'My information is he may have already done so. My men are keeping a tab on them both just like you said. They are in Caspia at the moment. He is showing her around some of the Caspoil sites, supposedly to prove he has nothing to hide. Before that they went through Moscow. They both checked in to the Ritz Carlton. Fine for her but why him? He already has a huge apartment in Moscow round the corner. The randy little snake must be trying to get in her knickers.'

Kornilov grunted with derision. 'I didn't think he would have it in him. I don't mind him screwing around with this American whore but I don't like the idea of her poking around in our business. Keep them under close surveillance. There's no saying what that fool Petrovna will do if he's got a hard-on for her.'

'Don't worry, I have,' said Romanov.

'Good,' Kornilov hung up the call and wondered how to amuse himself that evening. He could try and get another girl from the agency like last night, assuming Caesar's would let him. He was minded to play one of his rougher games. It had been a while. He wandered over to his desk and reached into a bag that was stored next to it and retrieved his precious knuckle-duster from within. It accompanied him everywhere he went almost as if the item held some talismanic allure. Now he toyed with it in the palm of his hand as he pondered whether there was a way he could procure a victim to use it on. Then he put it back in its case again, closing the lid with an irritated snap. Even little people had rights in the United States and diplomatic immunity has its limits. He would have to wait.

He could just pick a girl up off the street in Caspov. Sometimes, when he was in his motorcade, a girl caught his attention. He would tell his driver to slow down while he pointed her out to his guards. Later, she would be 'invited' back to his compound. Refusal was not an option. His favourite scenario was emotional blackmail. Last month, when a rebel militia man had fallen into his clutches, Kornilov had been delighted to learn about the existence of his twenty five year old sister. She had proven to be very accommodating as soon as she learned of her brother's predicament. It's touching what people will do to save a loved one. Kornilov smiled to himself. Seeing the look on her face when he broke the news that her brother was already dead had been almost as much fun as forcing her to strip and perform oral sex on him. Seeing the hot tears stream down her innocent face as she did so had merely engorged his merciless lust. It was such a shame that she had to spoil things by screaming and threatening to tell the press. As if they would even print it! Anyway, a session with knuckle duster had quickly put an end to all that nonsense. It had made a nasty mess but at least she was reunited with her brother now. How touching, he thought.

CHAPTER 20

Tanya woke early and instantly felt that horrible morning after sensation. She had a vague trace of a hangover from the champagne. The sight of Petrovna still asleep next to her told her everything else she didn't want to know. She had fallen for the oldest trick in the book. Big night out, alcohol, flattery and then she had screwed the person she was supposed to be busting. It was just so clichéd, and to make matters worse, she had an inkling that she had instigated the sex act. The details were hazy, which she thought might be a blessing.

She dragged herself out of bed, pulled off the top bed sheet and wrapped it round her midriff. The action of yanking the sheet caused the mass under the remaining bedclothes to groan and shift position. He twisted his head to look at her.

'Good morning,' he said nervously.

'Yea, hi,' she replied whilst beating a rapid retreat towards the bathroom with the bed sheet trailing behind her.

When she returned, now wearing the clothes she had grabbed on the way, he had already pulled on a shirt and slacks. She looked at him awkwardly and said. 'Look, about last night. That shouldn't have happened. I don't normally do that sort of thing it's just...'

He stopped her mid sentence. 'Don't worry about it. I understand. It's fine. Let's just pretend it didn't happen. Why don't you go back to your room and get some breakfast. I will take you round the Moscow office and then it will be time to fly down to Caspia.'

She nodded and looked at her watch. 'OK, I will see you in the lobby at nine thirty then.' With that she left the scene of the crime.

The Moscow office was vast compared with London. It occupied the entirety of a modern glass office building a few miles North of Moscow's centre.

'London is just a corporate office for meetings,' he explained. 'I have a similar satellite office in New York just to keep track of CES's North American investments. Moscow is the administrative hub and overall commercial headquarters. There are nearly five hundred people in this building alone, so you can see it's a serious international business now with an army of accountants, lawyers and engineers to keep it going. Most of the physical plant is still in Caspia, by which I mean the refineries, storage and drill rigs. I also have some assets in Siberia. The old head office is still in Caspov. I will show you that tomorrow, but that office is just a local branch now. The business as a whole is really run out of Moscow these days. Now, if you follow me, I have something important to show you,' he said, betraying a trace of smugness.

They walked through the centre of a large open plan room that must have contained at least a hundred people all labouring diligently in a collection of hutch like cubicles. They arrived at a cluster of desks in the far corner that seemed to be staffed mainly by women of about Tanya's age wearing earnest trouser suits. Most of these ladies were working on PowerPoint presentations or documents that looked like brochures or similar. Tanya peered over one girl's shoulder. The text was in Cyrillic but the picture of a large group of smiling children with the towers of an oil refinery in the background made the concept abundantly clear.

'This is our corporate social responsibility section,' he said triumphantly. 'Anya, this lady is an American journalist. Please explain to her what you are doing.'

The girl answered in perfect English. 'I am responsible for liaising with the local communities where CES operates. Caspoil is totally committed to operating in a sustainable fashion and working with local people to preserve the environment around them. We insist on fair and safe working practices. That helps not just to protect but also to develop these areas and help the local economy. For example, CES has just sponsored the construction of a new school next to one of its storage depots in North Caspia. The brochure I am working on here is designed to explain the benefits Caspoil has to offer to local people. You know, I am really excited to be working on a project like this,' she gushed, barely pausing for breath.

Tanya didn't know quite what to say. Obviously this whole thing had been well rehearsed. Nonetheless an immediate response eluded her.

'Wow. That's really great,' was the best she could manage.

'We are serious about protecting the environment and the communities we work with Tanya,' Petrovna said before ushering her away.

When they had finished touring the rest of the building they drove straight to the airport. They were served a light smoked salmon lunch on the G5 as they flew south to Caspia. As usual, a car was already waiting for them as they touched down. There were no visible immigration formalities. On the way to the hotel they stopped at a drab concrete industrial office complex. Petrovna pointed though the glass at the grim edifice.

'This is the old Caspoil head office. As I said, it is still in use for local administration. I use it myself when I am down here to review the local operations. We won't bother going in unless you really want to. There is very little to see there.'

'OK, let's just go to the hotel then,' she said.

They continued to the Hotel Grand Caspian. The building was now owned by CES and had been the beneficiary of an incredibly expensive make over. Whilst not quite as lavish as the Ritz Carlton, the building was at least back to its former glories.

'Would you like to have dinner again tonight?' he asked.

Tanya knew perfectly well what that would entail. She had calmed down a bit since the initial shock of discovering her professional lapse earlier that morning. Of course it had been a huge mistake. However, on reflection, she had enjoyed the mistake whilst it was happening and had to acknowledge that her role in initiating the proceedings had been quite enthusiastic. The truth of the matter was that she found him quite charming in an odd sort of way. And he was extremely rich. Not for the first time she dismissed that vulgar thought out of her head. She didn't want to reject him entirely but she needed time to think.

'You know what, I am kind of tired,' she said

'No problem. Tomorrow's a big day,' he said as he escorted her into the lobby and made sure she was checked in.

'Let's meet here at nine thirty tomorrow morning if that's all right with you. There's a lot to see tomorrow. Wear some sensible shoes. Remember, we will be in an industrial environment.'

She nodded and picked up her hand luggage before the porter could get it.

'Oh, by the way,' he added. 'It's probably best if you stay inside the hotel tonight. I am afraid Caspia is not completely safe, especially not for single women at night.'

'Thanks for the tip,' she said before disappearing into the lifts.

The next morning, she went down to the lobby at the allotted time dressed in jeans, boots and a smart top. She hoped these would be appropriate for an industrial environment. He was already waiting for her in the male version of similar apparel. She had to admit that for an older man, he did look quite handsome. They drove to a refinery near to the Caspov docks first.

'This is where the accident you are so obsessed with occurred. There's really nothing to see now. I had the whole thing rebuilt afterwards. There's a plaque round the other side of the site commemorating the men who died.'

'I think you said you were actually here on the day the accident happened. Surely you could have done something to prevent it?'

He let slip a sigh of exasperation. 'Obviously there was no way I could have known that the procedure I requested would actually cause an accident. That's the point about accidents, people don't cause them on purpose, it's just lots of small errors building up to a point where they meet to cause a tragedy. Not everything is a conspiracy like your Kennedy assassination.'

The car drove round the refinery. They remained inside it as he pointed out the site of the explosion and the joys of fractional distillation.

'How does that work?' she asked.

'Crude oil is just the raw material. You heat it up in these tall towers until it evaporates and separates into its constituent parts then you siphon them off from different parts of the column. You end up with petrol, chemicals and other products. Some of the gases are very volatile.' His voice tailed off

'Ah. I get it,' she said.

He also showed her the control room, which had been rebuilt since the explosion and was now just an underground room with CCTV and lots of computers. She had been expecting something more like Star Wars and was actually a bit disappointed.

Next they drove a couple of hours north to show her the new storage hub. This connected the Caspian gas supply network with Russia. It was also the site of the newly built school that the preppy social responsibility girl had shown her back at head office. The long drive north was through featureless landscape and they both dozed off for a while. Their driver awoke them when they arrived at their destination.

The storage facility itself was even less interesting than the refinery whose mass of steel pipes and towers at least had a certain metallic drama about them. This site resembled a giant barn with some very large gas silos and not a great deal else. Tanya did her best to stifle a yawn.

'Why was this site built here exactly?' she said, sounding bored.

'Ah. Several reasons actually. First, it's convenient for the intersection of the two gas pipeline systems. Remember we are only about ten miles from the Russian border. Secondly there is a small gas field under the site too. It's not very obvious but in addition to storing gas from the rest of Caspia before it's piped down to the coast or into Russia, we are also drawing fresh supplies out of the ground. There are dozens of small gas fields in Caspia. Not as big as the great reserves in the Caspian Sea but they are still worth exploiting.'

'And where is this famous new school?'

'It's a couple of miles down the road. We can head down there now. There's also a place we can get something to eat in the adjoining village.'

When they arrived the school buildings looked pretty much as depicted in the brochure, except there was no sign of any smiling children.

'I think it's a school holiday,' he said, correctly anticipating her next question.

She nodded but did not look totally convinced. The village itself looked strangely artificial. The narrow string of houses was simple in design and obviously newly constructed compared with the others she had observed on their drive up. They had cheap corrugated iron roofs and were little more than grey coloured boxes that suggested just about every expense had been spared. The overall effect was charmless and depressing.

'Is it safe, being so close to the storage depot? I mean what if there was another explosion like the one you had at the refinery?'

'Obviously we take every step to make sure that doesn't happen. If it did, then at worst a few windows might be blown out. We actually moved the village for that reason, that's why it looks so new.'

'That's nice,' she said.

'It's time we got something to eat. I think we can get a snack at that little cafe.'

The so called cafe was really just a gas station with some tables selling drinks and snacks from a big fridge. As they walked towards it Petrovna's phone rang. His expression clouded when he saw the number and he took the call. After a moment he put his hand over the mobile handset and said.

'I am really sorry but I need to take this in private. I could be ten, fifteen minutes or so. Please wait in the café. If you take a walk, don't go too far.' Tanya was actually quite relieved at getting the opportunity to have a wander on her own for a few minutes. She pointed down the road to indicate that she was going to walk further into the soulless hamlet. He remained at the side of the road. His face wore an pained expression as he clutched the mobile handset tightly to his ear.

Tanya walked for several minutes down the eerily quiet street until she came across a house with an old woman standing at the gate. She looked like some comic book Russian crone. Overweight, with a balding grey top, two rows of rotten teeth and a heavily lined face with more than a hint of facial hair. She was no oil painting but she gave Tanya a sad smile. Tanya dutifully smiled back at her.

It suddenly occurred to Tanya that thus far she had not had a single conversation with anyone in Caspia other than her host and the hotel receptionist. This could be interesting she thought. The woman stared at Tanya, obviously picking up on the fact that she was not from these parts.

'Where are you from?' she asked Tanya. She spoke in a Caspian dialect which was like an antiquated form of Russian. Tanya strained to understand her thick accent but they could just about converse.

'I am from the USA,' she replied in her best Russian.

The woman broke into a broad smile, clearly delighted that she had met a foreigner who she could actually talk to.

'I am Olga. Please, come see my house', beckoning that Tanya should come inside. Tanya hesitated for a moment. Was this a good idea? Then she mentally slapped herself. You are supposed to be a journalist. Can't you handle some peasant's shack?

When she stepped inside, the house was as expected, new but very austere with flimsy looking interior walls that screamed cheap prefab. The contents of the sitting room were not new at all, just some threadbare easy chairs and an old TV set in one corner. A few photographs hung from the walls, and that was it décor wise. The woman disappeared into a back room then reappeared carrying first a dainty china tea set and then an odd looking device that looked a bit like a metal urn. The women lifted a small pot off the top of the urn and used it to pour a few dribbles of very potent looking tea into one of the painted cups. Tanya took the cup with some trepidation and then watched as the woman filled her own cup and then diluted the brew with hot water from the bottom section of the urn. Tanya took one sniff of the tea concentrate and quickly decided to follow suit.

She took a sip. It was surprisingly pleasant. 'It's a real nice house you have here. Is it new? It looks quite new' she said, trying to avoid looking at the women's horribly visible moustache.

'Yes, it is new. The whole village is new. We all moved here about five years ago, what was left of us.'

Tanya considered her turn of phrase. Maybe she had misunderstood the woman's last comment. Listening to the dialect was a struggle.

'You live here alone?' she continued.

'Yes. My husband was killed during the rising against the Russians and my son was killed a few years later.' The woman turned and pointed at the photographs hanging from the back wall. 'And you? Why have you come here from America? No one comes here, especially not people like you,' she said with the first trace of bitterness as she added a drop more water to her tea.

'Actually I am a journalist for an American magazine. I am investigating a story about Caspia.' The old woman seemed momentarily lost in thought. Then she looked up and said.

'You want to hear a story?'

Tanya nodded enthusiastically.

'Here is a story. My husband, he was an honourable man, a proud man. When the war came he joined the local militia to fight for Caspian Independence. He said to me: I must go. This is the only chance we might ever have to be free of Russian rule. I never saw him again. The fighting was savage, even the militias that were supposed to be on the same side ended up fighting each other instead of the Russians. Then this man comes. He calls himself Kornilov. He comes and he terrorises us all. His men wear army uniforms but they act like wild animals. They go from village to village. They say they are the rulers of Caspia now and they will do as they please. They say they will kill us all if they find we are supporting any of the militias.

Some of the other villages were destroyed completely. They told us: that is the fate of anyone who defies the will of Kornilov. When Kornilov triumphed in the conflict, we were all heart broken. Then we thought, at least it would all be over and the killing would end. It did not. Men came from the oil company and told us that we must all leave our homes so that they could build a new factory or pipeline or something. We said that we did not want to leave our village. Some families had lived and farmed the land for hundreds of years. There was a meeting in the village with a man from the oil company who they sent to persuade us to move. Someone said to him that they must have found oil underground and we should all be paid a share of the money. The man from the oil company was angry. He said we were all greedy ungrateful peasants. He said that Kornilov would make us sorry we had been so difficult. Then, two days later a truck arrived with men in uniform.

Their faces we're covered with masks but we knew they must be Kornilov's troops by their type of uniform. They announced on a loud speaker that we had an hour to get our belongings and leave our homes or else we would be moved by force. My son and some other men refused to leave and confronted the soldiers outside. Then, without warning, the soldiers started firing. Our men were not armed but they just shot them like dogs. They killed my son and all the other young men that day. They just killed them in the street in full view of the rest of us. Then they went round the houses one by one, kicking in the doors, stealing what they wanted and then setting them on fire when they had finished. Some of the young women were dragged away and raped. They said it was to teach us a lesson and make us remember this day forever.'

Tanya sat aghast at the unsolicited anecdote. She had been hoping to uncover something like this but now she had, she felt sad. She wasn't sure why

'So, what happened next?'

'They put the bodies of my son and the other dead men in the back of the truck and drove them away to get rid of them. Then the rest of us were marched out of the burnt out village with what few belongings we could salvage from the ruins. They made us stand and watch while a bulldozer flattened the site, then the survivors were put in open trucks and driven away to a makeshift camp. We spent a year living like gypsies in a tented shantytown down the road. One day, a man from the oil company came again, a different one this time. He told us that President Kornilov had decided to forgive us and that we could move back to a new village. So we all came back to this place and everyone has to pretend that nothing had happened. When the leader of Kornilov's men first left us at the shantytown, he said, 'No one cares about scum like you, no one is interested in your lives. If you try and tell anyone we will come back and kill the rest of you just like we did your husbands and your sons. We believed him at the time. Now I think, Olga, soon you will die anyway, someone should know about what happened to your son.' The woman fell silent and stared into the dregs of her cup.

'Do you know what they did with the bodies of your son and the other men they killed?'

'I do. I have been taken there a few times to lay flowers. It's a short drive from here but I would need to ask someone else in the village to find the place for certain.'

'And could you arrange for me to be taken there?'

'Yes. Maybe. Would that help you tell our story if I did?'

'Well yes it would' Tanya said excitedly. Then, suddenly it dawned on her how much time had passed. She looked at her watch. She had been gone nearly half an hour. Shit, she thought, Petrovna will be going ape.

'I am really sorry but I have to go in a moment. I really want to come back and visit this gravesite. Is there any way I can contact you? A phone number?'

'No phone, but I am here until I die.'

Tanya got up and clasped the woman's veiny hand.

'Believe me Olga, I really want to tell your story. I will be back soon. I promise.'

She jogged back to the car and found an agitated looking Petrovna.

'Where did you go? I was really worried. Please don't wander off like that again. It's not safe here,' he said, sounding genuinely anxious.

They got coffee and a cake from the depressing gas station. Both were horrible. Not a place to linger. Back in the limo he seemed tense. The phone call must have been problematic. She toyed with the idea of confronting him right there with the old woman's story. Then on reflection she decided against it. After all, he could easily be involved and who was to say what he would do to her if he knew she knew. She was on her own out here. Instead she asked him an oblique question to see how he would respond.

'Are you sure everyone in the village is happy to be moved? I asked a woman down the street how she liked her new home and the school. She didn't seem happy at all. She seemed scared to talk to me. Is there something going on here you haven't mentioned?'

'Not at all Tanya. I have done everything possible to make these people comfortable. Lots of tragic things have happened in Caspia, especially during the insurrection so I am not surprised she was not cheerful. These people are not used to meeting strangers. You are probably an oddity to her. I am not aware of any problem with this village,' he said stiffly whilst staring straight ahead.

A few minutes into the journey he seemed to fall asleep again. For the time being at least, it absolved her from any obligation to have a difficult conversation. The details of the old woman's account of what happened in the village churned over and over in her head as the monotonous landscape sped past. She doubted very much that the story the woman had told her was fabricated. In fact it was very consistent with the other reports and rumours of what went on in Caspia. At worst her account could be exaggerated but it seemed highly unlikely that the woman would completely make up a story like that and tell a total stranger. She looked at the man slumped in the seat alongside her. Could he have ordered the atrocity and others like it? After all, it was his oil company that stood to benefit from moving the villagers. Obviously the company had little real interest in their safety beyond bad PR. They just wanted the gas field, so when the villagers started to be difficult and demand cash had the company decided to play rough? Had Petrovna actually ordered the action personally? That was possible even though he didn't seem the type. On the other hand it could just be Kornilov playing his games without Petrovna's knowledge or permission. That was also a possible scenario, albeit a charitable one. Alternatively, he may have known that this type of thing was happening on his watch and was just too chicken to face down Kornilov and put a stop to it. Maybe building the school was some form of private penance. She told herself that the last scenario was the most likely. It would have been risky to drive her all the way up to view that facility for a PR exercise, if he knew for a fact that an atrocity had taken place there. Yes, moral cowardice was surely the most likely explanation, she reassured herself.

CHAPTER 21

Tanya woke up just as their car was approaching the outskirts of Caspov. She checked her phone and was alarmed to see an avalanche of texts and missed calls from the boss. This didn't look good. She suddenly realised what day it was. When they arrived at the hotel Petrovna asked her what she wanted to do later.

'It is your last night,' he said wistfully. 'Besides which, I will need to explain the details of your travel back to London. I have arranged everything for you of course.'

'OK, let's have a drink here later. I need to freshen up. It's been a long day.'

'OK, shall we meet at nine then?'

As soon as Tanya got back to her room she put a call in to Chicago. Her editor took it straight away. She had a good idea of what was coming and was not wrong.

'Oh. You have decided to communicate with us at last. You know when I said you needed to file your story and get back here by Monday? Hey, guess what, it's Monday. No story. Oh, and you are not here. What have you got to say for yourself?'

'I am still working on the story. It's really hot. I think I am on the verge of a breakthrough.'

'A breakthrough, what sort of breakthrough?' The man's patience was audibly tapering out.

'Well I am in Caspia...'

'You are what?' he exploded. 'I told you. Don't go to Caspia. Which words in that sentence didn't you freaking understand? You did not have my permission to go there. You did not.'

'But it's not costing anything. He's paying for everything.'

'Tanya. That is not the freaking point. Actually. No. It is the freaking point. He is paying for everything so you can write a story that busts him? Really? Get real Tanya. This is your last warning. When this call ends, you file what copy you have and get straight back to Chicago or you really are fired"

Tanya said nothing.

'Are you going to do that Tanya? Talk to me.'

'You know what,' she said 'I am not sure I am.' Then she hung up on him. Now that she had dug her own grave all that remained for her to do was to lie in it. Petrovna came to meet her again at the allotted time. They found a table in the corner of the bar that was almost empty.

'So' he said, staring into his drink. 'What do you think of Caspia then?'

'It's certainly real interesting. I enjoyed looking round the first refinery but the rest of the country, it's...'

'Underdeveloped?' he suggested.

'Yeah, it kind of sucks. The place is ugly, the people look miserable and scared. It's just not nice.'

'I wouldn't disagree,' he replied. There was another long pause. Now that she had burned her boats with her employer, she pondered the wisdom of confronting him again. It was ill advised under the circumstances. She decided to do it anyway.

'You know what your problem is? You are like one of the three wise monkeys.'

'What do you mean?' Petrovna said looking blank.

'It means, you see no evil, you hear no evil and you do no evil. But if you know evil things are happening around you and you say and do nothing, then you are party to that evil too,' she said. 'You know some pretty nasty stuff's been going on here. Maybe you don't like it. If so, why for Christ's sake haven't you done anything to stop it? You could if you wanted to, with all that money of yours. Are you scared of your friend Kornilov? Or is it just greed, like that character in your beloved opera we sat through in Moscow? Which is it Mr Petrovna, greed or fear?'

A vacant expression spread across Petrovna's face, then he replied. 'How exactly do you expect me to answer a question like that Tanya? I can tell you this – I have never wanted to hurt anyone but I can also tell you there are two types of people in life, victims or victimisers. Actually, I have been both. I expect you have too. Then one day I saw my chance to be in control and I mean really in control. Because that's what money really buys you. Control. The greatest treasure is not a possession. It's the absence of fear. That's the greatest thing money can buy. I may not be proud of everything I have done but who is? Do you seriously think I wanted to get involved with Kornilov? I have played the hand I was dealt as best I could. Maybe I could have played it better but who amongst us is perfect? Are you honestly saying you have never made a moral compromise? Or maybe you have just never had to make a serious moral choice in the first place.' His voice was hardening for a moment.

She watched him purposefully avoid her gaze. Then she said, 'You say you never wanted to hurt anyone and maybe I believe you but people are getting hurt in Caspia everyday by the Kornilov regime. We are not just talking bribes or bad apple cops. We are talking about serious crimes. We are talking deaths. We are talking the kind of stuff that ends up at the International Criminal Court. And all the time this is going on you just get richer and richer. How can you just sit there and say that you are just playing your hand? This isn't a game of cards, this is people's lives.'

'Tanya, I did what had to be done and I have to live with the consequences everyday.'

'Oh. Poor little you,' she cooed mockingly.

'Look,' Petrovna shot back with the first hint of steel. 'Kornilov is not the only one who is vicious. Haven't you seen how most people behave? One minute they seem reasonable but then they turn on you like a pack of wolves. Even people you consider friends. At least with Kornilov you know what you are dealing with. The only difference is, he has the power to inflict his will on others and the only certain way to protect yourself from the cruelty of others is to amass as much power and wealth of your own as you possibly can.'

He looked at her despondently as she shook her head.

'Tanya, I am sorry if this offends you but that is how it is.'

Then that strange vacant expression descended across his face again. 'You know I am in love with you so why do you ask me these things?' he said.

She looked startled by his revelation. After a moment she replied.

'I am asking you these things because I think I might be in love with you too but I need to know what kind of a person you really are. That's why I am questioning you. What are you Nicholas Petrovna?'

'I am what I am but you make me want to be something different Tanya. Something better. Look, I don't really care what you say in your article anymore. If you don't believe me you can leave right now if you want. My driver can pick you up at ten and then the plane will take you right back to London or Chicago even. Is that what you want Tanya?'

Her head was spinning again. She could just cut her losses and take up his offer of returning to London. The story wasn't completed to her satisfaction at all. She did have something to file even though it wasn't great. If she got the next flight to the States and pleaded for her job back she would probably get it. That was the sensible option. Then she thought about the old woman in the village and her words "No one cares about us" echoed once again. Then Tanya knew that if she did not try to tell this story no one else would. Sticking with Petrovna was the best tactic if she wanted to do that. She could always sell the story freelance afterwards if it was big enough. Then there was Petrovna himself. If she was being honest with herself, her response to his romantic declaration had not been entirely cynical. After the night in Moscow, she had fallen for him just a little bit. It was complicated.

With her mind made up, she looked up at him and said. 'No. Actually I don't want to leave. But I want to know more. I think you are a decent man at heart. Naive maybe. The thing that gets me is, with your money, you really could change everything. I mean like really make a difference. I just don't get this whole Kornilov thing. Nobody has to associate with someone like that, especially not you.'

'Tanya, I have told you I love you but you are right. This is no game. If you think it is then you should just go home right now and file your story before it's too late. I will just have to take my chances. You Americans think you can just change the world like in the movies. But you can't. This isn't Hollywood. This is the real world and it's not that simple. Doing the right thing doesn't always mean a happy ending you know.'

She paused again. 'But maybe it is. I am not asking you to save the world I am asking you to save Caspia. You know you could do that if you wanted to. You already own half the place at least.'

He suddenly changed the subject 'Have you ever been to Venice?'

'No,' she said tentatively, wondering where this was going.

'Well, I have a villa on an island in the Venetian lagoon. We could go there for a while to talk and get to know each other better. Perhaps you can tell me how I can save the world,' he said smiling for the first time.

'OK. You just got me interested,' she said.

CHAPTER 22

The Gulfstream jet did not return to London. Instead it flew a different leg with the pair of them on board. It was early evening when the plane made its final approach over the Venetian lagoon. Tanya was amazed at the sight of Venice from the aircraft's large portholes. The city looked like a scale model mounted in the looking glass of water.

'Wow, is that even real?' she said.

After they had landed, a car picked them up from the foot of the aircraft and drove them the short distance to a landing jetty at the edge of the airport where a small motor launch was waiting. Petrovna got in first.

'Jump in,' he said, before offering his hand to assist her as she stepped off the jetty into the rocking boat. The boatman placed their meagre luggage carefully in the back.

'You need to sit one on each side to balance the boat,' he added.

The engine roared into life and they cast off. At first the boat moved slowly as it left the area around the jetties. Once it was in open water it picked up speed, thudding and bouncing over the wakes of the other vessels as it made its way down the path laid out between brightly painted wooden stakes protruding from the water. Venice loomed in the distance. In the foreground a smaller island came into view and as they drew closer she observed that it was exclusively given over to a cemetery. Before they reached the necropolis, their boat turned sharply left towards a tiny islet that sat apart in an expanse of open water.

'This is it,' Petrovna announced, pointing at the rapidly encroaching tuft of land. 'My favourite European bolt hole.'

The launch manoeuvred alongside the landing jetty where the boatman quickly secured it to the mooring posts. Petrovna leapt out first and proffered his hand to Tanya by way of gallant assistance. She grasped it gladly and carefully disembarked the launch.

'Thank you,' she said. 'I take it the whole island belongs to you.'

'It does. Let me show you round. It's not that big.'

They walked up a short flight of stone steps leading up from the jetty to the main villa complex that occupied most of the islet. The boatman followed behind dragging their cases up the steps as best he could. The islet consisted of a flat plateau of agricultural land, a smattering of trees and some buildings. The centrepiece was the large villa. The main building was a simple two-story affair painted in a well weathered sepia colour that gave it a rustic look. It was connected to single story outbuildings that looked as though they might have once been in agricultural use but had now undergone a modernist conversion.

'The island has been occupied and abandoned several times since the sixteenth century,' Petrovna explained. 'Most of the buildings you see here now date from the nineteenth century. It was last used as a vineyard. I have kept some vines going for that reason,' he said, pointing to an expanse of land in the distance given over to trellised bowers.

They entered the main building through a heavy wooden door. The rustic luxury theme continued indoors. The walls were mainly bare stone with thick wooden beams supporting the roof. The furniture and decor were strictly modernist and had no doubt been shipped in at great expense from fashionable designers in Milan or London. Someone had obviously gone to a lot of expense achieving the designer peasant look.

He led her up a flight of stone steps to the second floor.

'This is where the bedrooms are,' he said, looking rather sheepish.

They entered into one of the rooms. It was substantial and airy with a king-sized bed in the middle of the wooden tiled floor. Light streamed in through two large windows that overlooked the lagoon. There was a smaller door in the far corner that led into the obligatory spa like bathroom complete with a freestanding bathtub on steel legs fashioned like lion's paws.

'Ooh, it's lovely,' she said, genuinely charmed by the setting.

'You can take this room if you want to, I am in the next room along,' he said.

'What's upstairs?' she said.

'That's the staff quarters. I have three full time who live here: Silvio, who picked us up in the boat, his wife who is housekeeper and a Romanian maid. Come back down, I will show you what I have done with the outbuildings.'

The single story buildings Tanya had seen earlier had indeed previously been used as part of the working vineyard. Petrovna had hired a Swedish architect to refurbish the main house and convert the rest of the buildings into a lavish leisure complex. A single covered corridor now connected all the outbuildings. One contained a small gym. Another was a cinema room. The largest construct was an indoor swimming pool entirely encased in glass. Immediately outside this there was a second larger swimming pool on an adjoining veranda area.

'The glass wall can open out onto the veranda. It's nice to have it like that in the summer. In the winter you definitely want your pool area to be indoors. Even though it's rarely as cold as Moscow you can still get snow in Venice occasionally.'

Tanya was struggling to take it all in. She had never seen a set up like this before and the effect was almost overwhelming. However, she did her best to maintain her customary air of cynicism.

'I really like what you have done with this place. It's totally cool. Is it not, like, a bit lonely being stuck out on this island in the middle of the water?'

He shrugged. 'I like it that way. I feel calm when I am here. Anyway, you can reach Venice in fifteen minutes on the launch. Silvio can take you there anytime you want or you can just get a water taxi.'

'I think I will have to do that if I am going to spend any time here. Besides, I will need to get some more clothes just for starters.'

'Not a problem, we can go there tomorrow. I can show you the main tourist sites then we can both get some lunch at Harry's Bar and afterwards you can do your shopping. There are plenty of boutique near St Mark's Square.' Tanya had to admit, that sounded fun.

'Anyway, I had better let you settle in. Your bags have been left in your room. It's easier if we eat here tonight. Silvio's wife is a wonderful cook. She does all the classic Italian dishes beautifully.'

Tanya climbed the stairs back to her new-found boudoir. As promised her belongings were waiting for her but before she unpacked them, she had one other task she wanted to complete. She pulled her phone out of her pocket and switched it on. She knew that what she was about to do was rash to put it mildly but what were the alternatives? Abandon her Caspia story half-finished and throw away the most exciting romantic opportunity she was ever likely to encounter? Make a grovelling apology to the boss to keep her job and all for what – a career as a provincial journalist? No. That made no sense. With that thought buzzing in her head she texted her resignation to Chicago. It felt better doing it that way round, so much more satisfying and decisive than waiting to be fired, so much more in control. Petrovna might have been onto something about control, she thought.

That evening at dinner, she said nothing about her career move. They dined on a tasty spaghetti dish made with black squid ink. It was accompanied by thick crusty bread and washed down with some very drinkable Chianti. It was simple but delicious. There was a lovely lemon sponge cake for desert.

'So' Petrovna asked as the meal neared its conclusion. 'What do you think of this place?'

'Oh, it's absolutely gorgeous. I love the way it's so like, simple and at the same time really lavish and modern. It's so romantic as well.'

'That's great. I so glad you like it. I suppose you are tired after the day's travel. I think I am going to retire myself in a few minutes,' he said.

'OK. I guess I'm a bit tired too.'

He emptied the last of his glass of Chianti and headed up the flight of stairs. She followed a few steps behind. Then they both went their separate ways.

Tanya spent a few minutes undressing and then took a quick shower. She lay on her bed for a short while and then made another big decision. She padded barefoot down the corridor and tapped on the door across the landing. She opened it tentatively without waiting for a reply and crept inside clad only in a loose fitting tee shirt.

'I guess I wasn't as tired as I thought,' she said as she leapt onto his bed in a nimble cat like move that positioned her so that she was straddling him. Then the tee shirt came off. Seconds later his hands were reaching up and caressing her pert bosoms, her tiny nipples immediately engorging at his first touch. Then their lips met in a languorous kiss. She pulled away.

'Please fuck me' she panted. He grasped her waist and seconds later, he was on top. She groaned, her glistening petals expectant for his arrival. He eagerly obliged.

———

The next day was spent very much as promised. After a breakfast of coffee and patisserie, Silvio took them into

Venice on the launch. Once they were back onto the open water it didn't take long for the boat to reach the shore of the northern section of the city. The vessel slowed down as it approached and eventually turned into one of the narrow canals. Their passage continued at a regal pace as they navigated the narrow waterways that separated the aged and sometimes crumbling buildings. After a while they reached the Grand Canal itself. Tanya absorbed the stunning vista as they cruised down its centre with baroque palazzo on either side. It was a wonderful early summer's day, warm and clear. The sunlight reflected off the water giving the whole scene a bright lustre that seemed almost unnatural.

They disembarked just in front of the Rialto Bridge and walked hand in hand down through the maze of passages that led to St Marks. After the previous evenings coupling, anything else would have seemed remote and prudish. Any casual bystanders observing the couple would have probably have assumed them to be honeymooners or newly minted lovers at least. That was not an unusual sight in a city like Venice and was hardly worthy of anyone's second glance. Except, one man was giving them a second glance as they walked together under one of the mighty arches leading into St Marks. Dark haired and thick set. He too was indistinguishable from the many other Russian tourists who flock to the world's great attractions. This man was different in only one respect. It was not the great Basilica that he was photographing. Although his camera pointed in the direction of that building and the famous campanile, the digital viewfinder was firmly focused on the couple he had been following. As they continued to stroll through the square in the direction of Harry's bar, he made a call on his mobile phone. Then he seated himself at an incredibly expensive tourist cafe just round the corner to wait.

On the way back to his Island, Petrovna had taken a call on his phone. It was brief and terse. 'OK, OK,' he had said. 'I am with someone now. I will call you back later with my answer.'

Tanya noticed his demeanour visibly change again after the call. Lunch at Harry's bar had been great fun even though she had been very relieved that he was paying the bill. He had even seemed to enjoy their little shopping excursion, the expensive fruits of which were stacked high in the back of the launch. Now, he seemed distracted and withdrawn, just like in Caspia. Whatever had been said over the phone had not been welcome tidings.

That evening over dinner he announced that he needed to travel to London urgently on business.

'I am really sorry. It's literally just for one day. I am going to fly up first thing tomorrow morning and hopefully come straight back again in the evening if my business is concluded.'

'Is everything alright?' she asked, reaching across the table and squeezing his hand.

'Of course. It's just a business problem I need to deal with in person. It's nothing you need to worry about. I will be back late tomorrow night at worst. You just stay here and make yourself at home' he said.

That night they slept fitfully in their separate rooms. As predicted, Petrovna's phone call had been disagreeable. Conversations with Sergei Romanov usually were. When he had called him back from the islet, the situation had become unpleasantly clear.

'Look Petrovna. You need to make a decision on this right now' he had said. 'Kornilov's onto me. I think he must have got wind of the fact that I left Caspia while he was in New York. He's on your case real good too. You are being followed now by the way. I am sitting at my desk looking at photographs of you playing lovebirds in Venice. Great tits by the way. Have you drilled her yet? She looks nice and tight.'

Petrovna ignored Romanov's crude line of questioning and let him continue. 'Kornilov authorised that operation personally so it's not looking that good for either us right now. If we don't act soon it could be too late and once it gets to that stage, I can't help you anymore. You need to help yourself while you can. The time is now, so you need to make up your fucking mind. Are you with us or are you not?'

Petrovna had agonised over his response. He just didn't want to get involved. Besides which, the spy chief was a highly unsavoury character in his own right. It was debatable whether Romanov was any great improvement on Kornilov at all. On the other hand, what he was saying rang true. Kornilov's behaviour had always been brutish and unpredictable but now it was growing not just erratic, but murderously erratic. Being blameless was no longer a guarantee of safety. Nor was it a good sign that Kornilov had arranged to have him and Tanya followed. Doing nothing could in itself be dangerous for him and her. And then of course there was the whole morality thing Tanya kept going on about.

She kept saying he should be able to make a difference. Would she regard getting involved in a military coup as moral? He wasn't sure but after a very brief moment of reflection, he decided she might if it meant getting rid of Kornilov.

'OK. What is it exactly you want from me Sergei?'

'All I need from you is to go to London and agree to pay for the whole thing. I have already done the groundwork. You meet a man called Hicks. His office is just round the corner from you. You tell him you will act as financial backer and provide him with any upfront cash he needs. That's it. You don't have to shoot anyone yourself. I will send you the address. It's that simple.'

Petrovna sincerely hoped that it was that simple as his plane descended through the early morning haze to London City airport. Once on the ground, he headed straight for his own office where he knocked back an espresso and gathered his thoughts before walking the short distance to the offices of 'Affirmative Outcomes'.

On arriving he was surprised to see the outfit's name clearly displayed on the brass name plates in the foyer of the Edwardian office building. He climbed the flight of wooden stairs to the first floor and nervously pressed the buzzer. The door clicked open and the heavily made up receptionist of a certain age greeted him breezily.

'Go straight through, Major Hicks is expecting you.'

Hicks was already holding the door open for him when he reached it. He was tall, quite thin but muscular. Petrovna guessed he was early forties. He wore a blazer, striped shirt and what Petrovna guessed was one of those old public school ties that the English always bang on about.

'Come in, come in,' Hicks said. 'Sit you down. Have you been offered a drink yet? Do you want one?'

Petrovna shook his head as Hicks grasped his hand in a very forceful handshake. The office was small with only enough room for a desk and two chairs. There were a lot of photographs on the walls. Most of them seemed to be of formal military type gatherings although one of them was a school photograph with the words Eton College written on the bottom of the frame in an elaborate font. Hicks followed his gaze and answered his unasked question.

'Sandhurst and Lifeguards. Twenty years of my life.'

To Petrovna's enormous relief, Hicks cut the small talk and launched straight into it.

'Now. I understand you know that I have already been having discussions with an associate of yours, a Mr Romanov, about a very delicate issue you want resolved.'

'That's right,' Petrovna confirmed, nodding some more.

'I presume you are also aware that Mr Romanov has proposed that you are prepared to, how shall I put it, financially underwrite the action in question. I really just wanted to meet with you face to face to discuss what terms those might be and how the arrangement as a whole might pan out.'

'Sure, Major Hicks, that's why I am here.'

'Forgive me for saying this Mr Petrovna but unlike your associate, you don't look like the sort of person I usually deal with. This is an extremely grave and serious enterprise with considerable risks for all of us. I think perhaps for the absolute avoidance of any misunderstanding I should start by asking you what exactly you hope to achieve personally from what is being proposed.'

Petrovna's knew exactly what to say next. He'd carefully scripted and mentally rehearsed the whole routine just like he always did on these occasions.

'Well, as I am sure you are aware I have very substantial business interests in the Republic of Caspia. These are mainly in the oil, gas and petrochemical areas. I do also have very strong personal links with the government of Caspia, including President Kornilov who is a long-standing acquaintance of mine. However, I have become increasingly concerned in recent years about the political stability of the regime in general and the state of mind of President Kornilov in particular. His behaviour has become very unpredictable and there have been a number of very disturbing incidents involving some of my business colleagues including sudden deaths and disappearances. In general the actions of the Kornilov government have become an embarrassment and a bar to inward investment. Some of us are also beginning to fear for our personal safety. We have reluctantly concluded that it is necessary to bring about a regime change. As I am sure you are also aware, Caspia is not a Jeffersonian democracy. In the absence of any voting procedures to remove the incumbent we have been forced to seek your services.'

Hicks sat back in his chair grinning broadly. 'That was rather elegantly put Mr Petrovna and delivered without the aid of an auto queue. Very impressive. However, I must again make myself plainly understood. Your friend Mr Romanov has proposed that I hire and equip a group of professional mercenaries to launch an armed intervention into Caspia that removes President Kornilov. That will effectively leave the field clear for your man Romanov to launch a coup and declare himself President instead. When I say remove, I mean permanently. You do fully comprehend what I mean by that don't you? We are going to blow that fucker's head off' he said in his perfectly clipped English accent.

Hicks' patronising bedside manner was beginning to grate with Petrovna. He gritted his teeth and nodded as Hicks continued.

'At the moment we have only discussed draft proposals. What we have established so far is that a small military force will be required to fly in to Caspia and make a surgical strike on the Presidential compound. We have already been supplied with detailed plans of the Presidential compound itself. The objective, as discussed, will be the removal of the subject, permanently. The infiltration team will adopt the dress of ethnic Caspian insurgents in order that your friend Mr Romanov can claim it was a revenge terrorist attack and thus avoid being implicated in any way. The team will infiltrate by plane. Then my friend, it is down to you to pick up the political pieces.'

'Fair enough,' Petrovna replied. 'That was very much in line with what I was expecting. It does leave the question of your fee.'

'Indeed it does Mr Petrovna, indeed it does. As you can imagine, setting up an operation like this is a hugely complex and expensive undertaking. We run a highly professional service here and we always insist on the very highest standards. That costs money, a shit load of money.

Not to mention the enormous risks for which we of course expect to be adequately compensated.'

'OK, Major Hicks, I get you. It's expensive. Exactly what sums are we talking about here?'

'Well let's see. I will require from you an upfront cash deposit to meet the basic working capital requirements. Lightweight military transporter, that's half a million dollars straight off, same again on weapons and ammo. We will need at least two dozen men for an operation of this nature, that's another three million dollars at least. Add in some other contingencies and let's just call it a round five million dollars upfront. That just leaves the issue of our performance related carried interest.'

The size of the upfront fee came as no great surprise to Petrovna. Something like this was never going to be cheap. He shuddered to think what demand was going to come next. Hicks did not disappoint on that front either.

'In terms of our profit on successful completion, I was thinking that this might take the form of a five year security consultancy with Caspoil. The annual retainer for this consultancy would be equivalent of one per cent per annum of the company's gross revenues.'

'What,' spluttered Petrovna. 'Are you quite insane? I know they call you people soldiers of fortune but that could run to more than a hundred million a year in fees. I can't pay you that sort of money even if I wanted to. International investors would query it for sure. Ramberger's auditors are nobodies fool.'

'With respect, that's not my problem. As I said, this is a hugely risky business. We need a reward to match. I would be leading the operation myself you know. I could easily be killed if it went wrong.

As regards the bonus, you can always suggest an alternative arrangement. After all, you are a businessman,' Hicks said breezily.

It was perfectly obvious to Petrovna, who was a veteran of numerous multi-billion-dollar negotiations, that Hicks was trying it on. The problem was that Petrovna was in a weak bargaining position. It wasn't as if he could just pop next door and get a cheaper quotation.

'Look, it's just not possible to pass off a payment of that magnitude through the company accounts, even in a corrupt country like Caspia. The most I could pay you is five million a year for the consultancy and even that is rich. I am prepared to offer you fifty million dollars cash bonus immediately on success. That would come straight out of my pocket so no one will query it. That's a lot of money Major Hicks and I don't see any other partner's names on the plaque here.'

Hicks smiled again and folded his arms. 'Sterling' he said. 'Fifty million sterling. Not US dollars. Please bear in mind, I have to reward my boys as well. This is not a charity shop.'

'OK, sterling it is then,' Petrovna growled. 'Strictly payable on success only you understand. I want Kornilov gone you hear me, gone for good. No collateral damage either. This has to be clean if it's going to work.'

'Let me assure you Mr Petrovna. My boys are surgically thorough.'

'Yes, you say that but have you ever actually completed an operation on this scale before?' Petrovna said, looking sceptical again.

'We have done very similar ones, admittedly nothing quite this large. Similar though, very similar,' Hicks said folding his arms tightly in front of him.

'So what happens next? I mean how long is this going to take to organise?'

'Oh, several months at least. You can't rush something like this. Everything has to be arranged with the utmost discretion or else we are all screwed. It goes without saying that you must not breathe a word of this to anyone. You even need to be careful how you communicate with Mr Romanov. Just because he is the intelligence chief, it doesn't mean someone else isn't bugging his phone. An old school friend of mine tried to do a show like this a few years back. He was careless, word got out and he ended up in an African jail. Not good. From what I hear I wouldn't want to end up in one of your Caspian jails. I take it your President Kornilov is no great respecter of human rights.'

'No he isn't,' Petrovna said smiling weakly. 'So what do I do now then?'

'You go to one of your homes. You lie low and you wait further instructions. Nothing will happen until September at the earliest. In the meantime, I will arrange to have payment details sent to you. Might I suggest you dress the deposit up as the first instalment of a consultancy agreement? That's what most clients do. It might actually look less suspicious that way. When I receive the payment, the touch paper is lit and there is no going back. Do you understand?'

'I understand perfectly Major Hicks. Are we through now?'

'I believe we are. My secretary will show you out.'

Another bone crushing handshake and then it was over. Once back at his own office he rang Romanov who picked up straight away. No sooner had he dialled the number than Hicks' warning about being careful on the phone sprang to mind. Thankfully Romanov was suitably cryptic. 'How was your trip to London?' he had asked innocently.

'Oh, it all went fine. The usual business, a couple of meetings and a few financial issues, you know.'

'And was your main business concluded successfully?'

'Yes it was, thank you. All settled,' Petrovna replied.

'Good,' said Romanov.

CHAPTER 23

They spent the rest of the summer on their secluded island retreat. It took her surprisingly little time before she fell into a pattern of pleasurable torpor. Some days she would take the launch into Venice to spend the day in languid exploration of the city's baroque treasures. Other days would be spent reclined on the veranda or swimming in the elegantly landscaped pool. Petrovna's morning routine was to stay in his study dealing with business matters she never asked about. If she was home he would always join her for lunch. The afternoons were spent talking and reading. The evenings were spent making love. Occasionally he would have to fly to London or Moscow to attend a board meeting or similar event. He would rush back as soon as he could so as not to be away from her a moment longer than he had to.

For her part Tanya had been doing her best to use his absences productively. Now that she had cut her ties with her old employer she had decided to try some freelance writing. She reasoned that this would keep her hand in while she figured out where this whole thing was going. However, one troubling thought persistently intruded on her fairy tale romance. A whispered breath of conscience, a voice from over the sea. Call it what you will, she had let down the woman in the village. She had persuaded herself that she was relentlessly pursuing the story, but whom was she kidding? She had become Petrovna's lover and now she was shacked up with him on his private island. She wasn't relentlessly pursuing anything. Then there was the new 'little' problem. Her pregnancy. The pangs of nausea had struck her after the first month on the island. She had said nothing to him as of yet but sooner or later she would have to. She had been horrified when she first discovered. How could she have been this stupid? She had briefly considered getting rid of it. Then she had heard her father's voice again. 'So you are killing my grandchild because you were careless. Is that how we brought you up?' He wouldn't have approved of an abortion that's for sure. This must be fate, she thought. Petrovna might even be pleased. She resolved to tell him that evening over supper.

She waited until they were on their cassata deserts, safe in the knowledge that plenty of alcohol had been consumed. She was just revving herself up to drop the bombshell when he pre-empted her.

'I need to talk to you about something really important Tanya. I need to make some major changes to my businesses. It's going to involve me being away for a few weeks next month. Meetings in Moscow, site visits in Caspia. You are always saying I should make changes, but these changes, they are different. They are big changes. They may cause problems that you read about in the newspapers. I can't go into any more details with you at this stage because they are confidential but I promise you that when you see what I have done, you will be proud of me.'

Tanya wondered what the hell he meant. He was talking like a press release again but it sounded positive. 'Wow, that sounds really exciting,' she said. 'I mean what sort of changes. Do you mean like a corporate restructuring?'

'Well, yes. I suppose you could say it is a type of corporate restructuring. It certainly involves some reorganisation and I will be making some leadership changes. As I said, the details are confidential and you must not even tell a soul we have discussed it all,' he said, silently relishing his choice of words.

'I guess that means I can't come with you then,' she said.

'I am afraid it does. I will be travelling all over the place and there are bound to be some local problems. Maybe even some political fallout. I think you definitely need to stay here.'

'OK,' she said tentatively. She was now wondering whether it was still a good time to hit him with the baby news. Was there ever going to be a good time? 'I think you need to know that I am pregnant,' she said in as matter of fact a tone as she could muster. His initial response was silence, just as she had expected. Then she waited, carefully searching for any sign of emotion his inert body language might betray. Then, at last she saw the trace of a smile spread across his thin lips.

'Well in that case, you definitely need to stay here,' he said in his normal measured way. 'We will have a lot things to talk about when I get back. Obviously I will want us to be married but I want you to know Tanya, that whatever happens, I will always care for you both.' He stretched out his hand across the table awkwardly and patted hers.

'If that is your romantic proposal, then I accept' she said, bursting into a fit of relieved giggles.

Petrovna spent the next day behind the closeddoor of his study until after dark. Tanya spent hers wallowing in her own deliberations. The previous night's conversation had gone far better than even she had dared to hope. However it had also set a time frame that was potentially forcing her hand. Once she had married Petrovna and born his child, she would be very much his chattel, however expensive and desirable a chattel that might be. For sure, she could carry on with her journalism. Knowing Petrovna he would probably buy her a magazine to edit or even set one up especially, if she asked him nicely. The fact remained that none of these things resolved the issue of her unfinished business in Caspia. And if the issue was ever going to be resolved it had to be resolved pretty much now before her pregnancy advanced.

In practice that involved her traveling back to Caspia alone, locating the village and hoping she could find the old woman who claimed that she quite literally knew where the bodies were buried. She would have to do it while he was away on his mysterious business trip. The risk was that if she discovered he was involved in atrocities it would really take the shine off the romance. Bearing the offspring of a human rights violator might be awkward but exonerating him once and for all would clear the air. Whichever way, she needed to know for certain. She wondered for a moment what her father would have said. Then she heard his voice again. 'Never give up Tanya. Always persevere if you want something and you know it's right.'

The remainder of the morning was spent on her phone, working out the logistics of how she might get back into Caspia. That would be easier said than done without the benefit of Petrovna's private plane, which she was already becoming alarmingly accustomed to. A little research suggested that the least bad option was a flight from Milan to Baku in neighbouring Azerbaijan. From there she could get a short connecting flight to Caspov. There were no formal visa requirements for Caspia so it should just be a case of talking her way in and getting the job done and getting the hell out again.

Finally the moment came. Petrovna casually informed her over lunch that he would be leaving the next day. 'It's that thing I told you about,' he said matter of factly. He kissed her on the head. 'Don't worry about anything. I will only be gone a week or so and when I get back, I promise everything will be better.'

That night she discretely started to put her travel arrangements in place. Then she went to his room and they made love.

CHAPTER 24

Petrovna finally departed on the Saturday. Before he left he had spent his few last moments in his study where he conducted a ritual he had performed on many occasions over the years. Immediately behind his desk hung a copy of Delaroche's famous portrait of Peter the Great. Petrovna had a fascination with the historic ruler who modernised Russia. For sure, he had been a tyrant. So had all the Tsars of note but Tsar Peter had got things done. He was enlightened, by the the standards of the age at least. If trains had existed in the seventeenth century, he would have made them run on time. That's what mattered and Petrovna admired that. If the original portrait ever came up for auction at Sotheby's, Petrovna would bid for it. For now though, the replica would just have to do.

He gently lifted the picture off its hook revealing his private safe. A few twists of the dial and it opened. There were only five items inside: a Canadian passport, a small bag of Krugerrand gold coins, a scrap of paper with his Swiss bank account number, an old photograph of his parents and his mother's wedding ring. The Canadian passport clearly had its uses, as did the access code but the significance of the last three was largely symbolic. The gold coins, valuable though they were, wouldn't sustain him for long if the whole edifice of his life really did come crashing down but for some reason they made him feel better knowing they were there. As for the photograph and the ring, as far as he was concerned, they were the only things he owned that were of any true value. All his other possessions, the yacht, the jet, the gilded mansions like the one he stood in now. To him, all these glorious trophies were little more then chimera that could fade away at any moment, like a desert mirage. In the ritual, he would inspect these objects and consider whether he should carry them with him whenever he faced a perilous situation. The outcome was always the same. He would always end up returning them to the confines of the safe. This time it was different. He inspected the items one by one and carefully replaced them just as he always did. But then he added a sixth item, a small photograph of Tanya that she had recently given him. He shut the safe door and restored Tsar Peter to his rightful place.

———

On the Monday morning Tanya told the housekeeper that she was going to Milan to do some shopping. If the weather held up she might even go up to have a look at the Lakes. She would only be gone for four or five days at the most she told her. The woman flapped her arms and told her in her broken English to be careful not to tire herself out what with the bambino coming. Tanya assured her that she would not. Just for good measure she logged onto Facebook and posted a status report that simply said 'SHOPPING!'

Silvio took her across the lagoon to the railway station in the launch and dropped her off at the foot of the great flight of steps that swept down from the station's modernist facade to the edge of the Grand Canal.

'Call me when you know what train you will return on. I pick you up from this spot,' he told her. She waved goodbye and strode up the steps purposefully. She was soon settled down into her seat by the window. The so-called express took a good three hours to lumber its way into Lombardy. The old style first class compartment felt cramped and stuffy after the luxury of Petrovna's Gulfstream. She put on her iPod headphones and did her best to ignore the passengers who boarded at Vicenza and Verona. The southern slopes of the Dolomites and then the Alps slid past on the right until eventually these morphed into the Milanese suburbs.

On arrival at Milan's grandiose terminus, rather than switching straight onto an airport train she took a cab to a very pleasant but not too conspicuously grand hotel near the station. She had booked a room online for five nights. The plan was to spend two nights there and then tell reception she was sightseeing at the Lakes. If Petrovna rang and asked her where she was, she could claim to be at the hotel. If he checked with the hotel she should at least show as being on the register. Although the ruse was not infallible it would buy her some time if he started to check up on her. He wasn't usually possessive but there was a first time for everything and it pays to be prudent she thought.

The next day was taken up with the highly pleasurable ruse of acquiring a range of costly designer clothing from Milan's assorted fashion emporiums. It was important to make her story look completely convincing she told herself. On the way back from her expedition she spotted some finely tailored men's shirts in the window of one of the designer stores. She decided that Nicholas would look very handsome in them. For all his cash, fashion was not really his strong point, so she went in, guessed his neck size and bought three shirts in different colours. Back at the hotel she spent some time rearranging her luggage. Only the bare minimum would be required in the bags she would take to Caspia. Everything else would stay in this room until her return. She stacked her newly purchased items neatly in the chest of drawers with the shirts taking pride of place on top. Picking up these trophies would be something to look forward to when her mission was accomplished.

First thing next morning she informed the woman on reception that she had decided to head up to the Lakes for a day or so while the weather was still fine. However, she was not checking out, so her room should be kept on until her return in a couple of days' time when she would finish her shopping and collect her expensive purchases. Like most Italians, the receptionist was happy to chat and eagerly lapped up Tanya's concocted tale. They both agreed that it would be crazy to lug all that shopping up to Lake Maggiore and back. Her new clothes and Nicholas's finely cut shirts would be perfectly safe in the room, which was anyway already paid for. With her backstory in place she returned to the Central station to catch the train to

Malpensa airport. This turned out to be even slower than the express the previous day. Then, at long last, she found herself on the Azerbaijan flight.

The flight landed in Baku during the late afternoon and there was time to kill before the connecting shuttle to Caspov. She made sure no one else was looking before rummaging in her bag and pulling out a tightly rolled wad of twenty dollar bills bound by an elastic band. There was exactly a thousand bucks in total. These and the very expensive fully flexible air tickets she had purchased had eaten up the last of her savings. She had figured her savings wouldn't matter that much anymore given she was bearing a billionaire's child. She peeled off two hundred dollars and replaced the rest of the bundle in her hand luggage.

She was travelling light, just a change of clothes, some maps, a camera and a normal notebook. That should be sufficient. She had thought it best not to take all of her electronic gadgetry, in case her bag was searched and it aroused suspicion.

The shuttle flight turned out to be a 'Caspian Airways' twin prop. She wondered if Petrovna owned the flag carrier. It wouldn't be a great surprise if he did, given that he seemed to own almost everything else in Caspia. As she boarded the plane, she noticed most of the other passengers were male and many were wearing overalls emblazoned with the names of American firms, presumably contractors working for US oil companies.

The flight from Baku to Caspov was mercifully brief. No sooner had the aircraft reached the top of its climb, it seemed to commence its descent through the fast darkening evening sky. Soon she was waiting dry mouthed in the short queue at immigration. The official at the desk took her passport and after a cursory glance at the pages, started punching away at his dirty looking computer terminal. His uniform was scruffy, his face unsmiling. Then he paused and took a second look at her for longer than seemed necessary. 'Why do you want to visit Caspia again, you don't work for an oil company?' he said.

'My family are from here. I just want to spend a few days visiting some places I missed last time' she said squeezing out a smile.

He typed something else into his keyboard then stamped her passport without a word.

Once clear of the desk she breathed a mental sigh of relief and headed for the nearest bureau de change to swap the two hundred bucks into roubles. The dollar was still king in Caspia but it was always worth having a bit of local currency. When the notes were handed to her she noticed that they were local versions of the rouble with the image of Kornilov's head emblazoned prominently on them. She smiled and put them in her pocket before heading for the grungy airport hotel where she had reserved a room for the night. The establishment was modern but Spartan and was already beginning to look frayed at the seams, nothing like the Grand Caspian at all. There were some oil worker types waiting to check in behind her. She felt their eyes measuring her up as she went through the reception formalities. Heading for the lift, she heard laughter and wisps of lewd comments trailing in her wake. Once inside her room she immediately locked the door and put the chain on, then for good measure she the dragged the single easy chair over to the entrance hall and wedged it up against the door.

She awoke with a start very early the next morning having barely slept, her heart already racing from the first moment of consciousness. She stuffed her toiletries hurriedly back into her carry bag, anxious to get on her way as quickly as possible. The hire car had already been booked. By the time she had grabbed some breakfast downstairs it would be time to pick it up. She threw on some practical clothes, jeans, T-shirt and a light sweater. Settling on light slip on shoes for the drive and she stuffed her trainers in her holdall. The camera and notebook soon joined them. Everything else went in the case. She went downstairs to the dreary restaurant to swallow a bit of breakfast and a coffee. Hunger eluded her but it was going to be a long day so she forced down some stale patisserie. Then for good measure wrapped a bread roll in a paper napkin and stashed it in her bag which already contained the complimentary bottle of water from her room. Now, it was time to get the show on the road.

Tanya trudged back to the car hire office at the airport terminal. The small Toyota was not exactly the latest model but as long as it didn't break down on her it would do. The airport was located on the outskirts of Caspov, so it didn't take long to find the main road heading inland. She had done her homework and had worked out as best she could where the village was likely to be. They had driven for at least two hours down this road when she had been with Petrovna. Although she had not managed to pinpoint the name or exact location of the village, she did remember that it was very close to the site of the gas storage facility. That was quite a prominent landmark so once it had been located her target should surely reveal itself soon after.

The road itself was reasonably straight albeit heavily potholed. There was little else in the way of traffic, just a few lorries transporting building materials and the occasional car. She made good time and by late morning the silhouette of the Caucus mountains began to loom on the horizon. Then, bang on cue, the Caspoil storage depot reared its ugly head on the right hand side. Her heart leapt when a little further down the road as she recognised the filling station with its awful cafe attached followed closely by the make shift school a minute or so later. This was it. She slowed down and parked up a narrow lane just off the main road. Now it was simply a case of finding the house with the ageing Olga in it.

She decided to do a quick circuit of the village first just to get her bearings. Like the previous occasion the place seemed to be almost deserted. The school was once again suspiciously empty given it was the middle of the day. A very long school holiday for sure. The whole setup felt like a scene out of a Hollywood zombie movie. She could remember roughly, but not precisely where the woman's house was. There was nothing for it other than to start knocking on the doors of the soulless dwellings. The first two she tried yielded no reply at all. At the third attempt a balding middle-aged man opened the door. She explained in her best Russian that she was looking for an old lady called Olga who she had met here earlier in the summer. He stared at her suspiciously for a moment and then told her that Olga lived three doors down, before slamming the door shut in Tanya's face.

When she knocked on the door in question, no one seemed to be answering. Tanya was about to give up and try another house when she caught a glimpse of the curtain twitching behind one of the windows. A face was peering through a parting in the lace. Tanya smiled and waved. Moments later, the front door of the cottage slowly began to open.

'Hi,' said Tanya breezily. 'We met three months ago. I am an American journalist. I hope you remember?'

The old woman ventured her neck halfway out of the door to take a surreptitious look up and down the empty street. Then the door swung fully open and she gestured that Tanya should quickly come inside. 'You should not have come back here,' Olga said. 'Why have you come?'

'When I came here last time, you told me about things that happened here, very bad things. I had to go but I promised you I would come back. I really wanted to tell your story, so I have come back to keep my promise. Will you help me please Olga?'

The woman seemed startled that Tanya had remembered her name. 'What is it that you want? '

Tanya showed the woman her phone. 'I can make a recording' she said. 'Tell me the story of what happened at the old village. Show me where it happened. It would be really good if you could show me where the bodies of the victims are buried,' she said breathlessly. Olga sighed and scrunched her eyes shut.

'I can tell you the story but the old village itself was completely destroyed. Part of the gas plant was built on top of it after the houses were bulldozed. I am not sure about showing you the graves. It is a special place for us you understand, a very sad place. I need to talk to some other people about that.'

'Please can you do that Olga? It's really important that I see where these things happened. I can't help you properly otherwise and I don't have long. I only have today.'

'Maybe I think about it. But I tell you the story first OK?'

Tanya set a voice record function on her phone as Olga proceeded to recount her grizzly tale of the day Kornilov's men had run murderously amuck. She carefully noted the most important details on her jotter pad, asking the occasional question as the account unfurled. When the interview was finished Olga told her to wait in the room while she fetched someone else who would be able to help. A short while later she returned with the bald headed man who Tanya recognised as the one whose door she had first knocked on.

'This is Victor. He is one of the few men left in the village. He won't talk but he has agreed to take you to where the gravesite is. He says it's best if we use your car,' Olga said.

'Olga. Would it be possible to speak to one of the girls who was raped?' 'No. That is not possible. These women never wish to speak about what happened to them. Do you think they want others to know about their shame?' she said, glaring at Tanya who had already concluded they were best on their way.

Once the three of them were in her car it wasn't far to the burial site. They got out and Victor led Tanya up a short path into a cluster of tall trees. They weren't pines but the densely intertwined upper branches cut down the light lending the place a gloomy air. Soon she found herself standing in a clearing. The earth in the centre of this space was slightly elevated and the vague outline of a trench was still just about discernible. At the far end of this a roughly hewn wooden cross was jammed into the soil. Surrounding it were a few shrivelled bunches of long dead flowers. Tanya whipped out her camera and began furiously snapping away at the scene. The artificial sound of the electronic shutter pierced the eerie church-like silence. Some startled birds fluttered from a bough above their heads shedding a sprinkling of the first autumn leaves as they went. Then the oppressive quiet ebbed softly backwards and Tanya suddenly felt self conscious about offending the solitude. She lowered her voice to barely a whisper than said to Victor 'Is this like, it, then?'

He turned to her and replied 'Of course, what did you expect to see?'

'Well, I was kind of hoping we could see something a bit more dramatic. I am really sorry but I need strong evidence so I can bring home to readers what has happened here. I got some shots of the cross but did anyone take a photograph of the bodies before they were buried? Or maybe I can just remove a bit of the topsoil so I can see some bones. It will be totally respectful I promise.'

Victor's face twisted into a rictus of utter rage. 'No we cannot do this. These are the graves of our families. We did not photograph them when they were bloody and violated and we will not desecrate their graves so that you can take photographs for your paper.'

'I am really sorry,' Tanya spluttered.

He gave her a pitying look. 'You know, you Americans are all the same. You think you can just go somewhere and solve everyone else's problems. Well you can't. What do you think will happen to us after you print this story when you are safely in America? Do you think Kornilov will just hold his hands up and say "Yes I did it. I am sorry". No. Kornilov does not say sorry. He does not care about what people in America think. No. He will send his men to kill the rest of us as a warning to others. That is what he will do and there will be nothing you can do in your nice office in America to stop him. Olga should never have spoken to you. I regret even taking you here.'

'But Victor, don't you understand? Once I print the story, I will get you justice. I can protect you.'

'No you can't. All you can do is get us all killed. You are just a silly American girl playing at being a journalist. What you don't see is that you are also playing with our lives.' With that he turned his back on her and started to walk in the direction of the car. Olga shook her head and followed him while Tanya stood rooted to the ground, momentarily stunned. Then she followed too with the heaviest of hearts. None of them spoke in the car as she drove them back to the village. When they arrived Victor immediately stormed off muttering angrily in Caspian.

Tanya twisted round to face Olga and said 'I am really sorry,' in a hoarse voice that was close to cracking.

'It's alright,' Olga said, reaching forward and putting her shrivelled hand on Tanya's shoulder. 'I know you mean well but for everyone's sake you really need to leave now. It was a mistake taking you there. You can't help us. You can only hurt us. Please, just go, and forget what you have seen here.'

Tanya gave Olga an awkward hug then climbed back into the car. As she watched the old woman slowly shuffle the tears she had been fighting finally seeped out. All she had managed to obtain was an uncorroborated story that was barely useable. Even worse, Victor had a point. Even if she did run the story there was no guarantee the consequences would be good and actually, they could be disastrous for Nicholas. Olga had been right, she should never have come back. So much for her intrepid journalism, this had been a complete disaster. She stayed slumped on the dashboard for several minutes until the sobbing died down to a manageable level.

Then she pulled her mobile out of her bag and did something she had barely done at all in recent months. She rang her mother. Ever since she had rocked up at Petrovna's island retreat she had been avoiding any contact with her family in the States. She told them where she was and that she was still working freelance on a big story but very little else. Her mother had a habit of asking the sort of probing questions that she just didn't want to answer at the moment, but now she was dialling her number. She got the answer phone. 'Hi, Mom. I have been away on a business trip for a couple of days. I just called to say I was fine and I will be on my way home soon.' She paused. 'I guess I kind of wanted to hear your voice too,' she said as her own voice started to thicken. 'I love you, Mom.' She hung up and started sobbing again.

When her composure finally returned, she fired up the car's engine. She just hoped she could get back to Italy before anyone important really missed her. That way, Petrovna would never find out what she had been up to.

CHAPTER 25

Most of the journey back to the airport was uneventful. The road was straight and the traffic was sparse. Tanya couldn't wait to get the hell out of this place and put the whole incident behind her so she squeezed the gas pedal as hard as the potholes would allow. Go faster. Get this retreat over with. Occasionally progress would be delayed for a few minutes by a crawling tractor or truck. The journey seemed almost interminable. Then at last she breathed a sigh of relief as the first signs for the airport appeared. Another twenty minutes and she would be fine. She eased back on the accelerator ever so slightly.

Then she noticed in her wing mirror that another car, a black Saab, had appeared behind her in the distance. There weren't many fancy vehicles like that in Caspia and it was going at one hell of a speed, even faster than her by the looks of it. Within seconds it had screamed up to within a few feet of her back bumper. Then with another roar from its engine, it sped right past before slotting in just in front. Jerk, she mouthed as she slowed down to make a bit of space. Almost immediately, another vehicle appeared in her mirrors, this time a small van, also black. This was also tearing along at a ferocious pace and was soon right alongside her.

At that moment the Saab suddenly decelerated forcing her to do likewise. 'What the fuck has got into these guys,' she yelled in exasperation at no one in particular. As her Toyota slowed to a near walking speed the overtaking van slowed too. Then the Saab halted completely forcing Tanya to jam on the breaks hard to avoid a collision. As the Toyota ground to a halt the van pulled in right up alongside, then, before she had time to act, it noisily reversed and turned in behind her and stopped. The van and the Saab had boxed her in. The doors of the van swung open and three men jumped out wearing dark overalls and ski masks. The surge of panic rose in her stomach.

She quickly checked that the locks on the door were already down. They were. She reached into her bag for her smart phone. She had turned it off to save the battery. Shit. No time. One of the masked men was already tugging at the car's locked door handle. She would just have to try and ram her way out. She frantically crunched the gears and let out the clutch. The engine sputtered and died. Then was a dull loud thud. One of the men had attacked the window of the driver's door with a crow bar. The impact made a small crack but bounced off. He grunted and swung the implement again. This time the small dent from the first attempt blossomed into a spider's web of fractures. On the third swing the glass finally broke. Tanya screamed as the fragments of crystal confetti showered all over her. A gloved hand reached in and opened the car door.

The first man grabbed her arm and yanked her out onto the road but Tanya saw her chance and lashed out at his groin with her right foot. Her aim was bang on and he emitted an animal roar as his body contracted and he momentarily loosened his grip. She tore free of his grasp and just ran. She didn't know where, she just ran away with all her strength. Legs pumping, heart pounding. She felt the little stab first. Then the massive jolt of pain seemed to rip through her entire body. She screamed again. Then all control of her muscles was lost and she plunged head first towards the roughly tarmacked road. There she lay sprawled, face down, bloody, grazed and twitching as five masked men towered over her laughing. One was holding a device in his hands that sprouted a trail of wires terminating in Tanya's convulsion racked body. The controller of the device touched a button on it again. This sent her into another agonising spasm. The men laughed hysterically as she writhed and screamed. The button was pressed a couple more times before they seemed to tire of the spectacle. A man smelling of sour tobacco knelt down with a reel of heavy-duty gaffer tape. He quickly bound her wrists and ankles and then for good measure taped her mouth shut. He stuck his tongue in her ear.

'Playing hard to get,' he said.

With that, he tore the Taser wires out of her body, slung her over his shoulder and carried her back to the van where she was unceremoniously dumped. Then the doors were slammed shut and the men returned to their respective vehicles. They drove away leaving Tanya's car with its broken window the sole silent witness to her abduction.

In the back of the van Tanya lay helpless and panting on the floor Her three assailants looked down at their captive from the benches at the side. She was struggling to control her breathing. The interior of the van reeked of diesel and body odour, which did not help. She fought hard against the waves of nausea that threatened to engulf her. If she vomited with her mouth taped like this, choking to death was a real possibility. At least two of her captors seemed to be in a jovial mood. They were amusing themselves by making fun of the man with the bruised testicles who was still not seeing the funny side of it. He turned

'I will make you pay for that you little bitch,' he shouted down at her.

'Don't worry Miss America,' the Taser man said in a tone of mocking reassurance. 'You won't be raped yet. Someone else wants to meet you first.'

CHAPTER 26

Sergei Romanov slammed the phone down in exasperation. Apparently Petrovna's little American girl had just entered the country. Her timing could hardly have been worse. The assassination operation was scheduled for the following evening so the last thing he wanted was Petrovna's love interest screwing up his meticulously planned coup.

Romanov paused for a second then he picked up his phone again and started dialling a man he could definitely trust, his second in command Uri Prokina who was already part of the coup team because Romanov could trust him absolutely. The basis of that trust was not some great noble loyalty but rather the knowledge that Romanov possessed certain photographs of his deputy, the type of photograph that you never want anyone else to see. Romanov never ceased to be amazed how much could be achieved by a good old fashioned honey trap with some pretty girls or in the case of Prokina, pretty boys.

Numerous foreign businessmen had fallen victim to his little ruse over the years. It was so simple. She approaches them at the hotel bar at the grand Caspian.

'Do you mind if I practice my English?

'What are your hobbies?'

'Oh. You like Manchester United too'

It was all so very innocent and non-threatening. Then back to her room. Always her room at the Grand Caspian, because that's where the recording equipment was. Then things get frisky for the camera. Most of the victims panicked when confronted even if they weren't married. Romanov never asked for much, just some low level information and absolute compliance. And of course some cash.

The only exception to this rule was Petrovna who seemed to be largely immune to such simple inducements, even though he had succumbed to temptation on at least one occasion in the distant past. Romanov had tried to entrap him several times with various women in London and Moscow. He had even tried with a man as well, but to no avail. Petrovna, though seemingly unworldly, was just too standoffish to take the bait. But this time it was different. If he really was in love with this American girl then that could change everything.

His deputy answered.

'We need to talk about tomorrow night, we may have a problem' Romanov said.

'What kind of problem?

'His little American bitch has just entered the country a few hours ago. She could really fuck us up. If Petrovna gets wind of this there is a risk he calls the whole thing off.'

'Not if we fuck her up first,' Prokina replied deadpan.

'That's right. I like the way you are thinking, but everything needs to be timed perfectly. We are going to game this my way. So, Hicks and his crew will fly in at approximately 22.00 hours our time. Their convoy will drive' into Caspov from the airstrip as soon as I give the signal. I tell Kornilov that I have received intelligence that a coup is imminent. He heads for his private bunker at the compound and then Hicks' crew hits it as soon as we know he's there.'

'Yeah. I have got all that. The arrangements are in place. We lift up the security barriers at the compound when Hicks arrives. I have told my boys it's just a drill. They suspect nothing. Hicks kills Kornilov and flees, you take the credit for repelling the terrorists and then you become President with emergency powers and I become your new minister for internal security, like we agreed. But what do we do about the girl?'

'Your men take her today then we use her as live bait, that's what. I have been trying to work out how to deal with that fool Petrovna. He's already paid for the mercenaries so we don't need him anymore. The last thing we want is to have him hanging around afterwards, spouting democracy shit and expecting favours. A straightforward assassination could be messy though. With someone as rich as him, people will ask questions. I thought about poisoning him afterwards but his doctors are bound to smell a rat and we know that always attracts publicity. A show trial is way too dangerous, there's no knowing what he might say. Anyway, we need to keep things quiet so we can loot his fortune as easily as possible.'

'So what are you proposing then? You said you were going to use the girl.'

'Yes. I have a more elegant solution. If we tell Petrovna his lovebird is in peril from Kornilov himself, he is bound to come running with Hicks, just as it's all getting nicely violent and chaotic. If we can lure him here, we can kill him too when it all kicks off. Once Kornilov and Petrovna are both dead, it's happy days. We can blame Petrovna for planning the whole thing. Brand him a traitor and seize all his assets as reparations. Then, you can do what you ever you like with the girl. Oh, sorry, I forgot you're a queer. She is sexy as hell, so I am sure your men will enjoy using her. Get this right my friend and you can have as many rent boys as you like at your new ministry.'

Prokina ignored the insult. 'I will have my men go out and pick her up immediately. If she's in a hire car she will be easy to find. There are only about four main roads she can be on and the CCTV network at the airport should tell us which. We will have her by this evening Sergei Romanov. You can have no fear of that.'

'Good but listen carefully my friend. She needs to be kept alive for the time being at least and she must make no contact with the outside world. Keep her in one of the coffin cells. Whatever you do, don't let Kornilov get to her until tomorrow night. Maybe let him know you have her early tomorrow evening. It would be useful to get him out of the compound for a few hours while we prepare but remember, he needs to be back there before Hicks is due.'

Romanov put the phone down. Next, he needed to deal with Kornilov.

'I need to speak to you about something urgently' he said almost casually. Kornilov had agreed to see him right away. It was early evening so the President had already consumed an ample quantity of vodka and was slouched back in his presidential chair. He greeted his subordinate with narrowed eyes.

'What is it Sergei my friend? Can't you see I am busy,' he said without a trace of sarcasm.

Romanov cleared his throat. 'Actually it's a personal matter. It's about your friend Petrovna.'

Kornilov nodded his head sagely as if he knew what was coming. 'Ah. Little boy Petrovna. What about him? Is he still fucking that little American bitch?'

'He is. That's the problem. He's become obsessed with her and I think she's brainwashed him with a load of human rights crap about how evil you are. I met him in Moscow a couple of months back. We had a few drinks. He went on and on about Caspoil and then as it got later he started coming out with all this other shit.'

'What sort of shit,' said Kornilov, suddenly more alert.

'Well, he was mumbling stuff about how she had shown him the truth about Caspia and how someone should do something. When I tried to just laugh it off he got angry and started shouting about how he was the only person who really made things happen in Caspia and that I should show him more respect. He was really making a scene. I had to tell him to keep his voice down. It was embarrassing. I didn't say anything to you at the time because I thought it might just be the drink talking. He called me the next day and claimed he had been drunk and didn't mean anything he said. I accepted that then but now I am not so sure. I know you have been like a father to him so I say this with a heavy heart, but it is my duty to inform you that I think you may have a problem with Petrovna. He seems to be planning something' Romanov said solemnly whilst carefully avoiding Kornilov's eye.

'Planning what? Stop talking in fucking riddles,' Kornilov snorted dismissively. 'Anyway, Petrovna couldn't organise an orgy in a whorehouse.'

'Well you say that but you should know that his journalist bitch entered Caspia a couple of hours ago. She is alone and she has hired a car. Do you think she just wants to go sightseeing without Petrovna? I don' think so. She might just be planning an exposé but I am sure there's more. I thought all that stuff he came out with was just the drink talking but now my sources tell me that he's contacted a known mercenary in London. That's not talk. That's action. Why would a man like Petrovna be meeting a mercenary?'

Kornilov leapt to his feet with a frightening burst of energy that sent his chair toppling backwards.

'That ungrateful little snivelling runt, I made him out of nothing and this is how he repays me. And all over some little bit of American pussy, flashing her tits and spouting her Western crap. She must have poisoned him against me. You follow her, find out what she's doing, who she's seeing and then you bring her in.'

'I am already having her followed. We will take her tomorrow once we've seen what she is up to,' Romanov said.

'You do that and then you tell me when you have her. I want to see this bitch myself,' he spat.

'I will,' said Romanov. When he returned to his own office he had one last call to make. He dialled Petrovna's private number and waited. The conversation only took a couple of minutes but by the time the receiver had gone down he was satisfied that the call had achieved its desired affect.

CHAPTER 27

Somewhere in the Turkmen desert an ageing Antonov airplane stood waiting at a long abandoned airfield surrounded by dusty trucks and jeeps. The Antonov was a workhorse, a sturdy transporter plane capable of shifting men and machinery from the shortest airstrips in the roughest terrain. With its fat body and twin propellers it wasn't pretty. Neither were Hicks and his crew but like them, it was reliable and tough as hell.

The rear-loading ramp was down as they packed the last of their equipment. This was mostly weaponry and a heavily built armoured transporter. Other larger vehicles would already be waiting for them at the other end. The crew of thirty-five mercenaries were assembled beneath the Antonov's wing, making last minute checks to their kit. Hicks stood at the bottom of the loading ramp surveying the scene with a certain degree of satisfaction. The two squad leaders were both former NCO's in his old regiment. Most of the rest were ex SAS though it had been necessary to draft in a handful of foreign legionnaires to make up the numbers. This operation was the biggest he had done to date and there was serious booty at stake. Looking at his men, he afforded himself a wry smile as he recalled the comment of a very famous old boy from his school. He didn't know what effect these men had on the enemy but they really did scare the hell out of him.

Then, as he gazed up, something caught his eye. A twinkling star seemed to be descending from the fast fading twilight. That couldn't be right and it was too fast for a satellite. As it drew closer Hicks began to discern the vague outline of an aircraft. Slowly it revealed itself to be a small jet, rapidly approaching the desert runway with its landing gear lowered. Hicks shouted a warning to his men who cocked their weapons in unison and adopted defensive positions around the Antonov. They trained their weapons on the uninvited plane as it touched down heavily and drew to an abrupt halt in a cloud of dust. As the scream of the jet engines faded into a whine, the dust cloud disappeared revealing a Gulfstream executive jet. The door at the front opened and a set of steps appeared. Hicks could only look on in disbelief as the distant figure emerged. It was a man. He advanced briskly towards them, his casual jacket flapping in the breeze. Finally, as he approached the ramp, Hicks saw that it was none other than Petrovna who was striding so purposefully in his direction.

'What in the name of fuck are you doing here?' he roared.

Petrovna replied in a state of agitation.

'There is a major complication. My fiancée has been arrested in Caspia. I need to come with you to find her.'

'Well you bloody well can't,' Hicks snorted. 'This is a professional operation. You have no idea what you are getting into. This is an armed coup not some frigging relationship service. If there is a problem with your girl-friend we can sort it out afterwards.'

'You don't understand,' said Petrovna gesticulating wildly. 'Kornilov has taken her. She is in terrible danger. If we wait until afterwards it may be too late.' He stepped onto the ramp of the plane. Hicks grabbed him firmly by the arm. 'I said you are not coming,' he snarled. 'You will jeopardise the integrity of the operation and most likely get yourself killed in the process.'

Petrovna pulled his arm free from Hicks' grasp and continued defiantly up the ramp. Hicks started to follow but Petrovna held up his hand and said 'In England you have a saying 'He who pays the piper calls the tune.' I come with you or the operation is cancelled.'

Hicks threw up his arms in exasperation. 'Fine. You want to get yourself killed. That's your damn business. I have already banked the advance.'

The mercenaries marched up the ramp to take their positions in the plane. Once they were all in, Hicks drove the discretely armoured vehicle into the belly of the Antonov. The ramp gradually lifted as Hicks checked his Tag Heuer watch. It was time. He gave the order to the pilots to start the engines, which were soon spluttering into life.

'Go,' Hicks screamed. As the pilot pushed the throttle levers forward the engines rose to a full throaty roar as the Antonov surged down the runway. After thirty seconds he pulled back the joystick lifting the plane into the evening sky. Moments later the barren expanse below faded into the haze. As it continued its ascent, the plane tacked northeast over the Caspian sea while the men in the back sat in nervous silence as they usually did at the start of an operation.

There was little point in attempting pleasant conversation above the deafening drone of the engines. Petrovna stared emptily ahead apparently lost in thought. Hicks glared back, silently fuming. Although the distance was not great, the heavily laden Antonov, which was not a fast plane at the best of times, made slow progress. After about forty minutes the incessant roar of the plane's engines lessened and its occupants felt the familiar sinking sensation of an aircraft descending. A few minutes later it banked very sharply left as it made its approach to a landing strip at a disused Caspoil refinery that had been prepared for their secret arrival. The men gripped the side benches tightly as the cabin tossed and bucked violently in the evening crosswinds.

When the engine noise finally ceased Hicks made one last desperate attempt to talk some sense into Petrovna.

'In the name of God do yourself a favour and just wait on the plane. You are not going to help yourself or this girl by getting yourself killed.'

Petrovna was adamant. 'I must come. She is my life now. Everything I have is worthless if I lose her.'

'Well you had better take these then.' Hicks thrust a pistol and a bulletproof vest at him.

'Don't forget to take the safety catch off if you are actually going to try and fire it. It's on the side' he added.

Petrovna spent a minute or so fiddling with the vest before flinging it aside in exasperation and following Hicks down the ramp which had already been lowered. Someone had driven the armoured vehicle off and it was now parked up next to two much larger vehicles that were already waiting for them on the tarmac as promised. These were more like normal trucks. Most of the mercenaries piled into the back of them. They had donned their balaclava hoods to complete the pretence of being terrorists. Petrovna joined Hicks and a couple of others in the smaller vehicle. Once seated, he practiced cocking the weapon to soothe his screaming nerves.

The three vehicles drove off the airstrip at full speed and charged down the empty road towards the lights of Caspov's newly built skyscrapers in the distance. Hicks had arranged with Romanov for most of Kornilov's security detail to be diverted to the security HQ itself to repel the false terrorist attack. This would leave the presidential compound thinly defended. The fake attack needed to be convincing. As the lead truck peeled off towards the security HQ, Hick's crew and the remaining truck turned into the main 'Victory' boulevard, which they tore down at break neck speed. In the distance the first sounds of gunfire could be heard as truck number one started to do its stuff.

Now, their own target was directly in front of them. The compound's heavy duty security gate had conveniently not been lowered enabling the boarding party to screech to a halt right in front of the presidential palace entrance. The men in the truck leap out the back spraying the perimeter fortifications with covering fire as Hicks charged through the front door with Petrovna and the others in tow. They all dashed through the building's entrance as a ferocious exchange of fire raged at the front. The noise was truly deafening but Petrovna heard nothing but the pounding of his own heart. The flashes and cracks simply became background noise, unreal, almost like a movie. He no longer felt fear, only adrenalin. She must be here. Romanov had told him that she was to be brought to Kornilov immediately. He had to find her before the inevitable happened.

Inside the palace, Petrovna found himself in the familiar surroundings of the reception area. This consisted of an oval entrance hall with classical columns round the outside. The floor and walls were decked in a marble fascia giving the whole place the appearance of a mid range Dubai Hotel. Another barrage of gunfire greeted them. Two of Kornilov's guards started to take pot shots at them from the mezzanine tier directly above. Hicks accomplices swung their weapons round and returned fire while he and Petrovna navigated round the perimeter of the lower level, diving from pillar to pillar for cover.

At the end of one side of the hall there was a large gap in the columns at the point where an adjoining corridor led off to the left. Romanov was supposed to be waiting for them in that corridor behind a set of double swing doors. Crossing the gap would briefly expose them to the line of fire from above.

'We need to just go for it,' Hicks rasped above the din. They waited a moment for the other two mercenaries to spray more covering fire then they made their move. This was greeted with another hail of white-hot lead. Seconds later they both crashed through the doors into the connecting corridor. To their immense relief they found Sergei Romanov leaning nonchalantly against the wall with an automatic pistol in his hand.

'Follow me,' he said casually. 'He's in the panic room downstairs. He probably has a couple of guards with him. Nothing you can't handle I hope.'

They ran down the corridor for ten yards and then turned right through a door that led down another set of stairs into a very short service corridor. At the very end of that corridor there was a large steel door set in the wall. It had no visible handle but on its immediate right there was an electronic keypad with a digital display panel attached. Only two people knew the access code to open that door. Kornilov himself and Romanov.

'Right,' shouted Hicks above the continuing din.'Once you have got it open, we just charge in and shoot anything that fucking moves before they shoot us.' Romanov nodded grimly. Petrovna stood slightly to one side of the doorframe still grasping his pistol in a sweat soaked hand as the other two positioned themselves for the kill. When the last digit of the code had been entered, the box emitted a loud piercing wail and the door slid silently open. The two other men swung round the sides of the door firing furiously into the room as they did so. Almost simultaneously a barrage of bullets shot out of the room. Petrovna froze with his back pressed as flush up against the wall as he could as the bullets whistled past him just centimetres from his face. The deafening exchange of firepower punctuated by screams could not have lasted for more than a few seconds before suddenly everything stopped and both the room and the corridor filled with choking smoke. As Petrovna's paralysis ended, his fear surged back. He stifled the urge to flee. He waited a moment. After so much sound and fury there was now no sound or movement from the room all. When he could bear it no longer he cocked his gun and tentatively slid inside. Then from out of the smoke came a peel of laughter he knew only too well.

'So little boy. You want to play big boys with guns?'

The haze thinned sufficiently to reveal Kornilov on the floor with his back slumped against the far wall of the panic room. He was oozing blood from a shoulder wound. He was still brandishing his gun but was struggling to hold it up straight with his injury. As the smoke cleared the rest of the scene emerged. Petrovna was standing in a concrete box with a desk, a table, some communication equipment and a large map of Caspia on one wall. Sprawled on the floor next to the door were two bullet ridden corpses: Kornilov's body guard and Romanov. Hicks was lying prostrate in a swelling pool of deep black liquid. Little spurts of blood were pumping from a huge open wound in his neck. His vest had saved him from most of the bullets but not that one. He looked up at Petrovna and tried to say something. No words came out, just a burbling sound and bubbling blood from his nouth. Then his head fell forward and the neck wound ceased pumping. Three corpses now. Petrovna kept his gun loosely trained on Kornilov.

'Put it down,' Kornilov hissed. 'You are never going to fire that thing.' Petrovna lowered the barrel slightly but kept his finger on the trigger.

Kornilov continued in a forlorn tone. 'What did I do to make you betray me little boy? After everything I have done for you this is how you repay me. Was it the girl, your little American bitch?'

Petrovna didn't reply but inched closer trying to keep a firm grip on the weapon.

'Hey, I wouldn't blame you for that. I got you wrong. I always thought you were a secret faggot. She was real tough she was, your little bitch. Hot body, real tight pussy too. You know, I was fucking her just an hour ago. She squealed like a whore. Did she do that when you were fucking her? Maybe that was because she just liked me. Or maybe you haven't managed that yet.' He laughed again seemingly oblivious to the pain it must have been causing him in his gaping shoulder.

Then there was flash and a deafening crack as the cloud of pink mist engulfed the side of Kornilov's head. The white rage had surged through Petrovna like a bolt of electricity making his finger strong but the moment he had pulled the trigger he knew he had screwed up. Kornilov lay crumpled beneath a glistening patch of brain tissue on the wall. There would be no answers now.

Petrovna's frantic breathing slowed. He allowed his gun to tumble to the floor. The sound of gunfire from upstairs had ceased. He guessed that the remainder of Hick's motley crew would soon begin their flight back to the airstrip without their boss. At that moment two of Kornilov's men came bursting into the room screaming Russian obscenities and pointing their automatic weapons at Petrovna. Like him, they were rendered momentarily speechless by the sight that greeted them. The two soldiers stared at Petrovna as their tiny minds attempted to process what on earth had happened in this room.

Kornilov and his body guard were dead. Romanov and the apparent terrorist Hicks, who were both armed, also dead. The only living occupant in the concrete box was Petrovna, a man in a lightweight suit, apparently unarmed. He knew that what he said in the next thirty seconds would probably determine whether he lived or died. His desperate mind raced through every option. He turned to the soldiers and said in as measured a voice as he could muster.

'There has been an attempted coup by the traitor Sergei Romanov. He has consorted with terrorists and they have killed my dear friend Alexei. I tried to stop them but I was too late. President Kornilov is dead. Now we must find the other traitors and restore order.'

Then he waited to see if the extraordinary lie would stick. The more senior of the two soldiers, a captain, looked at him quizzically for an agonisingly long moment, then nodded his head in agreement.

CHAPTER 28

Tanya's journey ended when the van reached its destination, the compound at the rear of the security HQ in Caspov. They hadn't bothered blindfolding her, as in their experience it was never really necessary. It was starting to get dark as two men slung a thrashing human bundle out of the van and through a discreet side entrance. The men gripped her roughly by the shoulders and dragged her down a featureless corridor with her bound feet trailing limply behind. Then there was a painful descent down a flight of stairs, which made her scream into her tape gag. Finally, they stopped outside a small steel door that only went up to waist height. More like a hatch than a normal door except that it had a tiny grill in centre of it. It swung open. Someone started to remove the bindings from her wrists and ankles and also her watch. The tape was yanked painfully from her mouth before they slung her inside where she sprawled face down on the hard floor. Then the steel hatch clanged shut.

Now, she had the opportunity to absorb the full horror of her predicament. The cell was absolutely tiny, little more than a rectangular box that was devoid of any objects. It was wide enough to lie horizontal but with only four foot clearance to the ceiling, standing upright was impossible. The only other features were a red light in the ceiling and a grating in the floor. The grating looked ominous and was surrounded by nasty shit coloured splash marks. The air smelt damp and had the fetid tinge of drains. She glanced at the hermitically sealed hatch and suddenly found herself gasping for breath as her thoughts raced and her heart pounded uncontrollably. This was like a fucking tomb. She had read about this sought of thing in Nazis concentration camps. She could suffocate in here if no one came back soon. How long would it be before anyone knew she was missing? Nicholas would be gone for days and her carefully constructed story to cover her tracks could delay the discovery of her whereabouts longer. Long enough to die. The panic grew worse. She started to scream and kick at the hatch but no one came. Eventually, she slumped prostrate on the concrete floor, too exhausted to panic anymore.

She woke with a start, groggy, disorientated and wondering where the hell she was. With her watch and phone gone she soon lost all sense of time but she guessed she might have been out for a quite while. All was silent. She tried banging on the hatch again, but still no one came. At last, after what seemed like forever, she heard heavy footsteps advancing down the corridor. There was a metallic clunk. The hatch swung open bathing the cell in a stream of dazzling white light blinded her for a moment. Then a shadow loomed in the hatchway and she felt hands grasping hold of her ankles as they pulled her out into the open.

The same two guards from earlier hauled her upright and started to manhandle her unceremoniously down the corridor.

'Where are you taking me?' she yelled in English. 'I am an American citizen. This is bullshit, totally fucking illegal. I want to speak to the American Consulate right now,' she screamed.

The guards sniggered. 'You don't need to speak to your ambassador. If you don't like your treatment you can talk to the man himself,' one of them said

She didn't understand what that meant but they had arrived at another room and she had other matters to concern her than diplomatic channels. This room was quite big and had a high ceiling crisscrossed with metal pipes and beams. The only large item in this room was a single steel table with some nasty looking objects on it. Knives, pliers and a sinister looking box with wires attached to it. The room already contained four uniformed men. One of them tossed a coil of rope over one of the ceiling pipes. The guards held Tanya in a tight grip while the end of the rope was fastened around Tanya's wrists. They pulled the rope taut forcing her to stand upright with her arms above her head. Another man entered the room. He was a thickset man, dark hair, casually dressed to the point of being scruffy. There was nothing obviously impressive about him but she gathered that he must be in a position of some authority judging by the reaction of the others to his arrival. The uniformed men in the room had all leapt to attention as he entered. The others seemed highly deferential. As soon as he saw Tanya hanging from the ceiling his harsh face immediately cracked into a smile. He approached her and spent a minute or so inspecting her bruised dishevelled form.

'So,' he said in a strangely calm voice. 'You are the girl who has turned my friend against me.'

Tanya looked blank. Only now was it was dawning on her who this man actually was. The bull like face was now becoming familiar. She recognised it from the press cuttings and the snippets of TV footage. Now the weird deference of the soldiers made sense. It had to be him.

'They tell me he is in love with you, that you have bewitched him. Is that true?' She frantically shook her head.

'You don't understand. There has been a mistake. I am an American citizen. I came here legally. You have no right…'

Kornilov reached out and put his hand over her mouth whilst shaking his head and making a weird tssh tssh sound.

'No. It is you who do not understand. This is Caspia and we have our own way of doing things. Your American passport means nothing here. You sneak into our country. You start taking photographs and asking questions and you wonder why you are here. Stupid arrogant American girl.'

He removed his hand from her mouth and stood back a little. She looked around the room desperately, as if searching for some inspiration. Then she seemed to find some.

'I have done nothing wrong,' she said indignantly. 'My father was Caspian. All I wanted to do was to find out about Caspoil. I am not interested in the Caspian government I just wanted to find out whether my boyfriend has been telling me the truth about some stuff he said, that's all.'

Kornilov swayed his head from side to side as if he was carefully considering her statement. 'Ah yes, your boy-friend, Nicholas Petrovna. Billionaire Chief Executive of CES, economic advisor to the government of Caspia and a man who owes everything to me. And the way I see it, seeing as you seem to have turned him against me. That means that he owes you to me. I wonder though, what it is that he sees in you?'

For a moment Kornilov stepped back and surveyed Tanya as though she were a painting in a gallery. The he strode forward again, grasped the collar of her shirt and tore open the front in a single rough swipe that sent the buttons clattering onto the concrete. Then he reached over to the table, picked up an evil looking serrated knife and slowly approached her. She tried to twist away from him but one of the guards held her fast in a cast iron grip. She gasped as she felt the cold steel against her skin as he slid the knife between her chest and the front of her bra. A stream of hot yellow liquid began to percolate through the fabric of her trousers.

Kornilov paused to look down at the mess dripping to the floor. 'That's not very lady like is it,' he said, feign-ing a look of distaste. Then he continued to roughly saw through the front section of her sports bra, snarling as he did so. It took several attempts before he sliced through the last bit of fabric allowing Tanya's cleavage to burst out. This elicited a chorus of mocking cheers and applause from the onlookers. Kornilov grabbed her breasts and squeezed them hard before letting them go. Some blood was trickling down between them where the tip of the knife had scratched her flesh during the bra removal. He stood back to admire his work, nodding with satisfaction at what he saw.

' I can see why he liked you. Nice American girl, nice tits, nice talk about human rights. Then you start fucking him and feeding him a load of shit about me afterwards. And what did he say about me?' he said, getting right up in her face so close she could smell his foul breath

Tanya was panting again. It was a struggle to think straight. Her hands were already starting to go numb as the rope bit hard into her wrists cutting off the circulation. Sweat was beginning to pour down her back. She tried to think of the least inflammatory answer.

'He never talked about you much. He was only really interested in sex. I tried to interview him for my paper but it was hopeless. Then he offered me money and jewellery and stuff if I would be his mistress,' she stammered.

'Oh. So you really are a little whore who just fucks rich people for money. So why were you creeping around with a camera up in the north then? You were only here with him a few months ago.'

'I told you. I wanted to check out some stuff about the pipeline or something. I just wanted to see if he was telling me the truth about Caspoil being ethical that's all. I don't want to get involved in Caspian politics.'

Kornilov turned to the bystanders. 'Did you hear that. She doesn't want to get involved in Caspian politics.' A few of them laughed nervously. He turned back to Tanya. 'So, you don't want to get involved with politics but you start fucking Petrovna and suddenly he is conspiring against me. What can you tell me about that?'

She shook her head violently. 'I don't know anything about that.'

He grabbed her by the throat. 'Don't you fucking lie to me you little bitch. I know you've talked him into something. Where is he now?' He let go of her throat to let her answer.

'Please,' she screamed. 'I don't know where he is. He said he was away on business. He doesn't tell me anything about what he is doing.'

Kornilov shrugged his shoulders. 'Yeah. They all say that. If you're no good as a source of information then I guess you really are just a whore. But at least whores are good for one thing.'

He turned to one of guards and instructed him to lift her higher. The man loosened the rope from its mooring and heaved Tanya clean into the air. He refastened the rope leaving Tanya swinging helpless in the air, her feet a few inches off the ground. Then Kornilov undid his zip slowly causing further amusement from his henchmen then he approached Tanya's helpless form again, his eyes engorged with lust. As he bent down to open the top of her trousers she tried to kick out with her legs but succeeded only in losing one of her shoes.

Kornilov stepped away from her thrashing limbs. 'Now that's not very friendly at all. What's the matter?' Don't you want to know what a real man is like?'

'Petrovna is more of a man than you will ever be you disgusting ugly pig,' she screamed at him with the last dregs of her emotional energy.

There were several sharp intakes of breath and the atmosphere in the room seemed to chill. Kornilov's face had turned black with rage and the vein on the side of his neck had started to visibly pump.

'You think I am ugly. You little American whore,' he spat.

'Well I can show you what real ugly is.' He turned his back on her for a few moments and seemed to fumble with something in his pocket. He turned to her again. Now he held an object in his right hand. It glistened under the room's harsh lights like a piece of jewellery. Then he roared like an animal and swung his metal encased fist at her face over and over again until there was little left but flesh and bone.

CHAPTER 29

The presenter on the rolling news channel delivered his report from Baku. The channel didn't actually have any reporters on the ground in Caspia. The events had come more or less out of the blue. No warnings, no 'build up of tensions', so Azerbaijan would just have to do.

'Commentators are struggling to decipher exactly what has happened in Caspia in the last twenty four hours. The first reports that we received were that there had just been a terrorist attack by Islamic separatists. Then we were told that Caspia's Head of State, President Kornilov, had lost his life in the attack. Now it appears that there has been a coup of sorts in this oil rich but desperately unstable former Soviet republic. The current situation is very far from clear but we are hearing unconfirmed reports that the administration is now under the control of secretive oil billionaire, Nicholas Petrovna. If this is true, it will probably be greeted with a measure of relief in diplomatic circles. Many privately regarded the administration of the former President, Colonel Alexei Kornilov as little better than a gangster regime. It remains to be seen whether this is truly the case. This is Grant Barrett, Global News Channel, Azerbaijan.'

Petrovna turned off the television and fell back into his chair in what used to be Kornilov's Presidential office. He was struggling to come to terms with the events of the last day himself, nor were they ended. It was astonishing that Kornilov's guards had accepted his audacious lie in the blood spattered command room but once they had, everything else had simply fallen into place.

The rest of the mercenaries had fled the scene as planned and hotfooted it back to the airfield with a cohort of Kornilov's troops in pursuit. However, on arrival at the airfield they had been too slow to load and leave. Their pursuers were able to catch up with them while they were still on the ground. Hicks men soon found themselves under heavy fire. They boarded the plane and tried to make their escape regardless but as it had tried to take off, bullets poured into its engines and tires causing the dilapidated Antonov to cartwheel down the runway in a ball of fire. There were no survivors. With Kornilov, Romanov and Hicks all dead there was quite simply no one left alive to dispute Petrovna's version of events. He had reinvented history and apparently got away with it.

In the early hours of the morning a meeting of Kornilov's s former cabinet was called. He had attended in his capacity as Economic Secretary. He had stood at the table whilst coldly, calmly recounting the tale of Kornilov's death, the treachery of Sergei Romanov and how he had valiantly attempted to save the President. He had then announced that Kornilov with his dying breath had declared that he Nicholas Petrovna should succeed him as President. Much to his amazement, the inevitable cries of dissent never came. Maybe they genuinely believed his story. Maybe they guessed the truth but were relieved to have a leader who was not insane or maybe they were simply too tired and stunned to resist. For whatever reason, he had now assumed the mask of command and that at least would give him the authority to find Tanya.

There was a knock on the door that turned out to be Prokina, Romanov's newly promoted deputy from the security department. His first command as President had been to find and secure the safety of Tatiana Georgievna. The man looked very ill at ease in the presence of his new boss.

'I am afraid we cannot find any traces of her at all,' the man said guardedly.

'What do you mean you can't find any trace? That's insane. There must be a trace. Romanov himself told me she was only taken yesterday,' Petrovna replied, his voice rising to a pitch of exasperation.

'I am very sorry but there is nothing. The traitor Romanov only used a few special people for this type of work and they all seemed to have been killed in the terrorist attack.' Petrovna did not believe that for a second.

'We did find some items in Milan though,' Prokina ventured.

'What items exactly?' said Petrovna.

'Just clothes she left in her hotel room and some bags of shopping. Woman clothes, designer gear and a collection of men's shirts.'

'Men's shirts,' Petrovna repeated. He leant forward, silent. His eyes screwed tightly shut as if enduring a hidden pain.

'I know this is no help but I think,' Prokina continued cautiously, 'that after President Kornilov's personal interrogations, people were always removed very quickly. A body was removed early yesterday evening.'

'A body,' Petrovna shouted, his eyes wide open now. 'Whose body, where was it taken?'

'We cannot say who it was. Apparently it was in a mess, so we aren't sure of the identity or where it was taken. But we think it was a lady and she did not look alive,' he said guardedly, avoiding any eye contact with the new President.

'Not look alive,' Petrovna repeated in a tone of disbelief. He turned away and stared out of the window. Deep in his heart he acknowledged that Tanya was almost certainly dead. He knew Kornilov's methods. It all made sense, the security man's account, Kornilov's final words.

Outside, the day was bright now and the window afforded him a view of the cityscape down the boulevard they called Victory Avenue. The modern skyscrapers made for an impressive sun lit vista. One of Kornilov's last acts had been to encrust the domes of the Russian Orthodox Cathedral in gold leaf. Now they shone resplendently in the morning sunshine, their glittering grandeur ringing hollow as his own golden dream lay in a thousand broken pieces. He turned back to face Prokina.

'Someone must know more than this,' he said.

Prokina kept a straight face. 'I think maybe some of Romanov's surviving men do. I am sure they could be persuaded to talk if we used every possible method. Should we do that?' the security chief asked tentatively.

Petrovna looked back at him with hollow eyes and an empty spirit. He knew exactly what the man meant by every possible method. Was he now to become the beast Kornilov was, the last vestiges of his decency swept away?

He paused and thought of Tanya. She would not have wanted that. Then he coldly replied. 'Yes. I think you should.'

THE END

ABOUT THE AUTHOR

Owen Hollister is a well travelled London based financier who has dabbled in politics.

Printed in Great Britain
by Amazon